THE WITCH'S TEARS

Katharine and Elizabeth Corr have been writing since they were children. They keep in touch any way they can, discussing their work via phone, text and Skype, and have been known to finish each other's sentences – and not just when they are writing!

www.corrsisters.com

Books by Katharine and Elizabeth Corr

The Witch's Kiss

The Witch's Tears

THE
WITCH'S
TEARS

KATHARINE
& ELIZABETH
CORR

HarperCollins*Publishers*

First published in Great Britain by HarperCollins *Children's Books* in 2017
HarperCollins *Children's Books* is a division of HarperCollins*Publishers* Ltd,
1 London Bridge Street, London, SE1 9GF

The HarperCollins website address is: www.harpercollins.co.uk

3

Text © Katharine and Elizabeth Corr 2017

ISBN 978-00-0-818299-1

Typeset by Palimpsest Book Production Ltd, Falkirk, Stirlingshire
Printed and bound in England by Clays Ltd, St Ives plc

MIX
**Paper from
responsible sources**
FSC
www.fsc.org **FSC® C007454**

For our mum, who was beautiful both inside and out.

E.C.

In memory of Geoff, for his love and enthusiasm.

K.C.

PROLOGUE

Jack was sprawled on the grass, gazing up at the blue sky. Merry was lying next to him, leaning on one elbow. She had a paperback open in front of her, but she wasn't reading. Instead, she was studying Jack's face: the line of his jaw, the shape of his eyes, the curve of his lips as he thought of something and grinned.

'What's funny?' she asked.

'Nothing, really. I'm just enjoying the sunshine. Enjoying the fact that you are here, and Gwydion is not.'

'Gwydion?' Merry searched her memory. 'He was a wizard, wasn't he?' She glanced back at her book. The paperback had gone, replaced by pages of parchment bound together with a

leather cord. That was weird. But she didn't really want to read, anyway – she wanted to feel Jack's lips against hers. Tossing the manuscript aside, she shifted so she was lying right next to him.

Jack smiled, pulled her into his arms and kissed her.

Eventually Merry drew away and rested her head on his shoulder.

'I've missed that so much.' She shivered a little; the warmth of the day was fading and there were dark clouds gathering in the north. 'You know, I think it's about to rain. Let's go.' She sat up and reached for her bag.

But Jack didn't move.

'Jack?' She nudged him. 'Aren't you coming?'

He shook his head, not looking at her.

'You know I can't come with you.'

'Why not?'

'Because I'm dead, Merry. You killed me, remember? True love's kiss?'

He pulled the front of his shirt open and Merry saw a gaping wound across the centre of his chest, dark with dried blood.

'Oh God…' She pressed her hand to her mouth.

'There wasn't a happy ever after, Merry. Not for us.'

And now she could see that Jack's lips were pale and waxy, and his eyes were cloudy, unfocused…

★

Merry gasped and sat up.

It was a dream. Just a dream. Or at least –

She brushed her fingers against her lips. It had felt real. He had felt real.

Grief swelled painfully in her chest. She pulled the duvet back up and curled into a ball on her side, hugging her knees, waiting for the hurt to fade. It was nearly two weeks since she'd last dreamt about Jack, or had a nightmare about Gwydion. More than three months since she and Leo had escaped from the Black Lake. Sometimes – on days when she was busy, or surrounded by people – it seemed like longer. But then a fragment of memory would stab at her, make her catch her breath, and the whole thing could have happened yesterday.

There was a photo of Merry and her brother on her bedside table. In the photo, Leo was smiling. She tried – failed – to recall the last time she'd seen him look that happy. Today was the first morning of the summer holidays. But the brighter the sunshine, the more they both seemed to be lost in the shadow.

She wiped a tear away from her cheek. The day began.

ONE

MERRY WAS SITTING against the trunk of the oak tree in Gran's back garden, eyes half closed against the mid-afternoon glare, the bare skin on her arms and legs prickling from the grass and the heat. Her fingernails still ached from the surge of magic she'd just unleashed, and the back of one hand stung. When the potion had exploded, it had sprayed across the kitchen, a few drops escaping Gran's hastily conjured protective screen. Gran had been testing her, watching her make yet another healing salve. Twenty-plus herbs that all had to be correctly prepared and added in precisely the right order, supposedly. Merry had merely tried to… speed things up. It hadn't exactly gone to plan.

But it might have worked. If Gran had just let me finish what I was trying to do.

And if Gran hadn't suggested – for the second time in the last fortnight – that Merry needed to go back to the Black Lake. Right at the moment when she'd been trying to concentrate.

She ripped a tuft of grass out of the dry soil. Being a witch meant becoming familiar with hundreds of years' worth of spells and techniques and history. Merry understood the necessity, sort of. She had to be able to cast spells with the other witches so that she could become a full member of the coven. Witchcraft was a team sport. Or at least it was supposed to be.

But the endless, picky details were driving her crazy: a spell must be cast, and the results recorded, and each member of the coven involved in exactly this way, and this way only. Merry had done stuff by herself in the spring that none of the other witches in the coven were capable of. Not even Gran. Yet even spells that she could do almost without thinking had to be relearnt 'the proper way', which usually meant – at the very least – some sort of chant in a language that Merry didn't speak. Because that was how everyone else did it, and that was how it had always been done. No shortcuts allowed.

Even if you're powerful enough to use them...

Her fingernails were tingling again. She took a few deep, slow breaths, letting the frustration ebb away.

A tuft of dandelion seeds floated past, and Merry reached up to catch it. 'Wishes' – that's what Leo and she had called them when they were kids. They used to chase them around the garden. She examined the cluster of delicate filaments, remembering the sorts of things she used to wish for – more pocket money, blonde hair: all the really important things in life – and trying to decide what she would wish for now. Right this second.

Being allowed to concentrate on the types of witchcraft she was actually interested in – that would be her first wish. Healing was obviously important. Selfless, and all that. But it wasn't the kind of magic that she wanted to spend her life doing. Flying, or becoming invisible: *those* were the kinds of spells that made her heart beat faster. Or the Cinderella potion, one drop of which would transform the user into an utterly gorgeous version of herself. Gran kept promising they'd get on to the exciting stuff, but it never seemed to happen.

Her phone buzzed: a calendar alert. Probably reminding her about a coven meeting, or a practice session…

Merry grimaced. Being left alone for a bit – that would be her second wish. Because almost as soon as she'd recovered from the ordeal of fighting Gwydion – physically recovered, at any rate – her proper witch training had started. And the testing. Gran wanted to know why Merry's power was still unpredictable. That was why she kept trying to get her back to the lake: to see how Merry's magic reacted near the place where she'd first learnt to harness it. And the whole coven seemed obsessed with figuring out exactly how powerful she was, and whether the power would start to wane as she got further from the events of the spring.

Further from Jack.

She closed her eyes, shivering, remembering Jack as she'd seen him this morning: dead and cold at the edge of the water.

Merry never wanted to go back to that place.

But… But if I could go back to that time…

If she had a second chance, she might be able to do things differently. Find a way to keep him alive.

That's my third wish, then.

Perhaps there was a spell for time travel. Or perhaps

she could invent one. Though Gran would be less than impressed. Time travel was almost definitely not on the approved syllabus. Maybe it would be better just to wish for Jack to come back from the dead—

A wave of emotions – not hers, but somebody else's, someone nearby – crashed across her thoughts. Ever since her ancestor, Meredith, had left her that night beneath the lake, this kept happening. It was like... like there was some vacant space inside her head, just waiting to be filled up by other people's feelings. It was bizarre. Annoying, sometimes. But it was also intriguing. Merry opened her eyes and sat up straighter. The woman who lived next door to Gran was playing with her toddler in the garden. Merry concentrated, allowing her mind to float, to expand into the space around her. The emotions stopped being a random buzz of background noise and smoothed out into distinct strands of boredom and guilt. Or rather, guilt about being bored.

Merry drew back, trying to close off her mind. Before she could, another swarm of emotions surrounded her, as sharply delineated as ice crystals. Gran's emotions. Exasperation, a touch of disappointment and... nervousness? Gran hadn't exactly made a huge effort to hide her frustration at Merry's progress, or lack of it. But why should she be nervous?

Just as well Merry hadn't said anything about her new talent. Using magic to see inside other people's heads probably broke ALL the rules. Besides, if by some miracle mind-reading was allowed, the coven would definitely decide to test the extent of this power too. Or tell her to go away and learn how to do it using the official, ancestor-approved method.

It was too hot. She grabbed her phone and texted Ruby.

You around? Need to go out. Anywhere with air con.

She'd had enough witchcraft for one day.

By the time Merry left the cinema that evening the heat had faded, but the air was still sticky, clinging to her skin like damp washing. Ruby – because she was six months older, and because she had the type of gran who bought her grandchildren cars, rather than setting them magical homework – had dropped her home. Now Merry was sitting by the window in her bedroom, leftover popcorn bobbing in the air above her head like a flotilla of tiny spaceships.

The film had been all right. She'd let Ruby choose, so they'd gone to see a romantic comedy – definitely not what Merry would have picked. Fictional happy endings held zero appeal right now. But it wasn't just the film: the cinema had been full of couples being… couple-y. At least her mental barriers had held. Merry closed her eyes and tried to replay the evening in her head, imagining that she'd been there with Jack instead of Ruby. Jack, the screen-light flickering across his face, sharing her bucket of popcorn and holding her hand in the dark…

Merry swallowed and shook herself out of the daydream. Sitting here, imagining what might have been –

Jack probably wouldn't have understood the film in any case.

Sighing, she reached across to her desk, grabbed a chunky A5 notebook and flipped it open to where she'd jammed a pen between the pages. This was her first spell book – or rather, the first that she was constructing herself. Gran had given her copies of what she called 'the beginner's standard works'. Four printed spell collections (technically known as 'knowledge books'). Six books of instruction, stories and traditions ('wisdom books'). But apparently it was customary (read: obligatory) for every witch to keep her own set of notes on the spells she tried, the effects she observed, and any other magical occurrences. The official name for this was a 'journey book'. Merry had seen Gran's journey books: thirty volumes or more of closely-written text, plus sketches and bits cut out from other books. There were even little watercolours. Merry flicked back over the last few pages of her journey book. In contrast to Gran's neatly presented pages, her efforts so far were a bit… slapdash. There was a lot more underlining, crossing-out and arrows to show where something had been missed. The only colour so far came from fluorescent highlighters.

She pinched a piece of popcorn out of the air and popped it into her mouth.

So, where was I? Oh yeah –

She picked up the pen and added: *and apparently I should have stuck to the exact order and just been more patient. But there must be a way to speed the whole thing up. I mean, who has the time to spend THREE HOURS making ONE potion?* She chewed on the end of the pen for a moment. *In any case, why do these long recipes have to be learnt by heart? Why don't witches just save all this stuff to the cloud? Then I could look spells up on my phone.*

Merry sighed, snagged another piece of popcorn and threw the journey book back on her desk.

Being a full member of the coven should have been kind of cool. All the sisterhood, and that. But surely there were alternatives to everything that came with it? Better alternatives, perhaps. Maybe she could be a sort of… freelance witch? A witch with choices. Possibilities.

Jack would have understood. He would have had something useful to say, if only she could talk to him. He would have taken her mind off the future, at least. Her throat tightened with sadness, and the remaining popcorn dropped out of the air.

Merry swore, sang the beginning of a cleaning spell and sent the scattered popcorn zooming into the bin. Her biggest regret was that she'd never taken a photo of Jack. Right now she could still remember his face clearly, but would that still be true after a year had gone by? A decade? Merry knew she couldn't have prevented Jack's death, and she'd come to accept that. Most of the time. But it still hurt. And she still missed him.

Then again, a photo might just have made things worse.

She got up and stretched. Maybe she could talk to Leo instead – if she had any idea where he was. He'd told her that morning that he was going to the cinema tonight, but Merry hadn't seen his car in the car park. And he wasn't replying to any of her texts. Still, for a witch, there was always another way.

Merry jumped up, grabbed the drawstring bag that was hanging from the front of her wardrobe, went into the bathroom and started filling the basin with water. Ever since what had happened at the Black Lake, she'd found spells using water – hydromancy – particularly easy. What she was about to do was, theoretically, supposed to be used for talking to another witch when no ordinary method of communication was available. She was just going to tweak it a little. If Leo ever found out, he'd be furious. But…

It's his own fault for acting so weird, making me worried about him.

Merry had promised, after what they'd been through together at the lake, that she would always be completely honest with Leo. But now she couldn't shake the feeling that he was keeping stuff from her. Sure, she hadn't exactly told him how much she was missing Jack. But he hadn't exactly asked her. And she didn't want him worrying about her when he seemed to be going through so much pain. Leo still couldn't bring himself to even mention Dan by name. She'd begged him over and over to let her help him. But he just brushed her off. Every time.

The basin was full. Merry opened the bag; a small selection of stones – some cut and polished, some rounded like sea-washed pebbles – spilt out on to the bath mat. At least she'd remembered to cleanse and recharge the stones after she used them last. Merry selected a chunk of amethyst and a piece of tumbled aquamarine – both good for scrying – and placed them in the bottom of the basin together with her silver bracelet. She spread her hands wide above the water and sang part of the incantation Gran had taught her.

'The Moon I invoke, a light in the darkness; the Pole Star, eternally present; enable my vision, show what I seek, but shield the seer from all who would harm her…'

The surface of the water became mirror-like, reflecting her own features, before fading to black. Merry closed her eyes and pictured Leo's face.

Show me my brother…

And there was Leo, sitting in his car, hands on the steering wheel. But he clearly wasn't driving. Behind him, through the car window, she could just make out what looked like trees.

Oh no. He's at the lake. Again.

Merry stretched out her fingers, almost touching the surface of the water.

Poor Leo…

★　★　★

Leo gripped the steering wheel tighter and stared at the dark trees ahead of him. He knew he ought to leave. He knew he shouldn't be here. Perhaps it would have been better if he had gone travelling with Sam and the others, but then he was convinced that Sam had been… reluctant, when he'd invited him. Whatever. He didn't need friends like that. The result was that he'd stayed in Tillingham, and over the last few weeks he'd been coming to the Black Lake more and more frequently. It was like a scab that he couldn't leave alone. To be sitting in his car in the car park, rather than down at the edge of the lake, was better than he'd managed before. But still, he knew that none of this was healthy. And it wasn't going to bring Dan back.

The funeral had been difficult. He hadn't dared show too much emotion, hadn't dared risk revealing his true feelings in front of so many of his other friends. He'd gone home, tried to put it behind him, to carry on as if nothing had changed.

When in fact everything was different. *He* was different.

The future Leo had been planning in his head for so long now belonged to somebody else. He wasn't sure that he even wanted any of it.

Leo turned the key in the ignition and reversed the car out on to the road. Maybe university would still be the best thing for him. It would get him away from Tillingham, away from what had happened here. And it wasn't like Merry needed him any more.

He changed gear and accelerated, wondering whether Merry would ever learn a spell to see into the future, wondering what it would show. Him as a doctor, an overworked GP in some suburban practice? Merry still in Tillingham, running the coven? And would either of them be happy?

Leo pulled up in front of the house. The lights were on in Merry's bedroom, which meant she was still awake, probably waiting up for him. Thankfully, Mum was on a yoga retreat with a work friend until Friday, so at least there wouldn't be any awkward questions. But lately, Merry had been watching him closely, badgering him to 'open up' to her. Which wasn't going to happen. A tiny part of him had somehow become convinced that, eventually, Dan would have loved him back. But there was no way he could admit that. Not even to his sister. So instead he'd made even more of an effort to try to act normal. But tonight…

Tonight, he'd messed up. Even if he'd stayed out for a couple of drinks after the cinema, he should have been home ages ago.

The moon emerged briefly from behind the clouds, and silver light flooded the landscape. Leo got out of the car, locked it and stood for a moment, gazing through the branches of the willow that grew next to the garage, out across the lawn.

Somebody was there. Someone was standing right at the edge of the garden, just beyond the overgrown rockery, looking up at the house.

TWO

FOR A FRACTION of a second Leo was paralysed, staring at the figure on the other side of the lawn. Then the clouds came over, the figure disappeared and, just as though a spell had been lifted, Leo was running: tearing round the back of the car, sprinting across the garden until he got to the rockery and found –

No one.

He pulled his phone out of his pocket – noticing that his hands were trembling, that all of him was trembling – switched on the torch and shone it around. There was the hedge that separated the garden from the road and the neighbouring houses. There was the unused, partly boarded-up greenhouse that Mum could never afford to get repaired. There was the back of the house, all in darkness apart from a faint glimmer coming from the bathroom. The whole garden was still, not even the whisper of a breeze to break the tranquillity.

Perhaps it had been Merry. What he'd taken for short, darkish hair could have been a hat. Or…

Leo reached the edge of the patio and the security lights snapped on, their yellow beams illuminating the entire garden.

He was being ridiculous. If there had been someone in the garden, the lights would already have been on. And why on earth would his sister be wandering around outside at this time of night? A car sped along the road in front of the house. After it had passed, the silence rolled back again. Leo yawned and squeezed his eyes shut. He never seemed to get enough sleep these days – maybe it was all messing with his head.

Just to be sure, Leo did a complete circuit of the house before going back to the car to get his bag. He walked up the path to the front door – ran a hand through his hair, trying to dispel the fog clouding his brain – and fumbled in his bag for his house keys. He was just about to fit the key into the lock when the front door swung open. Merry was standing there in her pyjamas, frowning.

★ ★ ★

Leo didn't look especially pleased to see her. 'Oh. I mean, hey. Were you waiting up for me?' He shut the door behind him, locked and bolted it, put the chain on. 'You didn't need to.'

He sounded really tired. And tense. He didn't look good, either. There were dark circles under his eyes.

'I wasn't waiting up for you,' Merry lied, trying to make her voice light and casual. 'It's just that... I heard your car pull up, about ten minutes ago. I was wondering what was taking you so long. That's all.'

Leo picked up the post from the hall table and flicked through it, but he didn't respond.

Merry knew she should probably go to bed and leave him alone. But, after what she'd seen earlier, in the scrying water...

She tried again.

'Leo, is everything OK? I mean... was the film good?'

He turned and looked at her. For a split second he seemed to waver, an expression Merry couldn't quite identify flitting across his face. Then he shrugged.

'It was OK. Probably not something I'd bother to see

again. But the others enjoyed it.' He brushed past her and walked into the kitchen, stopping at the sink to fill the kettle. 'You want some tea?'

Merry's insides began to knot up as she followed Leo into the kitchen. She knew where her brother had been this evening. But how was she supposed to bring it up without accusing him of lying, or without admitting that she'd been using her powers to spy on him?

'No, thanks. If you're hungry, there's some leftover lasagne in the fridge. I could heat it up for you, if you like?'

Leo shook his head.

'I ate already. Went for a kebab after the film.' He smiled at her, but the anxiety didn't leave his eyes. 'Sorry I'm back so late, by the way. Lost track of time.'

'No worries.' Merry sat down and watched her brother as he made tea. He was fidgety, tapping his fingers on the kitchen counter, glancing out of the window every few seconds.

'So, why were you outside the house for so long?'

'Geez, Merry. Why don't you just get me microchipped and then you can track my every movement.' He opened one of the drawers, took out a teaspoon and slammed it shut.

'Calm down – I'm only making conversation. You're always out, I'm always training; I – I miss talking to you. Remember us talking? Remember when we used to tell each other stuff? It wasn't that long ago.'

'Fine,' Leo muttered eventually, turning round to face her. 'If you really must know, I thought – I thought I saw...' He closed his eyes for a moment. 'Forget it. It doesn't matter.'

Merry looked at him steadily.

'Leo – it's me, Merry. You can tell me anything. Right? Because after everything we've been through these past few months, I wouldn't be fazed if you told me you'd found a secret way into Narnia through the bottom of your underwear drawer. Trust me.'

That brought a genuine smile to Leo's face.

'OK. Well, it was probably nothing. But when I got home I thought I saw someone outside the house.'

'Oh.' That wasn't what she'd been expecting. 'You mean, a prowler?'

'Yeah, exactly. It was only for a second, but I could have sworn I saw... someone, standing in the garden. So I went after him. But there wasn't anyone there.' Leo went to the cupboard and got out a packet of biscuits. 'There's nothing else to tell. I must have imagined it.'

Merry shivered. The last time there had been an intruder in the house, it had been Jack. That night he'd crept into her room and threatened her with a knife – it was one of the times she'd spent in Jack's company that she really wouldn't mind forgetting. 'I dunno, Leo. Maybe… it was an animal that you saw? Like, a really big fox?'

Leo raised his eyebrows.

'Seriously? A really big fox. A giant mutant fox, in fact, stalking round the garden on its hind legs…' He shook his head and sat back down.

'Well, I don't see how it could have been a person. Mum put extra protection spells on the house and the garden. She even got the coven to strengthen the runes they carved last time.'

Her brother looked surprised.

'Really? I thought Mum was keeping a safe distance from the coven.'

'She is. But they still came here after school one day when you were at work. Gran said it was unnecessary, cos it's not like any more cursed Anglo-Saxon princes are going to show up. But you know Mum.' Merry shrugged. 'Anyone with "evil intent" couldn't have got anywhere near the house. They wouldn't get past the garden boundary.'

Leo just stared down at his tea, frowning. Merry nudged him.

'Perhaps it was one of your mates. Come to drop something off? Or – I know: I bet it was Simon. He probably came to apologise, then chickened out when he saw you.'

'No way, Merry. Simon hasn't forgiven me for punching him and hasn't suddenly become less of a jerk. He hates me. He made that abundantly clear when I bumped into him in town last week.' Leo downed the rest of his tea, dumped the mug in the sink and stood there, head down, hands gripping the edge of the countertop.

'Honestly,' Merry began, 'there has to be some other explanation. I'm sure if—'

Leo swung round.

'What if… what if it was his ghost? What if he's come back to haunt me?'

Merry's stomach flipped.

She opened her mouth to say that there were no such things as ghosts, but thought better of it.

Because, honestly, I don't know. I didn't believe in magic swords and cursed princes this time last year. And those visions of Meredith I had were kind of ghostlike…

'But why would Dan come back to haunt you?' she asked gently.

'Because it's my fault that he's dead. I should never have gone to Northumberland with you and Mum. I should have stayed here, warned people. Maybe if I'd said the words from the manuscript, I could have stopped Jack from... from killing...'

Merry got up.

'Don't you dare blame yourself for anything that happened in the spring, Leo. Don't you dare! We did what we could. We both almost died.' She put her hands on his face, forcing him to look at her. 'Dan was murdered when we were under the lake, remember? And if you hadn't been there with me, Gwydion would have won. And lots more people would have died. What happened to Dan – that was Gwydion's fault. Not Jack's, not mine, and definitely not yours.'

She tried to put her arms around Leo, to hug him, but he pulled away.

'But I could have warned him!'

'He would never have believed you!'

'I – we could have made him. We could have shown him your powers. He would have had to believe us.'

'You're wrong. People don't want to believe in things that are scary or dangerous, not really. And even if Dan had believed us, who else would we have had to tell? The whole town? Let them see what me and Gran and the rest of the coven really are?'

Leo stepped back.

'Is that all you witches care about? Protecting your damn secrets?'

'Protecting *you*. That's what I care about!' Merry grabbed her brother by his arm. 'You need to stop this. I know you miss Dan. But this isn't healthy. And −' the words came out before she could stop them − 'and neither is sitting by the Black Lake obsessing about what happened. You have to move on.'

Leo shook her hand away.

'What? How did you know?'

'I'm worried about you. Really worried. So I… I cast a spell that would allow me to see where you were tonight.'

Leo shot her a furious look, the colour draining from his face.

'You've been *spying* on me? I can't believe you, Merry. Why didn't you just talk to me, if you were that worried?'

'But I've tried to! You know I have. I've kept asking—'

Leo interrupted her.

'And as for me "moving on", I'll do that when I'm damn well ready to!' He turned and strode out of the kitchen before she could say anything else.

Merry smacked her palm against her forehead.

Way to go, Merry.

She sighed, put the biscuits away in the cupboard and unlocked the back door. Switching out the lights in the kitchen she stood on the threshold, waiting for her eyes to adjust to the darkness. The night air was heavy with the heat and the scent of roses blooming somewhere nearby, so still that every sound seemed muffled. There was nothing amiss as far as she could see. And yet...

She closed her eyes.

And there it was, like a single wrong note in the middle of a symphony, or a dab of jarring colour at the edge of a painting. Something barely discernible, but just not quite... right. So faint as to be almost not there at all.

There was something in one of the wisdom books Gran had given her. Something about certain times and places being... points of intersection. Points at which the boundaries between different realms of existence stopped being like solid walls and became more like Swiss cheese.

Merry locked the back door again and went up to her room. The summer solstice had been more than three weeks ago, and if there was something odd about their garden, surely she – and for that matter, Mum and Gran – would have noticed it before now? And even if they'd all missed something, the protection put in place by the coven had been enough to keep Jack out. The runes would hold against anything.

She was certain of it.

Besides, Gwydion and Jack were both dead. There was nothing left to be frightened of.

The next day Leo was out of the house before Merry was up, giving her no chance to apologise. In the daylight, she couldn't pick up any hint of the strangeness she'd noticed last night. The garden seemed to be exactly the same as normal: suburban, ordinary, extremely non-magical.

At least she had plans for the day: a trip into London with Ruby and Flo, which would give her something else to do other than obsess about Jack or how much she'd messed up with Leo. She'd been hanging out a lot with Flo over the last three months; it was kind of relaxing, having a mate who knew the truth about her secret life, who understood it. And they had more than witchcraft in common. Merry couldn't help wondering whether the last few years would have been easier if she'd been allowed to train, and if she'd had a friend who was going through that training at the same time. She really wanted Flo and Ruby to get along, and so far they seemed to be hitting it off pretty well. Her own relationship with Ruby was better, but it wasn't quite back to normal yet. Merry hoped that shopping, eating and sightseeing – with a third person to smooth over any awkward silences – might push things in the right direction.

They caught the train from Tillingham station, and an hour and twenty minutes later got off the tube at Oxford Street. After spending the rest of the morning trying on clothes and shoes they really, really couldn't afford, they bought some sandwiches and headed into Green Park. It was another beautiful day, sunny and cloudless. Ruby flopped down on the blanket she'd brought and stretched her legs out in front of her, face turned towards the sun. Flo arranged herself cross-legged on the grass, adjusting her huge floppy sunhat so that most of her was in the shade. Merry sat down in between the two of them and immediately rifled through her bag for her sunscreen. She squirted a big dollop of it on to her hand and began covering her arms and legs.

'Blimey, Cooper!' Ruby exclaimed. 'Why don't you live dangerously for once, let yourself develop a light tan? It's the middle of July and you're still Snow White's even pastier sister.'

Flo giggled.

'Gee, thanks,' said Merry, pulling a face. 'Flo's wearing a sunhat.'

'Yeah, but she's already a nice golden colour –'

'Thanks,' Flo beamed.

– 'whereas you…' Ruby shook her head sadly.

'Huh. You're just lucky, inheriting your mum's skin colour.' Merry grinned, 'Not to mention her dress sense…'

'Take that back,' Ruby scowled. 'Right now.'

'Yeah, yeah, all right.' Merry pulled her sandwich out of her bag. 'But while we're on the subject, why don't you tell Flo about your plans to take over the fashion world?'

'Oooh, yes, please!' Flo clapped her hands together and sat forward.

'OK.' Ruby put on her newly acquired, almost-designer sunglasses. 'Well, people are always telling me I look good. Always asking me what I'm wearing. Aren't they, Merry?'

Merry nodded.

'So, I've been thinking I could become one of those online fashion/make-up/hair-care gurus. Only, like, much better than the other girls who are already doing it. So I started a fashion vlog. Last weekend.'

'Fab, I'll google you. Sounds like it's going to be epic!'

Ruby laughed, and she and Flo began discussing the

various crimes against fashion that were currently being committed around them in the park.

Merry took a bite out of her sandwich. It was such a long time since she'd had a day like this. Looking around, she could see dozens of other people hanging out among the trees, sunbathing or chatting or listening to music. And apart from Flo, none of them knew she was a witch. It almost made her feel normal.

Almost.

'Hey! Are you still with us?' Ruby was waving a hand in front of Merry's face. 'I said, do you know yet what you want to do next year? After we leave?'

Merry shrugged.

'Dunno. Something to do with sports, maybe.' Perhaps she could really work on her fencing, even take it up professionally. Jack would have approved of that.

'PE lessons —' Flo interjected, 'one thing I'm definitely not going to miss.'

'Me neither,' Ruby replied. 'Can't wait for the day I no longer have to waste an hour a week being bored on a netball court. But seriously, Merry, what are you going to do?' She sat forward, closer to Merry, pushing her sunglasses back on her head. 'I know the spring term was hard for you.' Ruby glanced at Flo. 'Has she told you about what happened?' Flo nodded, her face carefully neutral, and Ruby continued. 'But you seem better now. Right?'

'Better?' Merry wasn't sure what to say. Ruby was still smiling, but there was something in the way she was looking at her – searching her face – that made Merry want to look away. She'd so wanted to tell Ruby the real reason for her weird behaviour the previous few months, for missing classes and messing up at school, for never being around when Ruby needed her. She wanted to tell her the truth about Jack and Gwydion and the curse, about being a witch and all that it meant. Apart from Leo, Ruby was her best friend in the entire world: it would be amazing to let Ruby see her for what she really was. But Merry didn't know how to begin. Perhaps she and Flo should just... show Ruby their powers. Turn the parched turf in front of them into a bed of multicoloured daisies.

Ruby tugged at the shrivelled blades of grass.

'I just mean, that since that guy left, you seem more yourself again.'

Jack. Even here, Merry couldn't get away from him. Not that she wanted to. Thinking about him, talking about him – even if she never used his name out loud – it kept a little bit of him alive. Somehow.

'Um...' Merry's throat was dry; she took a sip from her

bottle of water. Ruby tilted her head, her curiosity nudging at Merry insistently. 'Well… Yeah. I guess. I mean, it would never have worked.' She knew Ruby was about to ask why, so she rushed the words out. 'I think he was still in love with someone else. Someone from his past.' *With Meredith. My ancestor from fifteen hundred years before I was born.* Two witches from the same family, in love with the same boy.

'Really? What a loser,' Ruby commented, satisfied. 'I'd want to seriously injure anyone who messed me about like that. Hope you dumped him from a great height.'

Merry stared at her friend.

You have no idea what he meant to me. And no idea what we had to do to him—

She caught her breath and shrugged, trying to look unconcerned even as her heart ached. 'It was months ago. I'm fine with it now.'

There was a surge of sympathy from Flo; she knew a little of the truth about Jack, about how Merry had felt about him. But Merry could tell Ruby didn't believe her. Not one little bit. A hint of panic began to swirl in the pit of her stomach.

Ruby nodded.

'Good. So you can begin dating again. Prove to him

that you've moved on. And I know exactly the guy for you – he's completely lush.'

Ruby started swiping through the photos on her phone, looking for a shot of Mr Lush, talking about how amazing he was. But Merry couldn't take any of it in. How could she move on from a boy she'd been so desperate to save that she'd been willing to let him die? It felt impossible.

Guilt mingled with the panic.

I really wish I hadn't told Leo last night that he needed to move on.

It was time to change the subject. But her mind was blank.

Luckily, Flo came to the rescue.

'Ooh – speaking of lush, I spent most of last weekend binge-watching *Poldark*. Have you seen it, Ruby? Aidan Turner is *so* hot.'

Merry's hands unclenched as Ruby and Flo began a long discussion on whether people really used to work down mines with no shirts on. For now, at least, she was off the hook.

A few hours later they were on the train back home. Flo started texting a guy she'd met at a party a couple of weeks ago, while Ruby put her headphones on and seemed to fall asleep. Merry's phone had died, so she looked around for something to read and located a discarded newspaper a few seats down.

The headlines seemed to be the usual mix of regular news, human-interest items and celebrity gossip. A politician had been caught doing something dodgy, some poor guy had been murdered for his collection of antique knives, and yet another Hollywood couple had split up. Nothing interesting enough to make her read the rest of the article. Until a picture of a woman caught her eye. The woman looked like she was in her early thirties, and she was going for a seventies hippy vibe: multicoloured peasant blouse, flared jeans, fringed suede bag. She was smiling flirtatiously over her shoulder. For some reason, her face seemed familiar, though Merry was certain that she didn't know her. She looked at the headline next to the photo:

Birchover death: police believe Ellie Mills's body lay undetected for days

Merry read a bit more of the story and grimaced. *Ellie Mills*. The name didn't ring any bells. And where could she possibly have seen her before? After a while she gave up trying to figure it out and stared through the window instead. She watched the landscape streaking past, until her eyelids grew heavy.

THREE

MERRY WASN'T SURPRISED to be back at the lake again. Somehow, it seemed… inevitable. Whatever path she chose, she kept ending up in the same place. But today it looked different. The water wasn't sparkling, or reflecting the cloudless sky above. Instead, the lake lurked within its hollow: shrunken, dark, stinking of rotten vegetation. As she got closer to the edge, she saw that it was choked with algae, and she thought, This place is dying…

Finding a clear spot, she knelt on the bank, staring down into the water. She could see him there, gazing up at her, his blond hair floating about his head.

'Jack?'

He stretched out his arms towards her, struggling to reach her. Instinctively she leant forward – forward – until her face was almost touching the surface of the lake, until—

Terror suffocated her. Scrambling backwards, she froze the surface of the lake, trapping Jack underneath. But she could still hear him, beating on the underside of the ice, screaming her name over and over…

'Hey, Merry?' She sat up with a jerk. Ruby was shaking her shoulder; the train was just pulling into Tillingham. 'You OK? You were muttering something in your sleep.'

'Uh… no, I'm fine. Just tired.'

Flo was staring at her, frowning. Merry shook her head fractionally; she didn't want to start discussing her strange dreams in front of Ruby.

Merry stumbled off the train after the others. Flo said goodbye to them there as she lived on the other side of town and was getting a bus home. Merry got into Ruby's car and turned the air conditioning on to full, trying to blow away the cobwebs of sleep still clinging to her brain.

Thankfully, Ruby seemed happy enough listening to the radio as she drove.

Merry was supposed to meet Leo at Gran's house for dinner, so Ruby dropped her off there. Gran was in the kitchen, and despite the heat outside, the house was pleasantly cool.

'Hey, Gran.' Merry kissed her grandmother on the cheek. 'That smells good. Where's Leo?'

'I made a chicken pie. And he's not coming. He called and said he's not feeling well.' Gran gave Merry a searching glance, but Merry didn't offer any explanation. She was hardly going to tell Gran that she'd been misusing her magic to spy on her brother.

'Can I do anything?'

'No. Go and relax.'

Merry wandered into the living room, spent a few minutes playing with Tybalt – Gran's tortoiseshell moggie – then began browsing her grandmother's bulging bookshelves: fiction, political memoirs, history, lots of knowledge books and wisdom books. And in a separate bookcase, Gran's journey books. Merry opened the doors and ran her fingers along the spines. Gran favoured brightly-coloured, cloth-bound notebooks, though the bindings of the earliest books were faded now. As her nails bumped across the rainbow fabric, Merry remembered the photo of Ellie Mills, and that strange feeling of familiarity. And then she remembered an evening at Gran's house a couple of months ago when Gran had asked her to copy out a spell from one of the journey books.

Ten minutes later Merry was sitting on the floor, a jumbled pile of discarded notebooks by her feet, one open upon her knees. Here was the spell: a charm Gran had developed for getting rid of acne. And on the opposite page was a photograph. Gran, with a group of six or seven other women of different ages, all standing a little awkwardly among four large, irregular-shaped rocks. A younger Gran – it had obviously been taken quite a few years ago. The camerawork was a bit wonky, but Gran had helpfully written the names of the women underneath the picture. And at the edge of the group – her hair bright pink in this photo – stood Ellie Mills.

Merry took the journey book into the kitchen. Gran was laying the table.

'Gran, who's this?'

Gran glanced at the photo.

'Oh, it was taken at a convention in Derbyshire, held by a local coven. We went on a day trip to visit a nearby stone circle. About ten years ago, I think.'

'But why is she there?' Merry tapped the photo. 'Ellie Mills.'

'She's one of the local witches. I don't know her that

46

well. Powerful, but rather… scatty, as far as I remember. Of course, she was only young when that was taken. She might be more disciplined by now. Why?'

Merry hesitated. Gran didn't seem to know Ellie Mills that well, but still…

Her grandmother was peering at her over the top of her spectacles.

'Merry?'

'Er, the thing is… I think she's dead. There was a photo of her in the paper today, and it said…' Gran had gone sort of rigid, staring at the knife still in her hand. 'I'm really sorry, Gran. I s'pose it was an accident. I didn't read the whole article, but—'

'No. It can't have been. At least, not the kind of accident you mean.'

'But – you don't know that. Even witches have accidents. Mum told me about your sister and the car crash. So maybe Ellie Mills fell, or—'

'No!' Gran slapped the knife down on the table. 'You think you know everything, Merry, when you've barely scratched the surface of what it means to be a witch! I won't…' Gran clamped her lips together. Merry could almost taste her gran's agitation: an acidic fog filling her throat and her lungs.

'What's happening, Gran?'

'I don't know.' Gran sank into a chair. 'There are no more family curses. But—' The oven timer went off and Gran flinched. But she made no move to get up.

They sat for what felt like ages, listening as the *beep beep beep* split the silence of the kitchen.

The meal that followed didn't take long; neither of them had much of an appetite. Merry started the dishwasher then sat down opposite her grandmother.

'Well?'

Gran sighed and pulled the journey book – still open at the page with the photograph – towards her.

'Witches are… hard to kill. We can use magic to protect ourselves from ordinary people and to avoid accidents. We can heal ourselves. Usually, we prefer to expire in our beds: all our affairs in order, friends and family notified, and so on. Witches can't hold back time, and eventually we're usually ready to move on. But our deaths are expected. Organised.'

But Ellie Mills hadn't died of old age. Merry glanced up at the ceiling; it was getting dark outside and even with the lights on the kitchen felt gloomy.

'Unexpected deaths have three causes,' Gran continued.

'Usually, the dead witch has been experimenting with a dangerous or prohibited form of magic – that's why it's rarely discussed. Covens are embarrassed and try to cover it up. Or sometimes the witch has been killed in a fight with another witch. Or a wizard.'

Merry swallowed, remembering Gwydion: how he had controlled her and attacked her with fire runes. How he'd tried to kill Leo.

Gran brushed a fingertip across the image of the pink-haired girl in the photograph. 'Ellie isn't the first. There've been at least five unexplained deaths in the last year in the UK and Ireland. More abroad, before then. I'm just not sure…' She lapsed into silence, fiddling with the journey book, folding and unfolding the corner of one page.

'What about the third thing, Gran? You said there were three causes of unexpected deaths.'

'Well… There are stories. Myths, some would say. Or at least exaggerations. Very old stories. The sort that nobody wants to believe could be true.' Her grandmother's anxiety was palpable now, surrounding Merry like a winter mist, seeping into her pores and her bones. A thought flashed into her mind: *Maybe I don't want to hear about these stories. These deaths are not my problem. Not this time…*

She picked up her phone and pushed her chair back from the table.

'Sorry, Gran – I've just realised how late it is. Can we talk more tomorrow?'

'Oh…' Gran blinked and rubbed her eyes. 'Of course. I can lend you a couple of books, just in case.'

In case of what? Merry wondered. But Gran didn't say. Instead, she picked up the journey book and opened the elderly microwave that was sitting on the counter nearby. Inside – bizarrely – was a cardboard folder. Gran put the book on top of the folder, fiddled with the knobs and shut the microwave again. It pinged into life.

'What the hell?' Merry leapt up, hoping to stop the program before the book ignited. But there were no flames. In fact, when she opened the door, the microwave was empty. 'Where did it go?'

'It's a concealment charm. I use this microwave to store things. Come on, let's get you home.' Gran paused with her hand on the light switch. 'Honestly, sweetheart, prohibited magic is certainly the most likely cause of those deaths. I'm almost certain.'

Merry stared into her grandmother's blue eyes. And she knew she was being lied to.

★

Merry was back home now, sitting in the kitchen, drinking iced water and stroking one of the cats. In front of her were the two books Gran had lent her. One of them, it turned out, Gran had actually written. She ran her fingers over the words embossed on its front cover:

Wizards: Their History and Customs
A Witch's Perspective
by
Elinor Foley

Merry flicked through the first chapter, about how differently magic was practised by witches and by wizards. It was pretty dry and densely written, another big wodge of stuff to learn, by the looks of it. She pushed Gran's book to one side and turned to the other book. The title had worn off the old leather cover, but there were still traces of some sort of design that looked like lots of strangely drawn animals swirling around and intersecting one another. She glanced through the opening pages, then turned to a bookmarked section and started reading.

Once upon a time –

Just for a change, Merry thought.

– a young witch, living in a remote village in the north,

boasted of her skill at spinning and weaving. She claimed to be so magically gifted that she could spin ordinary flax into the finest cloth of gold, fine enough to be worn by the king himself. The earl in whose lands she lived heard of her boast and, pretending that he hated witchcraft, had her locked inside a cell. The floor and the ceiling and the walls of the cell were lined with mirrors, so the witch could not use her magic to escape. Then the earl revealed his true purpose: using only the flax that grew on his estate, he wanted her to weave a cloth-of-gold cloak that he could present to the king. If she succeeded in her task, he would give her a dowry and set her free. But if she failed, he would coat her in tar and burn her alive in front of the castle walls, as a warning to other witches and liars. The earl told the witch she had three days, then left her.

Of course, the witch knew no spell that would allow her to create cloth of gold from nothing more than flax. The best she could do was spin the flax into linen, which she could enchant to appear golden. But such an enchantment would only last a few days, and who knew how long the earl would keep her imprisoned?

The witch wept bitterly at her boastfulness. Then, on the third night, a man appeared in her cell. The witch was scared, because although the stranger was clearly magical, he seemed unaffected by the cage of mirrors. The visitor offered to help her by turning *the flax she had been given into gold thread, which she would then be able to weave into a cloak. In return, he asked that she should give him the life of her firstborn child. The witch hesitated and begged the visitor to choose another reward, offering him all she possessed. But he still demanded her child, although he relented a little, telling the witch that if she found out his name before he returned, he would consider her debt cancelled.*

'It's Rumpelstiltskin,' Merry said out loud, and the cat blinked in agreement. In the version Merry had read as a child, the girl wasn't a witch. And she ended up married to the greedy king. But presumably the ending would be the same: someone would figure out Rumpelstiltskin's name just in time, and the bad fairy – or whatever he was – would disappear in a puff of frustrated rage. She turned the page to read on.

So, in fear of her life, and thinking that she may never be a mother, the witch finally agreed. The visitor burnt an invisible rune into the witch's skin, just above her breastbone, and settled himself at the spinning wheel to begin his task…

The next morning, the earl was delighted with the shimmering cloak. And, much to the witch's surprise, he kept his word, releasing her from the castle and presenting her with a large bag of gold.

Now wealthy, the witch was soon married to a young man

she had long loved from a distance, the son of a local merchant. She forgot all about her promise to the mysterious stranger, until she fell pregnant with her first child. The witch began asking all the travellers she encountered for news of a man who could spin flax into gold, hoping to learn her visitor's name. But no one had heard of such a man. So instead she sought to protect her family from the stranger, seeking help from many other witches and wizards. And it seemed to work: no one appeared to claim the baby, and the little girl grew in wisdom and in power. Until, nearly twenty years later, the witch, now a widow, heard a commotion outside her house. Thinking it was her daughter returned from gathering herbs, the witch hurried to open the door.

It was the stranger, looking exactly the way he had all those years ago. And in his arms, he held her unconscious daughter.

'I have come to collect my debt,' the man said. 'Have you discovered my name?'

The witch, overcome with terror, could only shake her head.

The stranger smiled. 'Then I shall take what I am owed.' He laid her daughter on the floor and sank his fingernails into her face and began to draw out her power, while the witch, pinned in place by the rune on her chest, looked on helplessly...

Merry shuddered and pushed the book away from her, not wanting to read the last few lines.

That's not a fairy tale. It's a horror story.

There was a bad taste in her mouth. She drained her glass of water and stood up. At the same time a crash came from somewhere outside; fear bolted down her spine like an electric shock. She turned the light out and hurried to the window, peering into the darkness.

The lawn, the flower beds, the outline of next-door's house: as far as she could see, everything was as it should be.

Merry started breathing again, picked up her books and ran upstairs. Apart from the thumping of the blood pounding through her chest, the house was silent; there were no sounds from Leo's room.

And now she thought about it, there had been no sign in the kitchen that Leo – not usually the best at clearing up after himself – had cooked any dinner. She'd never known her brother to be too ill to eat. He was either seriously unwell, or lying his backside off. Walking to the other end of the corridor, where her bedroom faced his, she knocked on Leo's door.

'Leo?'

No answer. She turned the handle carefully, peeped inside. The bed was empty.

Anxiety chilled her skin, making her shiver. She went into her own room and texted him.

Where are you? Thought you were home sick???

She waited, then sent the same text again. And again.

After the fourth text, Leo replied.

I'm out. Don't wait up. If you're worried just use your magic to spy on me again.

Merry sighed. Leo was right: it *was* spying. She couldn't forget the angry, disappointed look on his face. So instead she got ready for bed, slipping into her pyjamas and under the covers quickly. She texted for the next hour with Ruby, then picked up a new book she'd just got from the library and tried to read. But she couldn't concentrate. Something kept niggling at her. Her gaze wandered over to the wardrobe in the corner of the room.

Merry, get a grip.

Don't even think about it.

She returned to her book, but found herself rereading the same paragraph. She glanced at the wardrobe again.

Come on. Don't be ridiculous.

But there was no resisting it. She jumped out of bed, went to her dressing table and fished the large key out of her jewellery box. Then she marched over to the wardrobe and opened the doors. At the bottom, pushed right to the back, was an old cardboard box. Inside that was the trinket box, the contents of which Merry had used to defeat Gwydion only three months ago.

She unlocked it. The braid of Edith's hair and the manuscript still lay inside. Mum had suggested burning them, to celebrate the fulfilment of Meredith's oath symbolically. But Merry couldn't bear the thought of destroying the only things that linked her, however tenuously, to Jack.

She hesitated, then picked up the manuscript and took a deep breath. Heart pounding, she opened it...

The pages were completely blank. Just as they had been ever since the day the manuscript had last been used. Ever since the day Jack died.

See? Nothing's wrong. No magical activity going on whatsoever. You can stop being an idiot now.

Her hands were shaking. She carefully replaced the manuscript in the trinket box and hid it in the wardrobe again.

It was really late now. She got back into bed and had just reached over to switch off the bedside lamp when she heard the sound of voices. There was somebody downstairs.

FOUR

THE FIRST THING Merry noticed was blood. Deep red blood glistening on Leo's face, matted in his hair, staining his blue shirt a dirty brown. Blood all over the hands of the guy who was helping him. Holding him upright.

'Oh my God – what happened? You need an ambulance! Why isn't he at hospital?'

'No –' Leo shook his head, wincing as the stranger helped him into the living room and lowered him on to the sofa. 'I'll… I'll be OK. 'S just… bruising.' He sank back against the cushions and closed his eyes.

'But what if you need stitches? What if you have

internal bleeding?' Merry heard the hysteria sharpening her voice. 'There's so much blood!'

'Not all of it's his.' The stranger spoke for the first time, his voice bearing the trace of an Irish accent. 'He gave as good as he got, didn't you, mate?'

'He got into a *fight*? I thought – I thought there'd been a car crash.'

'No. He was jumped. Couple of guys right on the edge of town. There's an alleyway that leads down to the river?'

Merry knew the place he meant. It was an unlit, unpaved passageway between a car park on one side and the blank wall of a shopping centre on the other.

'What the hell were you doing there, Leo?' Her brother didn't answer. Merry picked up the cordless phone from the coffee table. 'I'm calling the police.'

Leo opened one eye. The other was swollen almost shut.

'No. No police.'

'But, Leo!'

'Don't. Please…' He started trying to get up off the sofa.

The stranger reached over and pressed him gently back down again.

'It's OK, Leo.' He looked up at Merry. 'Maybe wait? Until he's less distressed.'

Merry gritted her teeth.

'Look, I appreciate your help, but this really isn't any of your concern. I need to find out who did this to my brother. And when I do I'm going to bloody kill them. I'm going to – to—' The ceiling lights flared brighter as pain lanced from her fingertips up the length of her arms. The phone slipped from her hands on to the rug. 'Damn it!'

The stranger was watching her, eyebrows raised.

'Sorry. I'm going to get some brandy.' Racing into the kitchen, Merry grabbed a cushion off the sofa and squeezed it as hard as she could between her hands.

I have to get a grip. I have to take care of Leo. Everything else can wait.

Gradually, the ache in her fingers faded. But when she let go of the cushion it was covered in burn marks: five on each side. Merry stuffed it into one of the kitchen cupboards, found the brandy and poured some into a glass. She returned to the living room just in time to hear Leo groan.

'Oh, Leo…' Thrusting the glass into the hands of the stranger she leant over her brother, pushing his matted blond hair back from his forehead, blinking away tears as she studied the mess that had been made of his face. 'I can't believe someone would do this to you.' Leo looked up at her with his one good eye, questioning. Merry understood what he meant: he wanted her to heal him. 'I'll try my best, OK? But it's not my strong point.' She glanced at the stranger, feeling some explanation was due. 'I, er... I did a first-aid course recently.'

The stranger nodded his acknowledgement and held up the brandy glass.

'Is he to drink this?'

'Yes. Please.'

'OK. I'm Ronan, by the way.'

'Merry. Back in a sec.'

In the kitchen, she pulled the old first-aid kit out from under the sink. It had bandages and plasters in it, not much else. But at least it would provide camouflage for the real medical supplies. In the cupboard above the fridge Mum kept various potions and salves made by Gran. One in case of poisoning, one for burns (the same lotion Merry had managed to explode the other day), one for cuts. Merry grabbed the latter – and a small glass vial of green liquid, labelled 'For Rest' – and put them into the first-aid kit. Then she found a clean cloth, ran some hot water into a bowl and carried the whole lot back into the living room.

Ronan was sitting on the edge of the sofa, watching Leo. He stood up as Merry came into the room.

'He drank a little. What else can I do? Or would you rather I just got out of your way?'

Merry hesitated. It was inconvenient having a complete stranger in their house, now of all times. But, on the other hand, if he had information about who had done this to her brother...

'Maybe you could make some tea?' Merry nodded her head towards the hall. 'The kitchen's that way.' She waited until Ronan had left before turning back to Leo.

She started by washing the blood off his face and hands, trying to be gentle. But some of the wounds were still oozing. Leo flinched as she touched him, and Merry had to bite her lip to stop the tears that threatened to blind her vision. As well as a black eye, Leo's mouth and nose had been bleeding, and he had ugly grazes across one cheekbone and over his knuckles. Removing the bloodstained shirt revealed bruises already discolouring his abdomen and ribs. She spread some of Gran's lotion on the cuts.

'That stings,' Leo murmured.

'Sorry. It'll wear off soon.'

On top of each blob of lotion she taped a gauze pad;

the grazes would heal and fade as the ointment sank into them, but she couldn't let Ronan see that happening. Then she turned her attention to Leo's black eye.

It made her stomach churn. The skin had been battered into a pulpy, discoloured mess, while the tiny slit of eyeball still visible was red with blood. There was a spell to deal with this kind of injury, but she'd never managed to get it to work properly. Gritting her teeth, she began to dab the lotion over the damaged skin. Leo moaned with pain and knocked her hand away.

Merry frowned, peering at his eye. Where she'd applied the lotion, the skin was reforming – but not in the right way. It was all puckered and lumpy. She swore and put the lid back on.

'This stuff isn't going to work on your eye, so you'll have to visit Gran tomorrow. Understand? You can't leave that untreated. And if Mum sees you like this, she'll have a fit.' She dabbed at a bloodstain on the sofa with the damp cloth. 'Several fits, probably.'

Leo nodded and gave her a wobbly smile. Merry swallowed the anguish in her throat and forced herself to smile back. At least she could help him get some sleep.

'Open your mouth.' She let three drops of the green liquid fall on to his tongue, repacked everything into the first-aid box, then leant over him again, studying her handiwork. Leo's good eye was still open, but he was gazing into the distance.

'Hey, big brother.' Merry ruffled his hair a little. 'Do you know who did this to you?'

Leo focused on her, his face flushing. Then he shook his head and turned away.

Merry knew he was lying. Just like she'd known with Gran, earlier.

'I promise I won't… do anything. Please tell me.'

'Not now.' He closed his good eye. 'Tired.'

Ronan walked back into the sitting room carrying a tray.

'Sorry, I needed to clean myself up. Bloody handprints all over the teapot might be a bit… off-putting. And then I burnt myself on the kettle.' He held up one hand, and Merry could see his fingertips were slightly red. 'But don't worry, I found ice cubes.'

'Oh. Right.' She spread a blanket over Leo, grateful to see he was already drifting off to sleep.

Ronan set the tray down on the coffee table and began to pour the tea.

'How is he?'

'Asleep, I think.' Leo was breathing more evenly now.

She picked up a mug of tea. 'So, did you see who it was? Can you describe them? He said he didn't know them, but—'

'Hold on…' Ronan pulled a phone out of his jeans pocket. Merry recognised it as Leo's, though the screen had a crack across it. 'It was lying next to him. I took a photo as they were running away, in case he wanted to call the police.' Merry thought for a moment, then entered the day and month of Dan's birthday to unlock the phone. The fact that it worked made her want to cry. She went to Leo's photos and looked at the most recent image. It was hard to tell – the shot was blurry – but she was pretty certain she recognised one of the men. Simon.

That emotionally stunted, homophobic bastard. I don't care what I promised Leo. He's not going to get away with this. I won't let him.

She scowled at the photo, trying to identify the second figure. One way or another, she was going to find out who it was. And then she was going to make both of them pay. Leo had been Simon's friend since they were small: how could he, of all people, do this to her brother? It made her want to be sick, to scream, to smash things—

Fault lines shot across the phone's screen, and as it

crazed and fractured there was the sound of shattering glass. The lamp on the side table next to her went out.

Merry froze, glancing at Ronan; she'd almost forgotten he was there. 'Guess the bulb blew. I'll fix it later.' She slid Leo's phone face down on to the side table, trying to breath slowly, hoping their visitor didn't notice her shaking hands or the cracked brandy glass that was now leaking amber liquid. 'Um, Leo was lucky you came along. God knows what they'd have done otherwise.'

'It was nothing, honestly.'

'No, it wasn't. Lots of people would have been too scared to get involved.'

Ronan shrugged. 'I can take care of myself.' From the breadth of his shoulders and the well-defined muscles in his arms, Merry could see that was probably true. His build reminded her of Jack; he had that same look of being physically self-assured, capable. For a moment, she let herself imagine it was Jack sitting opposite her.

I wish he was here.

And I wish – I wish the King of Hearts had killed Simon instead of Dan…

The thought shocked her even as it entered her head. But it was the truth. There was no point pretending.

'Don't worry about Leo,' Ronan was saying. 'I know

that eye looks bad, but I've had worse myself. It'll be better before you know it.'

'I hope so.' Merry fiddled with the edge of the blanket, staring at her brother's profile. Magic could help with Leo's physical injuries, but she didn't know of any spell that could help him deal with whatever was going on in his head. Let alone what was going on in his heart.

Ronan was still sipping his tea. She thought about asking him to leave, but this guy might have saved her brother's life; throwing him out seemed a bit harsh. 'Well, thanks for helping him. I'm glad you were in the right place at the right time. Do you live in Tillingham?'

'Just visiting. I'm kind of –' He pulled a face, like he was hunting for the right word – 'itinerant. A wanderer. I'm camping out in the woods, not far from the lake. Do you know it?'

Merry tensed up.

'Yeah. I've been there. Will you stay for long?'

'I might do.' He glanced over at Leo again. 'Tillingham is growing on me, aside from the brawling in the streets, obviously. I'm from Ireland originally; my mam and I left when I was nine and I've been back a couple of times, but I couldn't live there. As you might have heard, it's a bit on the rainy side. Not great for camping.' He smiled at her suddenly. It was a nice smile, Merry thought. Slightly lopsided. Cute, especially taken with his tanned face, curly black hair and dark brown eyes.

Ronan drained his tea and stood up. 'Well, I'll be on my way. D'you mind if I come by tomorrow afternoon, to see how he's doing?'

'Um, sure. If you like.' Merry stood up too, making a mental note that she'd have to tell Leo to keep the dressings over his already healed wounds. She led Ronan through to the hallway and opened the front door. 'Well, thanks again.'

'No worries. Did you recognise them, by the way? The blokes in the photo?'

'One of them, I think. He and Leo… they used to be friends. But then—' She stopped, uncertain how much Leo would want her to share. 'Then he turned out to be a jerk.'

'Poor Leo. I heard the names they were calling him. And I know what that's like – to be attacked for being different.' He shook his head. 'Well, goodnight then, Merry.'

'Night.'

Merry watched Ronan climb into a rather ropy-looking transit van and drive away. Once he was out of sight she locked the door and ran upstairs; it made more sense to sleep on the floor next to Leo rather than wake him up again. She grabbed her duvet and pillow and was about to leave the room when she noticed her wardrobe was open. Frowning, she twisted the key back and forth in the lock a couple of times. She could have sworn she'd locked it earlier. But of course the trinket box was still there, hidden at the back under a couple of bags. Locking the wardrobe door, she leant against it for a moment, squeezing her eyes shut, yawning.

She'd been meaning to put a warding spell on the wardrobe. It was definitely on her to-do list. But it could wait until morning. Proper morning, not middle-of-the night morning.

After all, the job the box was created for was finished. No one would be interested in it now.

Merry woke about three hours later with an aching back and cramp in one foot. Leo was still fast asleep on the sofa. Carefully she peeled back one of the gauze pads; underneath was fresh, unbroken skin, only slightly pink. His eye still looked terrible, though. Worse, if anything, than last night. Bile rose in Merry's throat.

That Simon is such a horrible, vicious, evil…

There weren't any adjectives bad enough. She went upstairs to get dressed.

Merry ran the whole way to Simon's parents' house, and with each step she planned her revenge, each scenario darker than the last: baldness – skin disease – crippling, incurable pain. Horns growing out of his head; horns and a long, forked tail, so everyone would know exactly what he was. By now it was a little past five, and she was standing on the driveway next to Simon's car – much newer and shinier than Leo's crappy black Peugeot. The sun had only just risen and no one was around. Simon's bedroom was the front right window. She could put a curse on him easily. As easy as breathing.

I haven't taken the coven's oath yet.

I can do exactly what I like.

Merry raised her hands. She felt the power building at her fingertips, pulsing underneath her skin. The air around her began to shimmer slightly in the pale grey light.

And yet...

And yet she hadn't ever actually cursed anyone. She'd defended herself against Gwydion, but that wasn't the same as deliberately choosing to hurt someone. Someone who had no chance of fighting back.

She gritted her teeth in frustration, nails aching with the build-up of magic. What was the point in being a witch, of having all this power, if she couldn't take revenge on the guy who'd beaten up her brother?

Get on with it, Merry. Do it. Punish him…

The pain got worse. Any minute now she was going to lose control. She wanted to lose control…

'Hell—' Merry jerked her hands downwards just as the power exploded silently out of her fingers, sending it across Simon's car, gouging deep grooves into the paintwork and the glass, warping the metal, taking chunks out of the hubcaps.

The pain faded to a tingling, fizzing sensation. When that had faded too, Merry lowered her hands.

The car was a wreck. As she watched, one of the hubcaps fell off and rolled away into the street. *Better than nothing*. But she didn't smile as she turned away.

Leo was in the kitchen when she got home.

'Where have you been?' His one good eye peered at her suspiciously.

'Er… out for a run.' There had been running involved, after all. 'I woke up early.'

'Want some coffee?'

Merry nodded and leant against the counter next to her brother.

'How are you feeling?' She studied his face. 'Everything looks normal again. Apart from your eye. Your eye is hideous.'

'Gee, thanks.' Leo put two mugs of coffee on the table and sat down. 'Hope I don't put you off your breakfast.'

'Don't be mean. I'm worried about you. Are you going to visit Gran?'

'Obviously.'

It was hardly obvious, given how argumentative her brother was being. But Merry let it slide.

'Want some toast?'

He nodded, so she went to get the bread out, wondering whether she should mention that she knew about Simon. Leo was just sitting there, slouched over his coffee cup. She watched him for a few moments. Maybe she should keep her mouth shut and let him bring it up when he was ready. Besides, if he found out what happened to Simon's car, and he knew that she knew…

Stick to casual conversation. That was a good idea. She put their breakfast on the table and sat down again.

'So… that was lucky. That guy coming along last night. Ronan.'

No reply.

'He said he was a wanderer. He's living in a tent in the woods. Near the lake.'

'I know. He told me about it while he was driving me home.'

'Oh.' Merry took a bite of toast. 'Not sure I'd fancy it, though, even if he'd chosen a different location: all the creepy-crawlies. Plus, not having a shower, or a washing machine.'

Leo pushed his plate away.

'You're so… judge-y. There's nothing wrong with not having much. I bet he's a nicer person than lots of the people round here with loads of money.'

Merry rolled her eyes.

'Give me a break, Leo. I didn't mean—'

'They were beating the crap out of me, Merry. I might have ended up in hospital if it hadn't been for Ronan. It was… terrible.'

'I know. I'm really sorry.'

Leo bit his lip, pressing the heel of one hand against his uninjured eye.

'I just…'

'What?'

He shook his head. 'Doesn't matter.'

Merry could almost hear her brother's agony, like he was screaming inside his head, reliving the betrayal and the pain. She wanted to hug him and shake him at the same time, to tell him that she knew the truth and that he didn't have to suffer on his own.

'Leo—'

'Don't, Merry.' He stood up. 'I know what you're going to ask. But I didn't see them properly. And even if I had recognised them —' He seemed to catch his breath, a quick, shuddering gasp that he turned into a cough — 'even if I had, I can fight my own battles. I don't need you to — to run around after me like I'm a child, like you're trying to fix my life.' He turned to leave the room, but stopped to add: 'Even a witch can't just wave a magic wand and make everything better. You should know that by now.'

He left the kitchen and stomped up the stairs. A few moments later, Merry heard the bathroom door slam.

She sighed and started clearing the table. So much for casual conversation.

They had to get a bus to Gran's house. Leo didn't feel comfortable driving with one eye out of use. The journey

– luckily – wasn't long. They sat on the top deck, Leo wearing his sunglasses, staring out of the window and drumming his fingers on his knees. Merry tried to talk to him about Ellie Mills and the other dead witches, and the story she'd read, but his replies were monosyllabic. Eventually she gave up and started looking at some new photos Ruby had posted on Instagram: her dad's parents on their farm, windswept on the north Norfolk coast, interspersed with pictures of her cousins in St Lucia, smiling and squinting in the sunshine. She scrolled up and down through the photos hungrily.

Must be nice, having a normal family. Without quite so much drama.

Fifteen minutes later they were on Gran's doorstep. As usual, the door opened as they approached. Gran was on the phone when they walked in, but she waved them through to the kitchen, finished her call and gave Leo a hug.

'My poor darling. Let me have a look.'

Leo took off his sunglasses and Gran tilted his head towards the light.

'Nasty. But easily dealt with. I'm surprised you couldn't take care of it, Merry.'

'Well, the lotion didn't work. And I have been practising

that spell you showed me, but I'm still not confident about actually using it.' She dropped her gaze. 'I fixed everything else, though.'

'Hmm.' Gran pursed her lips. 'Well, it won't take long.'

Merry and Leo sat down at the kitchen table. Gran got a tall green bottle out of one of the cupboards and poured a little of the liquid – violently pink and viscous – on to a cloth. Merry caught the scent of lavender, masking something else: something darker and more pungent.

'OK, Leo. I need you to hold the cloth over your eye. The spell is effective but rather painful, unfortunately. The liquid on the cloth will take the edge off.'

Leo blanched. 'Actually, maybe I should wait for it to get better on its own.'

'Don't be a baby. Sit still.'

Leo glanced at his sister apprehensively. Merry shrugged and tried to look sympathetic – *There's no point arguing, this is Gran we're dealing with* – and took hold of his free hand. As he pressed the damp cloth to his swollen eye, Gran placed her hands over his and began to sing.

Merry recognised the words. She'd sung them herself often enough, though with no discernible effect. The charm was in Latin, the rough sense of it being an order to the skin to knit back together, repair and renew itself.

And it seemed to be working: Leo was gritting his teeth, holding her hand so tightly her fingers hurt. Finally, the last note of the last phrase died away. Leo slumped forward, gasping for breath.

'Well done, darling.' Gran pulled his hand and the cloth away from his eye: the skin round his eye was slightly pink, like underneath a scab, but the cuts and the bruising had all but disappeared. As Merry watched, even the pinkness faded, until it was impossible to tell that he'd ever been injured. Leo blinked, opening one eye then the other.

'My vision's a bit blurry.'

'It will settle down soon.' Gran turned to Merry. 'That's what you need to aim for.'

'Fine, I understand.' Merry tried to keep the frustration out of her voice. 'But what about the guys who attacked him? Leo's refusing to go to the police.' She waved at Leo's face. 'And you just got rid of the evidence.'

'Merry—' Leo began, but Gran cut across him.

'Leo should have gone to the police last night. You should have called them when he got home.'

Merry huffed. So somehow this was her fault too?

'But,' Gran continued, 'since he didn't want to, the best we can do is put some charms on your brother, protect him from any further physical attacks. I'm sure you can manage it.'

'But that's ridiculous! He could have been killed. Even with the oath, there must be something you could do to – to find out who it was.' She felt her face flush. 'To punish them.'

Gran put her hands on her hips.

'What are you expecting, Merry? That we should choose which laws to enforce, decide who's guilty and hand out sentences? Those things can't be up to us. It would be too dangerous. Can you imagine a world where people with our kind of power set themselves up in judgement?'

Merry didn't reply. She understood what Gran was saying. But for Simon to escape scot-free after what he'd done to Leo – it was just wrong.

Gran was checking Leo's eye again.

'Vision better?'

Leo nodded. 'Thanks, Gran.'

'OK. Now, you can stay if you like, but I have a lot of work to get on with. I've had a visitor already this morning and he's put me terribly behind.' She turned away and started gathering up some papers that were spread out across the countertop.

'Anyone we know?'

Gran shook her head.

'A wizard.'

Merry's hands gripped the edge of her seat.

'A wizard? But why did he come here? And why did you let him in?'

Her grandmother finished putting the papers in order – murmuring something to herself as she did so – before turning back to them.

'It's customary, if a new witch or wizard moves into the area of an established coven, to visit the head of that coven. Out of courtesy.' Gran sighed, clearly exasperated. 'Honestly, Merry, there's no need for you to be quite so anxious. There are no wizards I trust, only a handful I can tolerate and perhaps two that I count as friends. And I certainly wouldn't be happy about you spending any more time with a wizard than was strictly necessary. But they are not all deliberately obnoxious. And I know no actual harm of the one who visited me this morning. He's young, and he obviously has only a slight idea of correct etiquette, but I suppose I shouldn't hold that against him.'

Merry loosened her grip on the chair fractionally. Obviously, not all wizards were going to be psychopathic crazy guys like Gwydion. Even so. She glanced at her brother, but he was yawning and looking deeply uninterested in the whole conversation.

'Fine.' She stood up. 'We may as well go – we have to catch the bus back. Bye, Gran.'

'Don't forget our training session.'

'I won't forget.'

Much as I'd like to.

But that never seemed to be an option.

FIVE

THE BUS TURNED up, eventually. As they queued to get on, Merry spotted one of Leo's old school friends already on the bus, but her brother didn't seem to notice him. He went upstairs to the stiflingly hot top deck, dropped into a seat at the back, pulled an ancient iPod out of his pocket and put his headphones on.

Merry did the same for a while, sinking into the music, singing along inside her head, tapping out the rhythms on her knee. The muggy air and the glare of the sun through the window was making her eyelids heavy. But she suddenly realised that having Leo next to her was too good an opportunity to waste: the way he'd been recently, she didn't know when she'd next get to talk to him alone. She paused her playlist and nudged him with her elbow.

'What?' He pulled one earbud out.

'I was wondering, when do you want me to put the protective charms on you? I need to look some stuff up, and I'm going to be working at the cafe this afternoon, but I could have a go this evening if you like.'

'Don't bother. I'll be fine.' He pushed the earbud back in.

Merry yanked it out again.

'Hey!' Leo glared at her.

'What do you mean, "I'll be fine"? You don't know that. I have to keep you safe, and witchcraft is the only way I can do it.'

'Witchcraft?' He groaned, running one hand through his hair. 'You all act like it's so great, but it isn't. Charms and spells and curses… It was magic that got you involved with Gwydion. It was magic that killed Jack.' He shifted in his seat, turning away from her.

Merry stared at the back of his head for a few moments. He was sort of right, but…

'What about your eye, though? And all the other injuries

you had?' She poked him in the back. 'Magic fixed you. Otherwise you'd still be lying in bed bleeding.'

Leo swung round.

'Well, that's another problem, isn't it? I'm going to medical school in September, supposedly. I'm going to have to study for five years and train for even longer so I can be a doctor. But what's the point?' He flung his hands up in a shrug. 'Why should I bother when Gran can throw some pink liquid around, sing a few bars of terrible music and heal me, just like that?'

Merry opened her mouth to reply, but Leo wasn't done.

'You lot have all this power, but who benefits? Your families, maybe. And a handful of locals who still believe the legends and stories, and aren't too proud to go to the resident wise woman when they need some help. Nobody else. Oh, you go on about protecting your identities like you're so many superheroes. But you're selfish, basically. You just want to keep the power to yourselves.'

'That's not true! You know it's not true. People would be terrified of us if we didn't keep it secret.' Merry looked around at the empty seats as if they might give her some inspiration. 'Helping people without them knowing that we're helping them is really hard. And the coven aren't perfect. But they try. You know they try.'

Her brother shrugged, crossed his arms and sank lower in his seat.

'They helped me, back in April.' She paused. 'Or would you rather they hadn't bothered?'

'Course not.' Leo was flicking the on-off switch of the iPod back and forth with his thumbnail. 'Of course I'm glad they helped you. And I'm glad you could stop Gwydion.' He stared at her, searching her face. 'You know that, right?'

Merry nodded. 'Yeah.'

'But I…' he sighed. 'I dunno. I'm tired, I guess. I need…'

'What?'

Leo twitched one eyebrow upwards.

'To get away from here, maybe. Lately, I feel like something about this place is sort of… sucking at me. Sucking away my energy.' He yawned and rubbed his eyes. 'Ignore me. Like I said, I'm tired.' He glanced out of the window. 'It's nearly our stop. Come on.'

They walked in silence back to the house, Merry trailing a few steps behind her brother, watching his hunched shoulders. It was hardly surprising he was in a bad mood, given what he'd just been through. She could still feel the pain she'd sensed earlier, like a long, continuous howl of anguish. Was it new, this agony? Or had it been there all the while and she'd just been too wrapped up in witchcraft and in her own loss to notice it?

I wish I could make him better. I wish, I wish.

Not paying attention, she turned off the road and bumped straight into Leo, standing motionless in middle of the driveway.

A transit van was parked in front of the house. And there, sitting on the front step, was Ronan.

He glanced up from his phone and smiled at them.

Leo turned and looked at her, his eyes wide, and Merry knew her brother was thinking the same thing: how on earth were they going to explain Leo's miraculous recovery?

Ronan was walking towards them. There were spells to alter perception and memory, but Merry didn't know them off by heart. Meanwhile Leo was fumbling in his bag for his sunglasses, but it was definitely going to be too late.

'Leo!' Ronan clapped one hand on Leo's shoulder. 'You look great. So much better than yesterday.' He scanned Leo's face. 'So much better than I expected, to be honest.'

For a moment nobody spoke. Merry could feel the blood rushing up to crimson her face. Leo, also scarlet, was staring at the tarmacked ground. She had to think of something. She had at least to say something.

'Um…'

'Are you a witch?' Ronan suddenly asked. 'Or do you just happen to know one?'

Leo's head snapped up. He took a step sideways to stand in front of Merry.

'What do you want?'

Ronan laughed.

'Relax. I'm not about to reach for my pitchfork and start trying to burn people at the stake. Not my style.'

Leo didn't move.

'I said, what do you want?'

Ronan backed away a little, holding his hands up, palms out.

'Really, I just came to see how you were doing. And I know about witches because I'm one too. Well –' he shrugged – 'a wizard. So can I put my hands down now? Please?'

A wizard?

Merry didn't know how to react. Sure, she was relieved that she didn't have to come up with some plausible explanation for Leo's unbruised features. But her brain was simultaneously sending a massive, flashing 'DANGER!' alert to the rest of her body. Her fingernails started to tingle.

Get a grip, Merry. Get a grip.

'A wizard?' Leo exhaled loudly, shaking his head. 'Sure, you can put your hands down. Why didn't you say something last night?'

'Generally, I don't go around advertising the fact to folks I don't know. They tend not to react so well. Besides, my healing spells aren't all that great, to be honest. I didn't think I could do anything to help.'

'Are you kidding? You saved my life.' Leo stuck his hand out. 'I owe you one.'

'It was my pleasure.' Ronan took Leo's hand. But instead of shaking it, he pulled Leo into a brief hug. 'Honestly, any time. So,' he glanced at Merry, 'are we good?'

Were they? Merry hesitated. Gran had told her – less than two hours ago – that wizards were untrustworthy. But this one had actually rescued her brother. Had turned up again today to visit him. And there was Leo looking all… smiley.

What wouldn't I put up with to have Leo happy again?

'Of course.' She nodded. 'We're good.'

'Grand.' He smiled. 'So, listen, I have to take off, but I wonder if you fancy watching the footy tomorrow? We could go to one of the pubs in town, have a couple of drinks…' He trailed off, looking enquiringly at Leo.

Obviously, the invitation wasn't meant for both of them. Leo was already nodding enthusiastically.

'Definitely, sounds great.'

'Excellent. Here's my number.' Ronan pulled a pen out of his pocket, took Leo's hand in his and wrote on the back of it. 'Text me later and I'll tell you which pub I'm going to.' He waved at Merry and climbed into the van. She watched as he reversed out of the driveway and took off in the direction of the Black Lake.

'Huh.' Ronan was not what she'd expected, when Gran talked about a visiting wizard. Because it had to be him; how many wizards could there be, wandering around an average market town at the edge of Surrey? Clearly, not all wizards were going to be like Gwydion. But she'd still expected someone… weirder. She turned to say as much to Leo, but he was gazing at the mobile phone number Ronan had scrawled across the back of his hand. Now that *was* weird – too familiar, almost, from someone he hardly knew.

'I wonder why he didn't just get his phone out and text you.'

Leo pulled a face. 'Why? This was just as quick.'

'I s'pose.' Merry turned towards the house, but her brother put out a hand to stop her.

'Hey – don't tell Gran that I'm going to the pub with Ronan. You heard what she said this morning, about wizards.'

He was right; Gran was unlikely to be thrilled.

'Sure. I won't say anything.'

'Thanks.'

A car turned into the driveway: their mother, back home from her yoga retreat. Merry waved at her and went to open the front door. 'And just remember,' Leo called out behind her, 'I'm allowed to have my own life. OK?'

No more spying on him, in other words.

OK, Leo. I'll remember.

'Mum, I'm going up.' Merry yawned and rubbed the muscles in the back of her neck. It was Friday evening – only 10.30, but she was definitely feeling a bit... bleugh. Lack of sleep combined with working all afternoon at Mrs Galantini's cafe in town (her new summer job) and all the drama with Leo. 'I think the cats are still outside.'

Her mother didn't reply; she just kept scrolling up and down through a document that was open on her laptop. It didn't look like she was actually reading any of it.

'Mum? You OK?'

'Huh?'

'I'm going to bed.'

'Oh, all right. Do you know where the cats are?'

Merry frowned. 'Outside, I think.'

Merry thought yoga was meant to relax you, but Mum had been restless all evening, fidgeting with stuff in the kitchen during dinner, rearranging cushions on the sofa while they were trying to watch TV. Leo had taken himself off upstairs at that point, having barely spoken two words to Merry since their conversation on the driveway earlier.

'Is anything wrong?'

'No, not really. I just feel a bit…' Mum scrunched her face up. 'You know that sensation of chalk squeaking against a blackboard?' She laughed a little. 'Probably not. Do they even have blackboards at school these days?'

'No,' Merry shook her head, 'but I remember from nursery.' And she remembered the feeling she'd had the other evening, that odd sensation of things being out of kilter.

'Ignore me.' Mum shut her laptop and got up. 'There's too much magic in the house at the moment, what with the cooling spells you're using and the extra protection runes I asked the coven to apply. It gets to you sometimes. Gets to me, at any rate. Makes my skin crawl.'

Too much magic? Merry wasn't really sure what her mother meant. She glanced out of the window, but all she could see was her and Mum, their reflections broken into a mosaic by the leaded glass.

'Do you want me to lift the cooling spells?'

'Course not. Not until this heatwave breaks.' Mum reached for the light switch. 'Bedtime. Night, sweetheart.'

Merry got into bed, but sleep wouldn't come. However tired her body was, her mind refused to switch off. After a couple of hours she got bored with lying in the dark, turned on the lamp and picked up her journey book from the bedside table. In the back she had tucked the list of spells that she was supposed to be practising before her next training session with Gran.

She glanced over the list and tried to pick the most straightforward: a shifting spell, which enabled the caster to make an object disappear from one place and reappear in another. Eventually, some witches got so good at this type of magic that they could transport themselves instantly – a charm known unofficially as the 'broomstick spell' – which sounded *really* handy. She leant on her elbow for a moment, imagining herself zipping around magically: no need for buses or a car, or plane tickets… Unfortunately, getting a broomstick spell wrong tended to have terminal consequences – Gran had made her swear not even to attempt it. Not yet, anyway. All she was supposed to do at the moment was to pick an object and move it a short distance by singing the charm and visualising the spot where she wanted the object to materialise.

How hard could it be?

Merry scanned her room and spotted – forgotten and dusty on top of her wardrobe – a unicorn snowglobe that she'd been given one Christmas several years ago by a would-be boyfriend of her mum's. The unicorn inside was pale pink, with a dark pink bushy mane and tail and an oversized gold horn. It looked a bit grumpy, unsurprisingly.

She placed the globe on the floor in the middle of the room, sat down cross-legged in front of it and began to chant the short phrase over and over. While she was chanting, she pictured the exact spot on the dressing table where she wanted it to appear. Gradually, the globe started to fade, until she could see the carpet through it. She closed her eyes, trying to get inside the spell, to feel the magic rippling through her, the power of the words...

Something skittered across the background of her mind, and as she winced and screwed her eyes tighter shut, trying to identify the distraction, her magic tumbled out of control. There was a loud thump and the brittle clink of shattering glass.

The snowglobe was embedded in the wall above the dressing table.

'Oh, for…' The glass orb had smashed and glittery water was soaking into the carpet. Half of the base and about two-thirds of the unicorn were protruding from the wall, as if the bedroom had been built and plastered around them. She tugged at the unicorn's head, but it wouldn't budge.

This wasn't a healing spell, or something with five hundred different components that she had to remember in the right order. It should have been easy. But she'd lost focus and her magic had gone wild. Again. She could imagine a couple of the less friendly members of the coven shaking their heads and tutting. *That Meredith Cooper. Calls herself a witch, but she still can't master her power. Can't be in the coven if she can't be trusted.*

Well. Maybe she didn't want to be in the damn coven. Gritting her teeth, she glared at the sparkling shards of glass scattered across the carpet, ordering them to *get into the bin*! A tiny whirlwind swept up the fragments and deposited them in the wastepaper basket.

So was it just that sudden distraction that had messed

up the shifting spell? Such a strange sensation, like a spider running across the inside of her brain. Merry paused by the window. Something on the other side of the glass caught her attention; some fluctuation of patterns or textures, out there in the darkness. Peering into the shadows, she picked up a hint of that same discord she'd felt two nights ago, standing on the threshold of the kitchen.

And there it was, at the edge of the laurel tree next to the gate: an indistinct shape that could almost, if she squinted at it, be the outline of a man. A patch of light that could just possibly be the moonlight reflecting off blond hair.

Merry unlatched the window so she could lean out, half opened her lips to call Jack's name…

But then clouds scudded across the moon, and her eyes watered a little from staring so hard, and the laurel tree was just a tree, after all.

She took a deep, jagged breath. Jack was dead. Dead and buried underneath the Black Lake. It had been too much, the last couple of days: the unexplained witch deaths and Leo seeing ghosts and being beaten up by Simon and—

She didn't want to do this again. To be the person who couldn't sleep because of strange dreams, the weirdo who saw visions in broad daylight.

Whatever was trying to happen – if anything *was* trying to happen – she wasn't going to allow it.

Merry went to her desk, opened one of the drawers and pulled out a knife. Her new silver-bladed knife, with an ash handle. Obsidian knives, like Gran had, were the best, but silver was still good for conducting magic and warding off evil. Returning to the window, she reassured herself that Mum wouldn't care, and carved a mark deeply into the sill: Algiz, the rune for protection and defence.

The fragrance of roses wafted through the open window, so cloying it made her feel slightly sick. She slammed the window shut, slipped into bed and turned out the light.

★   ★   ★

Leo was at the Black Lake again. It was late; the faint pearl sheen of moonlight slanted through the clouds. He could make out the shape of a tent a few metres away. As he watched, a figure emerged from the tent and walked towards him. He couldn't tell who it was. Until an orb of purple light appeared in the hand of the stranger, illuminating his face: Ronan.

'I'm glad you're here, Leo. He's been waiting such a long time for you to come back. To finally set him free.' Ronan raised an arm and pointed towards the lake. Another shadowy outline had appeared at the edge of it.

Leo gasped.

Dan.

Leo ran towards his friend, shouting his name. Dan took a few paces in Leo's direction before stumbling, falling forward into Leo's arms.

'Dan!'

But there was no answer, no heartbeat.

He lowered Dan's body softly on to the grass. Moonlight struck the sword hilt protruding from his chest, silvering the gold.

Dan was already dead. Once again, he was too late.

Leo woke with a jolt, his heart pounding. He collapsed back on the pillow and looked around his room. He reached over, squinted at his alarm clock and groaned. Time to get up for work already. He was almost tempted to turn over and go back to sleep, maybe call in sick. Prising himself out of bed just seemed like far too much effort. But then he remembered: that afternoon, after work, he was meeting Ronan. He lifted his hand, glanced at the faint trace of biro still left on his skin and smiled. For the first time in what felt like ages, he was almost excited about something.

★

Six hours at the farm dragged by, but eventually Leo was back home, taking a shower and having a bite to eat. Mum was around but Merry had gone out and, for some reason, Leo was relieved that his little sister wasn't there.

Ronan had suggested they meet at the Albany, a pub on the outskirts of Tillingham that Leo was able to walk to in twenty minutes. It was a Saturday afternoon and unsurprisingly the pub was heaving, people spilling out along the pavement in front. Leo went in and stood on tiptoe to scan the bar area, but he couldn't see Ronan anywhere. He pushed his way through to the back of the pub and the deck that overlooked the river: there was still no sign of him. Leo checked his phone, but there were no messages. Perhaps he had misunderstood the plan? Or… or what if Ronan just wasn't coming? What if he'd only invited Leo out of pity, and had now found something else to do, or someone better to hang out with?

Leo took a deep breath. He ordered a drink and found a spot where he could lean against the bar and wait.

Fifteen minutes later, he was still standing there on his own. His face began to burn: he'd been stood up. He looked around at the other people in the pub, laughing and chatting to each other, and sighed. This used to be one of his favourite hangouts, but he didn't seem to fit in any more. Not here. Not with his old friends. Not even at home.

Leo finished his drink and started to walk towards the door.

SIX

LEO JUMPED AS someone tapped him on the shoulder. It was Ronan.

'Leo – you're here.' Ronan swore and shook his head, laughing. 'I thought you weren't going to show. I've been waiting out front, but I must have missed you.' He frowned. 'Are you OK, mate?'

Leo started rubbing his eye, which allowed him to turn his head away and at least partially cover his face.

'Yeah, fine. Just a bit of hay fever, that's all.' He sniffed. 'One of the perils of working on a farm. That, and getting your leg chopped off by a combine harvester.' Hopefully Ronan would put the flush on his face down to an allergy, instead of a sudden burst of relief and happiness. 'Can I get you a drink?'

'My shout. What's your poison?'

'A pint of Hogs Back.'

'Anything else? You're entitled to three wishes, you know. By tradition.' Ronan winked and Leo laughed.

'Fine. A packet of crisps and a sports car too, please. Red, preferably.'

Ronan turned towards the bar.

'I'll see what I can do.'

Including injury time, the match lasted nearly two hours, but the time raced by. Ronan was entertaining and laid-back, and Leo let his guard down almost without meaning to. He hadn't felt this relaxed around anyone – other than Merry – for as long as he could remember. Of course, it didn't hurt that Ronan was also easy on the eye. More than once Leo found himself staring at him. Luckily, Ronan didn't seem to notice. Now, the post-match analysis was over and the pub was emptying out. Ronan stood up and stretched.

'It's still early. D'you fancy coming back to mine for a drink? I could probably pull together a bacon sarnie, if you're hungry.'

Leo nodded, ignoring the swirl of nerves in the pit of his stomach.

'Sure. That sounds good.' He tried to silence the almost-hysterical voice in the back of his head asking whether this was turning into a date. So far, the guy had been fantastically kind and nice to him. But that was no reason to assume he was gay. Maybe he was just lonely. Maybe he just needed someone to hang out with.

And that was fine. Leo had nothing better to do.

Ronan's van was parked in a side road. As they climbed in, he apologised for the mess.

'I've never got the hang of those instant transport spells, so I'm stuck with this rust bucket till I can save up for a Land Rover.'

'Don't worry about it.' Leo studied Ronan's profile as he started driving. 'I'd almost forgotten that you're a wizard.'

'Really? I'll take that as a compliment. So what's it like, living in a magical family?'

'Oh, you know. It's OK. Most of the time.' Leo didn't really feel like telling Ronan about Jack and Gwydion. Not yet, anyway.

'Your sister seems cool. Must be nice to have someone care about you that much.'

'It is. We're close and we get on fine.'

There was obviously something in the tone of Leo's voice, some shadow of hesitation, because then Ronan asked: 'Most of the time?'

'Yeah, well… We've had the occasional argument recently.'

'Ah.' Ronan shook his head, turning the corners of his mouth down in mock despair. 'Witches. Almost impossible to understand, reason with or control.' He waited for a lorry to go past. 'Treacherous creatures, my mam used to say.'

That made Leo smile.

'I think witches might say the same about wizards, from what I've heard. You don't have any siblings?'

'No. No family at all. But it's OK. I like my own company. And I occasionally run into other lost souls in my travels.'

They turned on to a dirt track leading into the woods. Ronan jolted the van along for a while – Leo expected a tyre to burst with every pothole they hit – until they came out into a clearing. He swallowed hard as the Black Lake came into view, just visible through the trees on the far side. In the middle of the clearing was a tent. A lone figure – a younger guy, perhaps sixteen – stood just outside it, putting the finishing touches to a small campfire.

Disappointment drenched Leo like a cold shower. Clearly, this wasn't a date. Embarrassed that the thought had even occurred to him, he considered just going home. But Ronan had already opened the passenger door, waiting for him.

'Leo, this is Ethan. He accosted me outside the off-licence in town last week, tried to convince me to buy him some booze. But now –' Ronan clapped a hand on Ethan's shoulder, as the younger guy laughed self-consciously – 'now he's agreed to stick to the straight and narrow, in return for me letting him hang around. To watch and learn.' Ronan grinned, whispered something under his breath and held out his arm. There was a rustle and a squawk from a nearby tree and seconds later a large black bird – a carrion crow, Leo guessed – dropped out of the sky and descended on to Ronan's outstretched palm. He ran one finger down the bird's back, and as he did so its feathers changed to a sparkling gold before returning to their natural colour.

'Awesome. You gonna teach me that?' Ethan asked.

'Once you've mastered the basics.' Ronan threw the bird back up into the air and watched it fly away. 'Have a seat, Leo.' The three of them sat down round the campfire, which luckily – magically? – didn't seem to be giving out much heat. Ronan handed Leo a beer and passed a can of Coke to Ethan. 'Why don't you show me how your levitation is coming along?'

Almost before Ronan had finished speaking, Ethan jumped up and ordered Leo to 'Look at this!' before waving his hands in the air above the chair he'd been sitting in. The chair began to float a metre or so above the grass.

It wasn't the most impressive magic Leo had ever seen, not by a long stretch. But still.

'Wow. So is Ethan a wizard too?' Leo glanced at Ronan, who chuckled.

'No. I'm just giving him an introduction to –' The floating chair dropped to the ground and Ethan swore – 'the magical arts. Are you all right there, Ethan?'

'Yeah.' Ethan sat down again. 'But I might be a wizard one day. That's what you said, Ronan. That I had a gift.' He cast an odd look at Leo, something between a sneer and a glare.

Ronan reached forward and patted the boy on the shoulder.

'For sure, one day. Just keep practising.'

After that the mood of the little party changed. Ethan clearly wanted to keep talking about magic, describing to

Leo all the things Ronan had taught him so far, but Ronan changed the subject each time and started chatting – mainly to Leo – about the football game that they had watched earlier. After another half an hour Ethan got up and said he was leaving, muttering something about an early start the next morning. Leo watched him traipse across the field and back up to the main road.

'I could teach you too, you know, Leo. If you wanted me to.'

'Magic? No. Merry's the one with all the power. I haven't got a magical bone in my body.'

'I'm not so sure. I've a feeling for these things. I can sort of… sense the power in others. And I think you could be like your sister. You could be one of us, with some training.'

'Me?'

'Yes.' Ronan leant forward. 'To be honest, Ethan's not special. I'm just teaching him a few parlour tricks to keep the poor lad happy and off the streets. But you… You've got magic in your blood. Imagine what you might be able to do, with a little training.'

Leo laughed. 'It's nice of you to say so, but I'm fine the way I am. I've seen what magic can do to people. No offence, but I'd rather not get involved.'

Ronan raised an eyebrow, but didn't push it any further and settled back into his chair. They chatted for another ten minutes or so. But then Leo glanced at his phone and wondered whether he was in danger of overstaying his welcome. He pushed himself up from the deckchair.

'Thanks for tonight, Ronan. It's been fun. But I'd better get going. It's a bit of a walk back home.'

'Are you sure? It's still early for me.'

'Well…' Leo hesitated. He wanted to stay. But it was late. And if he freaked Merry out too much she might decide to spy on him again. He definitely wasn't keen on his sister seeing him alone here with Ronan. 'Sorry. I really need to get some sleep. There's stuff going on tomorrow.'

'OK. But let me drive you back. I wouldn't want you to run into any more trouble now, would I?' He grinned. 'I know how hard you non-magical types find it to look after yourselves.'

★ ★ ★

'He's teaching people magic? Really?'

Merry was sitting on Leo's bed, eating ice cream straight from the tub. She'd lost the fencing match she'd taken part in earlier that evening. But on the upside, her brother seemed to be talking to her again. Leo grabbed the ice-cream tub and took a big scoop.

'Well, he said this guy Ethan doesn't have much talent, but he's clearly managed to teach him something.'

Merry snorted; she couldn't help herself. 'He's having you on, Leo. Magical ability is something you inherit.'

At least, it was for witches. She supposed it might be different for wizards, but that different? 'I doubt that any old nobody could suddenly learn how to do magic.'

'*Any old nobody?* Such as me, you mean?' He scowled at her. 'I didn't realise how superior you were, Merry. Must be a real drag for you to have to hang around with the likes of me.'

Merry groaned. 'Oh, come on, Leo. Can you think of a single member of the coven that has a son who's a wizard? It doesn't work like that. And I'm not being superior – I'm just being honest.'

Her brother didn't answer. Just dug more ice cream out of the tub.

Merry bit her lip as she watched him. 'Did he offer to teach you?'

'What if he did?' Leo paused, contemplating his ice cream. 'Doesn't matter, does it? According to you I'm too ordinary to be a wizard. So it would be rather pointless of him to try, wouldn't it?'

Surely he wasn't actually jealous? The possibility that

Leo might resent her abilities had never even occurred to her. He'd said often enough that he was the lucky one, that her power was more of a burden than anything else.

'But, Leo, magic is dangerous. You know that. If you—'

'Forget it, Merry. As it happens, I'm not remotely interested in learning magic, even if I could. Like you said, I've seen the damage it can do. But don't pretend this is about anything other than the fact that you like feeling special. You're the hero – I'm just the slightly useless sidekick. I get it.'

Merry could hardly believe they were having this conversation.

'That is not true. I just think that if you really had magical ability one of the many witches in your family might have noticed it by now.'

'I could have a shedload of magical ability and still no one in the coven would say anything because they hate wizards!'

They both stood up, glaring at each other.

'Sometimes you are just… impossible!' Merry grabbed the ice-cream tub, realised that Leo had eaten it all and threw it at him. She turned away too quickly to see whether he managed to catch it.

★

It took a good ten minutes of pacing in her own room before Merry even began to calm down.

I suppose I could go downstairs and tell Mum.

But what's she going to do? Forbid Leo to see Ronan again? Even Mum's not that ridiculous. Not any more. And Leo's nineteen. He's going to uni in a couple of months.

Besides, what was there actually to tell? So far Ronan seemed like a pretty decent guy. And she couldn't really blame Leo for fancying him.

God knows my brother could do with having some fun.

If he was having fun, he wouldn't have time to go around accusing people of being superior. Because it wasn't true. Yes, she liked having her power. She liked being powerful. But that was allowed. She was allowed to feel just a little bit proud of some of the stuff she could do.

Wasn't she?

How have I been acting superior anyway? I've barely talked to Leo about magic or the coven over the last couple of months. And I know he could read that manuscript when nobody else apart from me could, but surely that was just, like, a fluke…

In that instant Merry had a brainwave. Perhaps Ronan really liked Leo. Perhaps he'd made up the thing about teaching him magic to give Leo a reason to hang out with him. That made sense. So actually, she should either ask Ronan what his intentions towards her brother were – which seemed kind of awkward – or...

She got up and peered out of her bedroom. Leo's door was shut, so Merry tiptoed across the landing to the bathroom. She ran some water into the basin, realised she'd forgotten her silver bracelet and the bag of stones and went to open the door again.

No.

Maybe she was just being contrary, but Merry decided this time she was not going to bother with anything... unnecessary.

She turned back to the basin, held out her hands and just thought: *Show me Ronan.*

The surface of the water silvered and darkened again instantly. And there was Ronan, lying on his back in a sleeping bag, reading a book. Merry couldn't see the title, but it looked as though the book was funny. Ronan was laughing and shaking his head, and then...

And then, he lowered the book, turned slowly towards the perspective from which Merry was watching him – and winked.

She yanked the plug out of the basin. The scrying water

became just water again and gurgled away down the plughole.

It wasn't possible. He couldn't have seen her. But… had he *sensed* her, in some way? She thought about the last part of the incantation she should have sung: *shield the seer from all who would harm her.*

Damn.

But maybe it was nothing. He might have been winking at somebody else. And at least he was doing normal stuff. Not sitting in an underground lair, cutting out people's hearts. She shivered. Ronan was fine. No way would Gran let him stay in the area otherwise. And Leo? Ronan would probably do him some good. Give him something else – someone else – to think about.

Merry brushed her teeth, washed her face and poured herself a glass of water. Odds on, Ronan wouldn't be here very long anyway. But if he helped Leo get over what that bloody Simon had done…

There was a dull crack from the glass she was holding. The water inside had frozen solid. Merry carefully placed the broken glass and the ice in the bath and took a deep breath, waiting until the tingle of magic had ebbed away from her fingernails. She went back to her room, got into her pyjamas and switched off the light.

She could take care of herself and she could take care of Leo.

There's nothing to worry about. Nothing at all.

Merry didn't see much of Leo for the next few days. She worked three shifts at Mrs Galantini's cafe and went ice-skating with Ruby and Flo. The local gym was air-conditioned, so she went running twice too. And of course there were a couple of practice sessions with Gran. They were still – *still* – focusing on healing. Gran didn't ask her to try making the salve again, but showed Merry a spell for use on broken limbs instead. Merry tried the spell – this one was in Old English – on some fractured animal bones that Gran had got from the butcher. The first session didn't go well: the bones reassembled themselves, but they didn't knit back together, so they disintegrated again as soon as she touched them.

Merry swore and brushed the bone dust off her hands.

'Ugh. This is horrible. There's got to be an easier way. A quicker way. I bet I could figure something out.'

Gran made a disparaging noise and shook her head.

'Do you understand the construction of bones? Or the complex interweaving of the blood vessels and nerves that run through them?'

'No, but—'

'This spell was constructed, painstakingly, by a witch who did. You can't just order the bones to fix themselves and expect that it's going to come out right.' Gran sang a short phrase under her breath and the detritus covering the kitchen table came together in a heap, which then transferred itself neatly into the bin. 'Sit down.'

Merry sighed and dropped into a chair. Gran sat down opposite, gazing at her over the top of her spectacles.

'You may think, Merry, that the rules I'm insisting you follow are only there to make your life difficult. But that isn't the case. They're there to protect you too. You and others.' A shadow passed across Gran's face, sending a shiver down Merry's spine. 'You know that my sister Marianne and her daughter died.'

'Mum said they died in a car crash.'

'Well, that's what I told your mother. But it's not true. There wasn't any car crash. As I said before, witches tend not to have accidents. They actually died because my sister didn't follow the rules.'

'What?' Merry sat up straighter.

'Marianne had rather poor judgement, to say the least. She wanted to use a spell that wasn't in one of the knowledge books; something, I suspect, involving a form of prohibited magic. She wouldn't tell me exactly what she was trying to attempt, but we argued. I warned her not to do anything that would be against the rules of the coven. But she refused to listen. And –' Gran sighed and shook her head – 'she ended up buying a spell from a wizard. It was unstable, badly constructed, and when she used it…'

'It killed her?'

'It destroyed half her house. My niece was upstairs at the time, unfortunately.' Gran took her specs off and pressed her fingertips to her eyes.

'I'm sorry, Gran.'

Her grandmother plucked a tissue from the box on the table.

'It was a long time ago now. I didn't tell your mother because she was already resentful enough about inheriting the oath, and what that meant for her life. And it was too painful, admitting what my sister had done. Bronwen must have wondered, over the years, but she's never brought it up.' Gran put her specs back on and fixed Merry with a stare. 'Trading with wizards, using prohibited magic – it happens in the best families and the most organised covens. People don't like to talk about it. But most of us recognise the importance of following the rules. Do you?'

Merry nodded. She was starting to understand why Gran was so insistent on doing everything the right way, the way it had always been done.

'Are you sure, Merry? Do you realise that the rules are there for your own protection as much as for the protection of the rest of the coven?'

'I do, Gran.'

'Good.' Gran smiled and patted her on the forearm. 'Well, keep practising then, the way you've been taught. You'll get the hang of things eventually. I know you will.'

Merry spent most of the next couple of days practising the healing spell, as Gran suggested: memorising the words, pronunciation and even the correct points of emphasis in each sentence. The next time she tried it in front of Gran, there was a marked improvement. Even the worst-looking break, where the centre of the bone was fragmented into tiny pieces, came back together smoothly and cleanly. Merry picked it up and turned it over in her fingers.

'I can't believe I just did that.'

'But you did. Well done, darling. Time to try it on a person, I think.'

'What? No...' Merry backed away from the bone-scattered table. 'There's no way I'm practising on a real person. I mean, what if I make it worse, if – if their leg drops off or something?'

Gran clicked her tongue.

'Calm down, Merry. I'm not suggesting we hide outside the hospital and kidnap someone. But we're having a coven meeting tonight. It would give you the chance to practise in a controlled environment.'

Friday night. A normal almost-seventeen-year-old would be hanging out with her friends – if not a boyfriend – having a social life. Or at least hanging out online. But Ruby had left yesterday to visit her grandparents in Norfolk for a couple of days, and Merry hadn't remembered to arrange anything with anyone else. Hanging out with the coven was the only invitation she had.

Geez. I can't believe I'm agreeing to this, but…

'Sure. I can come tonight. Is it here?'

'No, Sophia Knox's house. Most of the coven will be attending.'

Great. A big audience to witness her probable humiliation.

Let's hope this time I don't blow anything up.

Mum dropped Merry off at Mrs Knox's house just after seven that evening. A lot of the witches hadn't yet arrived – apparently there was going to be some kind of late-night outing up on the Downs – but those that were there seemed distracted. Subdued. There was none of the usual smiling, chatting and catching up going on.

Gran waved over a younger witch Merry hadn't met before.

'This is Ilaria, Mrs Galantini's daughter. She's visiting from Canterbury and has very kindly volunteered to be your guinea pig.'

Merry said hello while scanning the woman's arms and legs. She couldn't see a cast or a bandage.

'Um, have you actually got anything that needs fixing?'

Ilaria laughed. She, at least, appeared to be completely unconcerned.

'Not at the moment. Elinor,' she nodded at Gran, 'is going to break my leg.'

'What?' Merry turned to Gran. 'She's joking, isn't she? You're not actually—'

'There's no need to be nervous, Merry. She won't feel a thing. Shall we begin?'

Ilaria nodded and went to sit in an armchair nearby, resting one bare leg on a footstool. Mrs Galantini came over and put a hand on her daughter's shoulder; in the other hand she held a long staff made of some dark metal; iron, perhaps. She started singing softly in Italian. Gran knelt on the floor next to the footstool and placed her hands on top of Ilaria's shin.

'Both ready? I'm going to count to three. One, two…'

Gran's hands remained rigidly still, but Ilaria's leg shuddered violently. At the same time Mrs Galantini gasped and the iron staff she was holding began to vibrate. Merry had to force herself to keep watching – the snap as the bone fractured made her squirm.

The other witches in the room stopped what they were doing and began to drift over.

'OK, Merry, dear.' Gran got up. 'In your own time. It's a simple, clean break, so do what you were doing this morning. Fix the bone, then I'll deal with the bruising and so on.'

Merry knelt in the spot Gran had just vacated. Ilaria looked completely unconcerned; she smiled at Merry and gave her a thumbs up, but Mrs Galantini was pale and frowning, still muttering words under her breath. It looked as though the pain had to go somewhere.

Huh. Shame Simon's not here. I should channel the pain into him. Maybe smash up a few of his bones for good measure.

Merry swallowed and took a couple of deep breaths. Her revenge fantasies weren't going to help right now. Laying her hands lightly on Ilaria's skin, she examined the leg. It was starting to redden and swell, and she could feel the break in the bone under her fingers.

Oh, this is so grim. Please let me not mess it up.

She cleared her throat and started to sing the words of the spell.

'*Ic singe be haele, ic sceal rihtan…*'

The broken ends of the bone began – very slowly – to come together. Ilaria didn't react, but out of the corner of her eye Merry noticed the iron staff give a sudden lurch. Gran put out a hand to steady Mrs Galantini.

'That's it, Merry. Keep going.'

She was over halfway through. The bone was correctly aligned; all she had to do now was knit it back together.

'*Séowe webteáhe, becnytte bán…*'

A sudden wash of emotions struck across the forefront of Merry's mind: jealousy, so intense she could taste its bitterness. Jealousy mingled with longing. And underneath, a deep note of hatred.

She faltered and glanced up at the other witches, but none of them seemed to have noticed anything.

Concentrate, Merry. Now is not the time.

She took another deep breath.

Um, where was I…

Her hands felt cold. She rubbed them together, placed them back on to Ilaria's leg.

But before she could say any more of the spell the bitter emotions were back, and this time there was a whispering, crystallised thought too –

Make them pay, make all of them pay...

– and an image flooded into her mind, blinding her: Gwydion, dead, with the King of Heart's cursed sword sticking out of his chest.

The half-healed shin rippled beneath Merry's touch.

Ilaria screamed, and Mrs Galantini collapsed, and Gran was pushing Merry out of the way. Because there was blood pouring out of Ilaria's leg where the bone had thrust upwards, piercing the skin.

SEVEN

THEY WERE WATCHING her, the other witches. They might think she wasn't noticing the furtive glances, or the whispered explanations to the witches who had just arrived. But she was. And maybe it was only in her imagination that the room was getting colder, but that's how it felt. Like a creeping frost was gradually building up around her, separating her from the rest of the coven – even Gran. Merry bit down on the inside of her cheek. She wasn't going to cry, not here. Glancing around the room, she found Ilaria watching her from the sofa where she was resting. Gran had fixed the compound fracture that Merry had caused and Ilaria was pale but composed. She began to raise her hand and Merry hastily looked away.

Gran and Roshni (her second-in-command) were still examining the shattered remains of the iron staff. More witches arrived. There were more hurried conversations in low voices. But no one spoke to Merry. No one came near her at all.

It wasn't my fault. I really worked at that spell. I followed all the rules.

Whatever had got inside her head – that's what caused the problems. But obviously nobody was going to believe her.

Roshni picked up the pieces of the staff and Gran – finally – came and sat down next to Merry.

'I understand that you're upset, darling. But... what happened to the staff, and to Ilaria's leg – both are consistent with the surges of power you were experiencing earlier this year. Surely, it's better just to admit you lost concentration and—'

'But I didn't, Gran, honestly. I heard this voice, like I said, and then – I couldn't see what I was doing any more. All I could see was Gwydion's dead body.'

She squeezed her eyes shut, trying to get rid of the picture inside her head. 'Do you think he's coming back? That somehow he's trying to get at me?'

'Gwydion is dead, Merry. The fact that you saw an image of him... it does suggest it was your own subconscious that caused the problem.'

Merry didn't reply. Could Gran be right? Perhaps doing magic her own way was messing up her brain, somehow. Or maybe it was because she kept listening in to other people's emotions. It wasn't exactly like she'd tried to stop it.

Gran patted her hand.

'We need to keep up your training, that's the answer. They – *we* – forget how new to this you really are. If you'd been properly taught from the beginning...' She paused, glancing at the witches congregating on the far side of the room. 'Well. There's no need for you to join in the ceremony later on. I'll drive you home.'

'Don't bother.' Merry stood and picked up her bag. It wasn't as though she'd even wanted to spend hours up on the Downs, singing to the moon or whatever they were going to be doing. She knew the rest of the coven were watching her. She could feel the weight of their gazes on her back, the sting of incomprehension and mistrust – so strong she didn't bother trying to close her mind to it.

'But, Merry...'

'Really, I'd rather walk.'

'All right.' Gran looked a bit hurt, and part of Merry was glad. 'Text me when you get home, though. I'm going away tomorrow for a few nights, but—'

'Where are you going?'

'Salisbury.' Gran bent closer, almost whispering in Merry's ear. 'There's been another unexpected death, and whatever Roshni says, I can't ignore it. I'm going to visit an old friend down there who might have some information.'

A few nights away meant a few days without any training. A few days away from all of this. Merry felt as if her eyes were brightening with relief, but Gran didn't seem to notice.

'Call me if you have any more… visions,' she continued, 'and keep an eye on Leo too.'

Merry nodded. She thought about saying goodbye to Ilaria – about saying sorry. But she couldn't. Facing any of the other witches at this moment was impossible. She kept her gaze fixed on the floor and hurried out of the room.

Mrs Knox's house wasn't that far from Merry's home; the walk usually took her about half an hour, so the lengthening shadows didn't bother her. There was no pavement; instead, she walked parallel to the road, keeping to the edge of the woods. She moved briskly, trying to clear her head and forget about what had happened at the coven meeting.

It wasn't really working.

Every broken tree branch reminded her of the bones in Ilaria's leg, twisting apart under her hands. The reeds that lined the tiny stream, standing up like spears, brought back the image of the sword sticking out of Gwydion's chest. And the rush of envy that had overwhelmed her still seemed to hang around her like a cloud; she could almost taste the bitterness at the back of her throat. It mingled with her anger against Gran, the conviction that somehow this was her grandmother's fault for not forcing Mum to let her train at the age of twelve, for allowing her to turn into some sort of magical freak. She ended up going over and over the healing spell in her head, hoping to pinpoint where she had gone wrong. It wasn't until she tripped on a tree root that she looked around and realised she was completely lost.

Merry turned, trying to work out how long ago she had strayed into the woods. Up above her the sky was a deep blue-black, the first stars shining vividly, just a hint of daylight far over to the west.

OK. This is annoying. But nothing I can't handle.

She conjured a ball of witch fire and set it bobbing in the air above her. This part of the woods was completely unfamiliar. Instead of the usual collection of birch, oak and Scots pine, the trees here were mostly dark evergreens, crowded together; a thick carpet of needles muffled her footsteps. Merry strained to hear traffic, anything that might give her a clue as to which way she should go.

There was something. A sort of... moaning. Following the sound, she pushed through a narrow gap between two thick-trunked yew trees, so close and spreading she had to duck down to clamber under their lowest branches. On the other side was a clearing.

Merry conjured two more balls of witch fire and tried to examine her surroundings. She was ringed by yew trees, black-needled in the darkness, apart from a glimmer of colour across the far side of the clearing. The sound seemed to be coming from there.

Roses. Deep, blood-red climbing roses, scrambling over – smothering – one of the yew trees.

The moan had become a loud whimper. It didn't sound human. She knelt down, trying to push aside the roses without touching the thorns.

A puppy was lying on the ground. There was blood

on its coat and every in-breath was a whine of pain. When it saw Merry it started trying to move towards her, but its back legs were dragging and useless.

Oh – its spine is broken, poor little thing.

The puppy was looking up at her. She had to do something.

Her hands were shaking as she placed them on the puppy's back. She started singing the spell she'd been practising all week. At the same time, she tried to visualise the puppy becoming stronger, fitter – better.

The puppy's breathing became less laboured, and under her fingers she felt the bones straightening out, fusing together perfectly. The animal's back legs twitched, flexed – and with a jerk the puppy was up on its feet.

Merry stopped singing and sat back on her heels, wiping the tears from her cheeks with the back of one hand.

'Thank God.' She stroked the puppy's head. 'Are you feeling better? Now all I have to do is—'

She stopped, holding her breath.

Because the puppy was changing.

It was getting bigger. Much, much bigger. As she watched, the muzzle and the tail lengthened, the ears became more triangular. The coat grew shaggier. The whole animal kept growing and growing.

Merry jumped up and started to back away, hands spread out in front of her. The dog – wolf? – looked up at her and snarled.

What the hell had she done?

Growling and baring its teeth, the wolf took a few paces forward, shook its head back and forth as if trying to dislodge something, then snarled at her again, the sound vibrating through the ground, sucking the strength from Merry's legs. She backed away further, muttering a shielding spell.

It's only an animal. You've dealt with worse, remember?

Sleep. She could put it to sleep. Her voice changed, singing soft and low: a lullaby. The wolf stumbled, its head drooping a little.

Merry sang a bit faster. If she could just get to the end of the spell…

The images came out of nowhere. *Jack, blood gushing from the wound in his chest; Carys and Nia lying dead on the floor of Gwydion's hall; the King of Hearts advancing on her with the broken blade in his hand.* And then the noise: only a whisper at first, an indistinct babble. But as the volume increased Merry could hear people crying, begging for mercy. More and more voices, swelling like a river in flood, so loud it hurt: drilling into her skull, driving out the words of the spell she'd been using, driving out all thought, until she was curled on the ground, hands clamped over her ears, weeping with agony. Through her lashes she could see the wolf crouching, about to spring, but there was nothing she could do about it, nothing—

'Enough!'

There was a flash of light and the wolf collapsed with a yowl of pain. The noise inside her head stopped, cut off as if someone had thrown a switch. Merry lay on the ground, trembling, too shaky to move any further. Someone was pulling her upright into a sitting position.

Ronan rested her head against his chest.

'Merry, are you OK? Are you hurt?' He started to run one hand over her back and arms, looking for signs of injury.

'No, I – I don't think so.' Her voice sounded muffled in her ears. 'Is it dead?'

'Yeah, it is. What happened? Where did that wolf come from?'

'It wasn't a wolf. It was an injured puppy. I wanted to help it, but…' She sat up and tried to brush some of the dirt and sweat off her hands. 'Something went wrong, obviously.'

'But what were you doing, wandering around in the dark all alone?'

'I got lost.'

Ronan's eyebrows lifted.

'You got lost? You need to be more careful in the woods, Merry. This place, this whole area is ripe with ancient magic. Saturated with it.' He gestured at the sombre trees around them, and Merry shivered. 'In places like this, boundaries break down. Worlds leak into each other. Gateways open up. It's all too easy to lose yourself entirely.' He leant closer to her. 'Or do witches not remember the lore?'

'We remember.' Merry bristled. 'I didn't exactly plan to spend my evening here.'

Ronan held his hands up in a gesture of peace.

'Sorry.' He looked at her thoughtfully. 'You and Leo certainly seem to be attracting bad luck at the moment, don't you?'

'Seems like it.' Merry reached up and pulled some straw out of her hair. 'Thanks for stepping in, by the way. Again.'

Ronan smiled, and it lit up his face. Merry could see why her brother was falling for him.

'You're welcome.' He stood up and bowed, then held out his hands to pull Merry to her feet. Once she was standing he looked her up and down and laughed. 'At

least you're dressed right for getting lost in the woods.'
He stared pointedly at her T-shirt.

'What?'

'Well… it's red, isn't it? With added bloodstains, by the look of things. And you've no actual hood, but still. Wearing red, attacked by a wolf – you're not on your way to Grandmother's house, are you?'

'Funny. I was meant to be on my way home.'

'Like I said, you should watch yourself, casting spells in the middle of the forest. You don't want to attract the wrong sort of attention.' He switched his gaze from her to the trees ahead, frowning slightly.

'What's the matter?'

'Probably nothing,' he said, still staring into the distance. 'Though you can never tell, somewhere like this.'

Merry turned in a full circle, slowly scanning the area around them. She didn't feel anything in particular. Not now. 'I don't see anyone.'

'It was just a feeling. But I think I should take you home.'

'OK. But can you wait a couple more minutes?' Ronan nodded, so she went back over to the dog, or wolf, or whatever it was, and knelt beside it briefly, running her fingers through its fur.

I'm sorry. I didn't mean for it to turn out like this.

The red roses beside the wolf were glowing like rubies in the starlight. Merry held out her hands and sang to them: of springtime and growth, and the sap propelling itself through stem and leaf. The roses trembled for a moment, as if caught in a gust of wind, then sent shoots and tendrils racing outwards. Within a few minutes the body of the animal was covered in a thick mound of flowers that looked like it had been there for many years. Merry turned and walked back to where Ronan was waiting.

'Nicely done.'

'Proper witch magic. For once.'

Ronan crooked his arm towards her, elbow out.

'Shall we, Little Red?'

Merry hesitated for a few seconds. But it had been a long and difficult evening. Having someone to lean on, just for a little, would be a relief.

They were back at Merry's house less than half an hour later. Merry hadn't felt like talking much on the walk, and Ronan seemed content to let her be silent. Now she was rummaging around in her bag, trying to find her house keys.

'Well, thanks for rescuing me, and for walking me home. I owe you one.'

'That's right. You do.'

She shot him a glance, trying to read his expression.

'And in payment of your debt,' Ronan continued, 'I'd like you to allow your brother to hang out with me.'

'Oh.' Not what she'd been expecting.

Ronan laughed quietly.

'You should see your face. Did you think I was about to ask for your firstborn child?'

'I thought you might ask for a potion or something you don't know how to make.'

'Ah. So you know about the illicit trade in magic between witches and wizards. In that case, you'll also know that witches don't much care for wizards, on the whole. And you'll understand why I'm...' He paused, tugging on one earlobe. 'Why I'm asking your permission to be friends with your brother.'

Merry didn't reply, so he continued. 'I've had no permanent home since I was fifteen. I've no family. And being a wizard tends to get in the way of relationships with plebs. Every now and then I get a little... lonely.'

'Plebs?'

'Non-magical folk. What do you call them?'

'I don't call them anything in particular. I mean, we're all just people.'

'But you know that's not true. We're not the same, whatever you might try to tell yourself. At what point do you explain to your mates that you have the power to turn them into frogs, and they can't do anything about it? I know it's a bit different for witches. But being a wizard... I'm not in a coven. Never even got properly trained, though that might have been a mercy.'

'Why?'

'Wizards are territorial and secretive, generally speaking. If a wizard finds a young guy with magical ability on his patch, he's almost as likely to kill him as teach him. At least, that's the way it used to be. Methods are slightly more subtle nowadays.' He shrugged. 'My point is, it's plebs or nobody, most of the time. But I can never really relax around them. Except – except perhaps with your brother. I feel like we could become friends. I like him.'

Ronan's shoulders were slightly hunched, and his hands were in his pockets as he scuffed the ground with the toe of his shoe. Yes, he was a wizard, but he was still a person. And a person who seemed to be romantically inclined towards her brother. Possibly. He'd said 'friends'...

'Sure. You can hang out with Leo: I won't try to put

a spoke in the wheel. But he's had a really rough time, recently, so—'

'I get it.' Ronan raised his hands reassuringly. 'I'll be careful. Promise.' He glanced at his watch. 'Oh – gotta run. Say hi to Leo for me, will you? Tell him I'll call him. G'night.'

'Night.'

Merry let herself into the house, dumped her stuff in the hallway (pulling on a hoodie to cover her bloodstained T-shirt), and wandered through to the living room. Mum and Leo were watching TV together: the end of an American comedy show that Mum really liked. They both looked relaxed, for once. Kind of peaceful. As the programme finished Mum glanced round and spotted Merry. She smiled at her.

'Hey, sweetheart. How was the coven meeting?'

'Oh, you know. Not great. The spell I've been working on didn't go exactly right.' No point worrying Mum and Leo with the details of her disastrous evening. Besides, after what had happened in the woods she was thoroughly exhausted. She really didn't want to think about magic any more, let alone dissect where she'd gone wrong.

Mum stood up, stretched and wandered over to her. She brushed a stray hair away from Merry's face. 'I know it's hard, but try not to worry. You're a very talented witch. Keep practising, do what Gran tells you, and you'll get your powers under control soon enough. And as for what the rest of the coven think… They do mean well, most of the time.'

Merry nodded and gave Mum a hug. Her mother squeezed her back tightly before pulling away.

'Right, I'm off to bed – I'm in London tomorrow, but I'll be back for dinner. And don't stay up too late: you're both looking like you need more sleep. Particularly you, Leo.' She ruffled Leo's hair, dropped a kiss on Merry's cheek and disappeared out of the room. Merry took her space on the sofa, curling up next to her brother. He was scrolling through the list of new film releases.

'So, I bumped into Ronan when I was walking home. He said to say hi, and that he was going to call you.'

Leo stopped scrolling and turned to look at her.

'When did you see him?'

'Well, he walked me some of the way home, and then—'

'You mean he was at the house? Just now? Why didn't he come in? Where did he go?'

'I don't know. He didn't say. Into town, I guess.' She wondered about it now. Tillingham wasn't exactly a hotbed of late-night entertainment. 'He said he had to go. But

I'm sure he will call you.' She hesitated. Somehow, she didn't think her brother would be that thrilled that Ronan had asked her permission to be his friend. Without thinking, she blurted out, 'He said he likes you.'

'Huh.' Leo scowled at the TV screen, then threw the remote at the armchair across the room. It bounced off and clattered against the leg of the coffee table. 'There's nothing on. I'm going to bed.' Without another word he pushed himself off the sofa and flounced upstairs.

Merry sighed, picked up the remote and turned off the TV. Bloody Leo. Bloody Ronan too. Had he already done something to upset her brother? Wizard or no wizard, if he hurt Leo...

She was getting ahead of herself. All Ronan had done was turn up in the nick of time to rescue them both from stuff. Merry flicked the light switch and turned to follow her brother upstairs. She'd been wishing for a way to help Leo. Maybe Ronan would help make that wish come true.

EIGHT

'WHERE ARE YOU going?' Merry asked her brother.

'Out. If you're going to stand in the way, can you at least help me?'

It was the next evening and Leo was in the hallway, storming around, pulling things out of drawers and yelling to Mum about the location of his car keys. Merry hummed the opening phrase of a finding spell; the keys leapt straight out of one of the plundered drawers into her hand.

'Here you are. Have you got a date?'

Leo scowled at her. 'I'm just going out. With some friends.'

'With Ronan?'

'With none of your business.'

'Leo…'

'Look, Merry, you don't tell me every minute detail of your social life, so I really don't see why I have to give you a blow-by-blow account of mine.'

She couldn't believe it.

'Is this about me spying on you last—'

'No.' Leo cut her off. 'You've said you won't do that again and I believe you. I just… I don't see why we have to share everything, all the time. I could do with some personal space occasionally. You've got your whole thing going on with the coven, so…'

'I always tell you about the meetings.' A pang of guilt rippled through her. 'When there's anything to tell.'

'I know that. But you tell me when you want to. I don't force the details out of you.'

'OK. Fine. I just like to know that you're safe.' In a flash Merry remembered that Simon was still walking around unpunished, and her guilt was swept away by fury. She swallowed it; now wasn't the time. 'What if – what if I need to get hold of you?'

'Text me. I'll see you later.'

'All right. Have fun.'

Leo made for the door. Merry bit her lip for a moment, then started after him.

'Just be careful, will you? Ronan seems like a really nice guy, but he's still a wizard. He's not like you—'

But it was too late. Leo had already driven off.

★ ★ ★

Leo drove as fast as he could along the road to the Black Lake, windows open, music turned up loud. He was heading back to the other side of the water, away from where Ronan was camping. He knew it was pointless – his bad temper was directed as much at himself as at Merry – but the urge to go back there was too difficult to resist. It had been OK earlier in the week, when he'd been either seeing Ronan or texting him or Skyping him constantly. But yesterday, all he'd had was a second-hand message from Merry. And today, nothing. It was obvious Ronan had got fed up with him. For some bizarre reason, being at the lake seemed like it would make the rejection easier to bear.

He parked the car and began walking through the trees. The glow of sunset was finally starting to fade, giving way to a blue-grey dusk. It reminded him of that terrible time he'd come here to meet Merry, to help her get under the lake. He kicked one of last year's pine cones away from the path. Perhaps he had been a little bit… harsh, this evening. But there was no way he was going to tell Merry what he was feeling about Ronan. He'd heard what she'd said as he got into the car:

He's not like you.

He's a wizard.

You have to be careful.

He thought back to what Gran had said the other day, after Ronan had visited her house: *none I trust, only a handful I can tolerate* etc. Which was so lame. And so unfair. The only thing Ronan had done was save him from being beaten to a pulp by Simon and his cronies. And he'd befriended him at a time when – let's face it – Leo didn't have too many other friends. At least in that respect Leo didn't think he and Ronan were really that different.

Leo kicked another pine cone into the undergrowth, remembering how the coven had tried to stop him from going with Merry to face Gwydion. How they'd said he would end up being a distraction; a liability, even. But then it turned out that Merry had needed him, that it had taken both of them to defeat Gwydion. OK, so mainly Merry. But he'd helped too. He was the one who'd destroyed the puppet hearts. Yet nobody seemed to want to acknowledge that now.

Damn witches. They thought they were so much better than everyone else.

The trees ended, and Leo saw the Black Lake lying ahead of him. The water level had fallen over the summer. He wondered how deep the drought would have to bite before the ruins of Gwydion's tower were revealed, or the petrified remnants of black holly that had not been sealed beneath the lakebed. Or what would be uncovered if the lake evaporated completely and the desiccated earth gaped open...

Only two bodies. But how many ghosts?

Movement caught his eye. Someone was walking along the edge of the lake. Leo remembered the dream he'd had a week ago, the dream in which he'd met Dan here, but had been too late to save him. His heart rate accelerated.

The figure got nearer. Leo squinted, trying to make out its features in the gathering twilight.

Ronan spotted Leo, and waved.

By the time Ronan got close Leo had decided to play it cool and distant. But then Ronan ran the last few metres and said, 'Leo, mate, I'm so glad you're here. I'm sorry about not getting back to you. I dropped my phone in the bog a couple of days back –' he wrinkled his nose – 'and I've only just this afternoon got a new one.'

Leo stared at Ronan. He really wanted to believe him.

'So why didn't you tell Merry that yesterday?'

'What can I say?' Ronan spread his arms wide. 'I was a bit distracted. Also, I'm an idiot. But I've been calling you for the last two hours.'

Leo pulled his phone out of his pocket and saw four missed calls. 'It was on silent.' He smiled at Ronan. 'Lucky I decided to come here.'

Twenty minutes later they were at Ronan's campsite. Ronan had set a fire burning again and was sitting with his legs stretched out in front of him, leaning against the front of the van, sipping from a bottle of beer. Leo, next to him, was making do with tea.

'What have you been up to, the last couple of days?'

'Not much,' Ronan replied. 'Popped into town yesterday evening, but otherwise… just sitting here on my own. Destroying my phone, that kind of thing.'

'Sounds lonely.'

Ronan shrugged.

''S OK, I'm used to it. It's all I've known since my mother died. Sometimes I meet guys like Ethan. Someone to pass the time with. Though we don't exactly have much in common.' He stared down at the bottle of beer in his hand and began peeling a corner of the label off. 'I haven't got much in common with anybody, really.' He looked up at Leo again. 'I think maybe you know how I feel? You're a bit of an outsider too, I reckon.'

Leo did know how he felt. *Exactly* how he felt.

'Yeah, I guess. Over the past few months I've sort of… grown apart from my old friends. Even my own family doesn't seem to quite get me any more.'

'Because you're gay?'

Leo felt himself blush, and wondered whether Ronan could see the colour that had flamed into his cheeks in the darkness. 'It is that obvious?'

'No. I guessed. From what those idiots were yelling at you the other night.'

'Oh.'

'And to be honest…' Ronan's voice was shaking a little and he hesitated for a moment, 'to be honest, I'm glad.'

Leo's heart practically stopped. Did Ronan mean what he hoped he meant? Up until now, he'd tried not to think about the possibility that Ronan might have feelings for him.

'You are?'

'Course. I'm not the most experienced guy out there. I haven't had many relationships, but...' he paused as their gazes locked. 'I really like you.'

'You do?'

'Why are you so surprised?' Ronan took another sip of beer. 'Being the only male in a coven family, being the only one who couldn't do magic – that must have been tough. But you seem totally cool with it. You must be very strong, to have turned out so normal while growing up in that environment. I think you're pretty amazing.'

Leo's face grew hot again.

'Thanks, but it's no big deal. I've always been around magic. I guess I'm just used to it.'

'You need to give yourself more credit.' Ronan glanced up at Leo, and the intensity of his gaze made Leo's insides flutter. 'You know, I'd have said something sooner, but I wasn't sure you'd want me.' He moved his hand so it was just resting next to Leo's. 'Not... not like I want you.'

'What?' Leo's voice almost broke.

Ronan didn't look at him. Just sort of... mumbled.

'I need to know if you're interested. In taking this further.'

Leo didn't have to think about his answer.

'Yes. Definitely.'

Ronan looked up, smiled and leant forward until his lips just grazed Leo's. It was barely anything, but Leo felt like his heart might be about to break open from too much happiness. Ronan sighed and sat back again.

'This is going to be amazing. But... d'you mind if I ask you something first?'

'Course not. Anything.'

'Well, I wouldn't know about this if I wasn't a wizard, obviously. But −' Ronan drained his beer and threw the empty bottle into the fire − 'it seems like there's a shadow in between us. Someone from your past.' He took Leo's hand in his. 'So I was wondering: why don't you talk to me about Dan?'

★   ★   ★

Merry texted Leo around midnight to ask if he was OK. All she got in response was:

I'm fine. Expect me when you see me.

He could be so bloody stubborn sometimes. She'd considered waiting up until he got back − even though she knew it would piss him off − but Mum told her to stop worrying and go to bed, reminding her that they would have to get used to him not being around when

146

he left for uni. Merry knew her mother was right, but she couldn't shake the anxiety in the pit of her stomach.

The morning sun, streaming in through a chink in her bedroom curtains, woke Merry around six thirty. She groaned and tried to go back to sleep, but after half an hour of lying there, stubbornly awake, she gave in and got up. Ruby was coming over later in the morning, so an early start meant she could fit in a quick gym session first. As she passed Leo's room on her way to the bathroom, she hesitated. It couldn't hurt, just to check.

Slowly, she turned the handle and opened the door a fraction.

Her brother was face down on the bed, one arm dangling over the side, still wearing his clothes from last night. He was snoring softly. She closed the door gently and went into the bathroom.

Merry worked out for a full hour at the local gym. The only cloud was seeing Simon on the way out of the building. He'd smiled at her: a taunting, malicious grin that made her want to rip his horrible, smug face off. She'd had to sprint out of the building, shaking her hands to get rid of the throb of magic in her fingers. Still, her anger had cooled by the time she got home and she was able to chat calmly with Mum over breakfast. Leo still hadn't surfaced when Mum was ready to leave the house, so she asked Merry to make sure he ate something when he finally did get up. There were some leftover boiled potatoes and some bacon in the fridge. Merry made a cheese and bacon frittata and put it on the kitchen table with a note that said, *Eat Me. There's some coffee in the pot too. Xx.* A peace offering, of sorts.

Ruby arrived just after eleven. They were sitting in Merry's bedroom, watching Ruby's latest vlog on her laptop when they heard the sound of footsteps across the landing and the bathroom door slamming. Ruby grinned.

'Another late night for Leo, then?'

'Something like that, yeah.'

'So tell me more. Is he dating anyone?'

'No, I don't think so,' said Merry, although she wasn't really sure. Leo was obviously crushing on Ronan in a fairly major way. And now it seemed that Ronan might feel the same.

Ruby sighed. 'Shame. He's such a nice guy. He deserves to find someone.' She picked up a bottle of deep purple nail varnish and shook it. 'Hold out your hand. This colour is going to look great on you.' Ruby began applying the nail varnish to Merry's fingernails. 'I still can't believe he's gay. All those years I spent obsessing over him. And he was completely unobtainable.'

'Well, I didn't know until last year. I don't think Leo knew himself. But once he told me, I did try to discourage you. Except you never really listened!'

'You should have chucked being subtle and laid it out for me. You know I can be pretty… focused, when it comes to stuff I want.'

'Yeah, right. Leo would have killed me if I'd told anyone before he was ready. Probably literally.' Merry gave Ruby her other hand and started waving the painted one around in the air to help it dry. 'Besides, didn't you ever think he might just not be into you?'

'No. Why would I ever think that?'

Merry laughed. 'If we could bottle your confidence, we'd make a fortune.'

'Now that's an idea. *Eau de Ruby – by Ruby…*'

An hour or so later, Merry had undergone a major style revamp. Ruby's attempts to do her hair and make-up, while not quite as effective as she imagined the Cinderella potion would have been, were nevertheless pretty impressive. Merry giggled at herself in the mirror. The make-up was quite subtle – for Ruby – although there had been a whole lot of time-consuming contouring going on. And her hair had been straightened, with only a tiny, tiny bit of backcombing.

'So, what do you think?' Ruby asked, leaning over her shoulder.

Merry tilted her head, admiring herself from different angles.

'OMG. I'm a babe.'

Ruby laughed.

'I've been telling you that for ages. I've also been asking you to let me give you a makeover forever. Years, in fact. But you never listened.'

'Guess that makes us even, then?'

'Almost. But to seal the deal you have to persuade your bro to be my arm-candy, if something insane happens and I don't have a date for next year's prom. I always enjoy walking around having other girls envy me.'

Merry grinned.

'No problem.' It was good to finally be open with Ruby, at least about one thing.

To be finally telling her the truth.

At least about Leo.

If not about the witchcraft.

She felt Ruby's mood change slightly; her friend seemed a little… apprehensive. Merry swivelled round on her chair. Ruby was still smiling, but her eyes were unfocused, as if she were thinking about someone far away.

'What? What's the matter?'

Ruby blinked, snapping back into the present. 'Oh, nothing. It's just that we never really, properly talked about what happened this spring, did we? I get the feeling that the stuff you were willing to share with me was only the *official* version. The edited highlights.' She picked up the piece of quartz from Merry's bedside table and twirled it around in her fingers, allowing each facet to catch the light. 'And I think, maybe, there was another side to the story of you and that what's-his-name. *Jack*. Stuff you haven't told me, even now.'

Merry sat there in silence for a moment, staring at Ruby.

Wow. I have seriously underestimated this girl. Perhaps it would be OK if I told her what I really am. Perhaps now is finally the time for the truth.

She took a deep breath and pretended to examine her newly-painted fingernails.

'You're right, Ruby. There's stuff I didn't tell you, about what happened earlier this year. And – and other stuff too. These… things that have been going on in my life for a long time. Things that I haven't ever mentioned before—'

'Merry, hold on a sec.' Ruby gave a strained sort of laugh. 'I, er… I didn't actually say that I wanted to know.'

Merry looked up, surprised. Panic began to rise in her chest. Had she completely misjudged this? Was Ruby about to say that she didn't want to be friends any more? Was she going to lose her, just like she'd lost Alex?

'But – but, why not?'

'Because something tells me I'm better off *not* knowing. That's why.'

It was hard for Merry to keep her voice steady. 'I don't understand.'

Ruby sighed and went to sit on the windowsill, tracing her finger over the rune Merry had carved there the week before. 'You're my best friend, right? Always have been. Always will be. I can't see that ever changing, no matter what. But I've known for a long time that you're a bit… different.'

Merry nodded mutely.

'You were never quite like me or Verity or Esther or any of the girls in our class. And I'm not saying that's a bad thing. You're just kind of, I dunno, off-centre. Not quite dancing to the same playlist as everyone else in the room. Does that make any sense?'

Merry shrugged, not daring to interrupt.

'Well, believe it or not, that's never bothered me. All the stuff about your family, the rumours about your gran – I've never been remotely interested. You're my friend, and that's all that matters. But last spring, something happened. And it really, really freaked me out.'

'What do you mean?' Merry murmured.

'You changed, Merry. Almost overnight. You went from being the sort of fearless idiot who jumps into rivers to being a – a frightened, helpless mess. And you were so sad. And distant. I don't want to even think about what could have done that to you.' Ruby turned to look at her again. 'Whatever it was that you and Jack got involved in, I really don't want to know. I'm just glad that he's gone. I brought all this up cos I want you to know that I love you. I've got your back, no matter what you do.'

And with that, Ruby rested her head against the window frame and closed her eyes.

Merry sat there, speechless. Ruby's relief was radiating off her like heat from a bulb. But she couldn't work out what her own feelings were. Ruby knew the rumours, but she wasn't connecting the dots.

Doesn't want to connect them, more like.

Ruby was still Merry's best friend, which was great. But a best friend from whom she would always have to keep secrets? How the hell was that supposed to work?

Merry thought for a moment about the other witches she knew. Mum, whose marriage had broken down, and who had a few acquaintances, but no close friends; Gran, whose friends were all other witches; Flo, who had a huge group of friends, none of whom (with the exception of Merry) she actually spent much time with.

And suddenly, Merry was able to identify the emotion that had crowded out her every other feeling.

Loneliness.

She felt totally and utterly alone.

NINE

MERRY WISHED SHE could straighten stuff out with Leo as easily as Ruby had straightened out her hair. But the situation between them was still out of kilter. Mum pulled Merry to one side after dinner on Tuesday evening.

'Have you and Leo had a fight?'

'No. Well… not exactly.' Merry carried on scraping the plates into the food bin. She didn't know what to say; if she told Mum about spying on Leo she would have to explain why she'd done it. And telling Mum about Leo's visits to the lake was not going to get Merry into his good books. 'We've both been busy. And you know recently Leo's been a bit…'

'I know.' Mum started scrubbing the lasagne dish. 'I thought he would begin to feel more comfortable about things over the summer.' She picked up a knife and jabbed at some burnt-on cheese. 'I'll sit down and have a chat with him. I was going to take him shopping tomorrow evening to buy some stuff for uni, but now he says he doesn't want to go. I do hope—'

The kitchen door opened.

'I've put the bins out.' Leo spoke to Mum; Merry was certain he was deliberately not looking at her. 'Anything else you'd like me to do?'

'No, love, that's fine. I was just saying to Merry that we still have a lot of things to organise before you go away. We should probably get some new towels in the sales when we go shopping.'

'Oh yeah… about that; I was actually—'

Mum didn't give him the chance to finish.

'Since you're off work tomorrow, would you drive Merry over to Gran's? The woman next door is going away and somebody needs to feed the cat.'

Their mother was still attacking the lasagne dish, so only Merry saw Leo roll his eyes.

'I'll do it. Merry doesn't need to come. I'm sure she's got important coven stuff she'd prefer to be doing.'

Merry waved at her brother.

'I'm standing right here. You don't need to talk about me in the third person. And I have to get another one of Gran's books, so I will come with you.'

That wasn't true, but she wasn't about to let Leo ditch her.

'Fine, whatever.' Leo got a glass out and leant past his mother to get some water. 'I'm going to leave at half eight, so you'd better be ready.' He kissed Mum on the cheek. 'I'm going up, Mum. See you in the morning.'

'Night, then,' Merry said, but Leo didn't reply.

Geez. When did he get so passive aggressive?

Mum was watching her.

'Don't worry. You know your brother loves you to pieces.' She started the dishwasher and put the kettle on. 'Still, if he's not talking to you at the moment, I hope he's talking to someone else. I don't blame him for not wanting to confide in me, but it would be good if he could open up to one of his friends.'

That hardly seemed likely, unless he talked to Ronan.

'By the way,' Mum continued, 'I hope you're not still worrying about that spell you tried to do on Friday. You're

157

not the first witch to get stuff wrong. That's why the coven system exists: you get taught the right way to do things, and mistakes are… contained.'

'But what if I can't do things the *right* way? Or – or what if I don't *want* to do them the way that everyone else does? Surely I can be a witch without having to be in a coven, can't I? You didn't have to.'

Her mother got a cloth out of the drawer and started wiping the kitchen table.

'Mum?'

'My case was –' Mum paused – 'different. I was trying desperately to avoid being involved with the ancestral curse of Meredith's oath, so I… went out of my way to underachieve. None of the other witches thought I had any real talent. So no one apart from my mother cared when I said I wouldn't be in the coven.'

Mum was getting anxious; the increase in tension was like a scouring pad being drawn across Merry's skin.

'Are you saying that people *will* care if I make the same choice as you? That if I wanted to leave, the coven would try to stop me?'

'I – no, that's not what I mean.' Mum finished wiping the table and moved on to the work surfaces.

'Then what do you mean?'

'I don't know. Nothing.' She threw the cloth into the sink. 'You're exceptionally gifted, Merry. The coven just wants to see you reach your full potential, that's all. Honestly, it's probably safer to let them guide you.' She smiled hesitantly. 'Now, are you going to watch some TV or…'

Merry shook her head. Her mum's words just didn't match the emotions that Merry was picking up, but she was too tired to think about it any more tonight.

'I'm going to bed. Don't want to oversleep and miss Leo's deadline. Hope work's OK tomorrow.'

'Thanks, angel. Sleep well.'

This time Merry wasn't sitting by the lake – she was underneath it, lost in the labyrinthine passageways of Gwydion's prison. Running from room to room, searching…

She reached the throne room. Jack was there, tied to that torture chair Gwydion had forced him to sit in. He was watching her.

'What are you looking for, Merry?'

The firelight threw strange shadows and colours across his face, hollowing his cheeks and eclipsing his eyes.

'I'm looking for Leo.' Merry turned, examining the room. 'Is he here? Have you seen him?'

'I saw him. But he's gone. Stay here with me.'

Poor Jack. She'd missed him so much. But she had to find her brother.

'I can't, Jack. I'm sorry. Which way did he go?'

'You don't understand, Merry.' The cords binding Jack to the chair fell away and he stood up. There was a single glowing glass jar standing by the long hearth; Jack picked it up and held it out to Merry. Inside was a heart, still oozing blood. 'Leo's gone. You see?'

Bile rose in Merry's throat.

'No... No – it was finished. We killed you.'

Jack put the jar carefully on one of the empty shelves. He turned back to Merry and drew the sword that hung at his waist.

'It is never really finished.'

Merry backed away, but Jack – the King of Hearts – kept moving closer.

'You're going to stay here with me, witch.' In the distance, someone was screaming. But the monster in front of her ignored it. 'I'm coming for you...'

'Merry – it's OK...'

She was screaming, and Leo's arms were holding her. Leo.

'You're not dead.' She pressed her fingers to his chest, felt the heartbeat. 'He didn't kill you.'

'Of course I'm not dead. It was just a nightmare.' Leo picked up the glass of water from the bedside table and pushed it into Merry's hands. 'A really, really bad one by the sounds of it. Do you want to tell me about it?'

Merry closed her eyes, but the vile images were waiting behind her eyelids. 'I don't think I can go back to sleep. Possibly ever.' She took a sip of water. 'I – I was back under the lake. And Jack was there. But not really Jack – it was the King of Hearts. He wanted me to go back.' Her brother straightened up and looked away from her. 'Leo?'

'Should we be worried? I mean…' He clenched one hand into a fist, tapping it on his thigh, and Merry saw that his knuckles were white. 'The other night I thought I saw someone outside the house, and now you've dreamt about Jack.'

'No.' Merry sat up too, tucking her hand under his arm. 'What was beneath the lake… it isn't there any more, remember? Everything collapsed. And the King of Hearts – he doesn't exist any more, either. Besides, I've had lots of dreams about Jack since then. It doesn't mean anything.'

'Are you sure? We killed Gwydion, but—'

'Yes, I'm sure, Leo. There was no one else left down there but us.' Merry yawned and looked at the clock – it was a little after six. 'Did I wake you?'

'No, I wasn't asleep anyway.' Leo looked tired, but Merry didn't want to risk another argument by asking what had been keeping him awake. 'Shall we go to Gran's now, then?' he asked. 'I'll make some coffee if you want.'

'Oh, yes – thanks.'

'There's no need to sound quite so surprised.' Leo sat there, gazing down at the floor, tracing an old scar on his knee with one fingertip. 'I know I've been… overreacting to stuff recently. A bit.'

Not exactly a gushing apology.

But at least he's talking to me again.

Merry punched her brother gently on the shoulder.

'Can we forget about everything that's happened over the last couple of weeks?'

'Course.' Leo stood up. 'I'll see you downstairs.'

Merry headed into the bathroom. The nightmare was fading now. Perhaps today was going to turn out all right after all.

It was nearly seven fifteen when Leo and Merry got to Gran's house. The street was quiet: sun shining on drought-withered front gardens, a light breeze stirring next-door's wind chimes, a couple of people on their way to work.

Leo stooped to pick up a package that had been left behind the plant pots on the front step.

'Oh – there's the cat. Hey, Tybalt.' He crouched down and held his hand out, but the animal didn't seem keen to emerge from its hiding place. 'You want to come and have some breakfast?'

'He'll come in once we put the food out.' Merry fished the door key out of her pocket, slotted it into the lock and pressed her hands against the woodwork to lower the defensive wards Gran had placed around the house. 'Maybe I should water the plants while we're here. D'you know where—'

She stopped.

'Where what? Leo was still trying to coax the cat out from behind the bush. 'Merry?'

'Something's wrong. The house isn't warded. The runes have been broken.' She turned the key in the lock and pushed the door open. 'Oh no.'

The hallway was full of debris: broken glass, bits of furniture, pages out of books. And some of it was floating.

They were inside the house now, the front door shut against the curious glances of any passers-by. Leo had wanted to run quickly from room to room, but Merry wouldn't let him. Instead, they were working their way slowly, carefully, through the ground floor, Leo behind, Merry in front, chanting: shielding spells, spells to detect intruders, spells to reveal magic. They hadn't found anyone else in the house – so far – but the characteristic signatures of different spells were showing up like glowing streaks of coloured light, marking the air all around them. It was like being encased in stained glass and sunlight. Leo prodded a piece of smashed china that was suspended in mid-air in front of him; it tumbled away across the room.

'All of Gran's stuff. Who would do something like this, Merry? And why is it…?' He waved a hand at the myriad glass fragments hanging in space like a miniature asteroid field, blocking their way into the dining room.

'I don't know.'

Merry's eyes filled with tears as she caught sight of Gran's wedding bouquet, carefully pressed and preserved behind glass for more than forty years, crumbling into dust on the floor.

Poor Gran. How is she going to cope with this?

Leo was trying to dodge past the glass fragments. Merry grabbed his arm.

'Hold on. Let me see if I can… make some space.'

She closed her eyes and stretched out her hands.

Um… gravity. That's what I need to use. All these pieces of glass need to be reminded of the weight of gravity sucking them down to earth, making them heavy…

The spell was a bit of a mess: words and phrases stolen from other spells, the tune as dirge-like as she could make it, speaking to the gently drifting debris of the earth, rootedness, pressure…

There was an enormous crash as everything that had been floating hit the floor at once – disintegrated – and skittered across the tiles. Merry and Leo flung up their arms, shielding their heads.

After a few moments the tumult subsided. Merry opened her eyes and waved a hand in front of her face: the air was full of dust.

'Well done, I guess.' Leo coughed and grimaced. 'I'll open the windows.'

'No – we should stay together. Let's check the kitchen, open the back door, then go upstairs.'

The kitchen was frozen. Literally. A thin veneer of frost sparkled across every surface, glazing the broken crockery on the floor. Icicles hung off cupboards and door handles. The magic used in here showed up as silver streaks against the arctic air.

Merry's teeth were chattering within seconds; Leo,

shaking his head, pushed her out of the kitchen and closed the door behind them.

Upstairs didn't seem quite so bad. They checked the spare room, the bathroom and Gran's workroom: drawers and cupboards had been pulled open, their contents strewn around, but there was less outright destruction.

'OK.' Leo pulled his phone out. 'Just Gran's bedroom – and the attic, I suppose –' he glanced up at the ceiling – 'but the bolt is still in place. I'm going to call Mum before she leaves for work.'

Merry nodded. She started singing a shielding spell again and pushed open the door of Gran's bedroom. Clothes were scattered across the room, the dressing-table mirror was smashed, and a broken string of beads lay on the floor by her feet. A sliver of something else was protruding from under the edge of the bedside table. Merry knelt, slipped her fingers into the narrow gap and felt the worn hilt of Gran's obsidian knife. Using her nails, she managed to ease it out. It didn't seem damaged. She turned the knife over in her hands, examining the carved oak handle, the inlay of polished moonstone set in silver. The last time she'd seen this knife up close was when Gran was using it to cut her hand open, before she went to the lake to face Gwydion. She hadn't realised then how darkly beautiful it was. Wrapping the knife carefully in a discarded scarf, she put it into her pocket, grateful that at least one of Gran's treasured possessions would be returned to her intact.

Sighing, Merry turned to go back on to the landing. And then she saw it.

Blood.

Smeared over the bedroom wall, spattered down the back of the door. Five lines, like somebody's bloodied hand had been dragged across the painted surface.

Oh my God.

'Leo! Leo, get in here!'

TEN

HALF AN HOUR later there were six more witches in the house: Mum, Mrs Knox and four other members of the coven. They were examining the residue of the spells that Merry had uncovered, as well as trying to restore some kind of order. Mum had been calling Gran non-stop on her mobile, but she wasn't getting any response. Merry and Leo were sitting with her on Gran's bed, trying to stay out of the way.

Mrs Knox popped her head round the door.

'Bronwen? Think you should come and see this.'

They all followed her down to the living room, where

Gran's desk was tucked into one corner. There were lots of different coloured streaks hanging in the air; multiple spells criss-crossing each other. A rainbow effect that might have been beautiful in other circumstances. Mrs Knox turned to Merry.

'Know what you're looking at?'

'I think so. The different colours represent the... enacting, I guess, of different spells. The colours fade with time. So here –' she pointed at a wide band of vivid purple – 'is where I cast a spell, and these fainter colours are from earlier on. Cast by whoever did this. And if you have enough experience you can tell what the spell was.'

Mrs Knox nodded.

'Basically correct. But it is also possible, if one knows how, to identify the person casting the spell.' She beckoned Merry nearer to the purple stripe and sang a few words of Latin. The spell residue seemed to shimmer for a moment. 'Now look closely. Can you see something else?'

Merry tilted her head, squinted – there was something, possibly. A smattering of darker-coloured dots and lines within the broader sweep of colour. Almost like notes on a musical score. At first the marks seemed random, but then—

'It's a pattern. It runs to here... ' she pointed at a place about ten centimetres from the beginning of the spell, 'and then it starts over.'

'Quite so. That's your signature. The precise arrangement of the marks, their intensity and so on, will tell an expert that you were the one who cast this spell.'

'Are you an expert?'

'Not at all. But I am very familiar with the signatures of a handful of witches.' She paused. 'Your grandmother included.' Mrs Knox turned to Mum and put one hand on her shoulder. 'I, er… I don't quite know how to break this to you, Bronwen. I'm afraid I don't think Elinor is in Salisbury. She was here when this happened.'

Mum gasped and clutched at Leo.

'No. That can't be right. She couldn't have been here.'

Mrs Knox shook her head. 'I'm sorry, Bronwen. I'll talk to Roshni, but I'm pretty certain.'

Mum started to cry. 'But why? Why would anyone attack my mother? It doesn't make sense.'

Leo glanced at Merry, then started to lead their mother out of the room.

'Come on, Mum. Let's call the hotel she's booked into.'

Merry waited until they had gone, then turned back to Mrs Knox.

'Are you sure?'

The older woman nodded.

'There's something else that worries me too. Whoever Elinor was fighting doesn't seem to have a signature.'

'You mean you can't read it?'

'No. I mean it isn't there. I can tell what most of the spells were – pretty damn violent on the whole – but the magic has been somehow... *anonymised*. I don't understand it.'

Merry turned cold. And then she thought about the last time she'd seen Gran, and how she hadn't even properly said goodbye.

Please, Gran, don't be dead.

It took hours to clean up the mess. Merry reckoned at least half of Gran's possessions had been destroyed. Most of her books had gone. The knowledge books looked like they'd been incinerated: nothing was left but the distorted remains of the covers. All the other books had been shredded, including Gran's precious journey books. Nearly sixty years' worth of notes and experiments and thoughts, turned into confetti. Merry got so angry when she saw this that she accidentally caused the ivy print wallpaper in the living room to spring into life, blanketing the ceiling in variegated foliage. She was sent home pretty soon afterwards.

Walking to the bus stop, it was hard to believe that the sun was still shining, that everyone else around her was enjoying a pleasant summer evening. She sat on the warm bench and waited, watching people in the windows of the bars and restaurants on the high street, all of them completely oblivious.

They'd notice soon enough if we stopped protecting them.

It wasn't fair. First Leo, and now Gran, and meanwhile these… these *plebs* were just walking around like nothing was wrong. Or worse, they were actively hurting people, like Simon had.

She knew he worked in the Waitrose on the corner. He could be in there now. She could go and find him, and hurt him, and make at least somebody pay.

Her fingernails were tingling…

Someone was calling her name.

It was Ronan. He sat down next to her on the bench, close enough that their arms were almost touching. Her face flushed and she clenched her throbbing hands into fists.

He shot her a quizzical glance.

'I reckon you're not exactly pleased to see me.'

'Sorry. It's been a really difficult day.'

'I wondered. You do look a bit…'

'Wrecked?' The sensation in her nails had faded, so

Merry tried to brush some of the dust off her legs, while pulling the fingers of her other hand through her hair. She hit a tangle, winced and gave up. 'Yeah. You've caught me at a bad time, again. Sorry.'

'You don't need to keep apologising.'

'OK. Sorry—' Merry swore and screwed her eyes shut for a moment. 'OK.' Time to think of something else to talk about. 'So, did you call Leo in the end? You said you were going to, on Friday.'

'I actually saw him, Saturday evening. And again, yesterday.' He grinned at her sheepishly. 'I guess you could say that things have kind of… progressed.'

'Oh.' Leo hadn't told her. How could he not have told her? 'That's, er… good.'

'Certainly is. For me at least.' Ronan's smile faded. 'I can understand that you might be rather nervous. About me and Leo. I'm a wizard and a stranger.'

'I'm not nervous. I really hope you'll be good for him.' She forced a smile. 'Besides, you know what'll happen if you hurt him. I'll have to come after you. Things could get messy.'

'I understand.' Ronan knocked a ladybird away from his arm. 'But I'd never do anything to damage your brother. He's very important to me, Merry. Truly, he is.'

Merry nodded. This was definitely not the sort of conversation she'd expected to be having right now.

'Well. Good.'

Ronan was watching her. 'OK. I'm out of here. You sure there's nothing you need help with, before I go?' He leant closer. 'Any straw you need spinning into gold? I charge very reasonable rates.'

For a couple of seconds Merry considered telling him what had happened. Perhaps even asking for his help to find Gran. But something held her back. Ronan wasn't family, and he wasn't in the coven. And Gran...

Gran doesn't trust wizards. So even if I think she's wrong, he shouldn't be involved. Not yet, anyway.

She took a deep breath to steady her voice.

'Just a bit of a family crisis. No gold-spinning required. But thanks.'

'Not at all.' He looked up and down the high street. 'How about this, though: my van is in the car park just over there. You let me buy you a coffee – to take away, mind – and then I drive you home?'

Merry was about to decline, but her stomach growled loudly.

Ronan smirked.

'I can stretch to a piece of cake too, if you like.'

She hadn't eaten since breakfast, getting on for nine hours ago now.

'Actually, coffee would be great. And some cake. And chocolate.' She stood up – too quickly, maybe – and stumbled, putting out a hand to steady herself.

'You OK?'

'Yeah – just dizzy for a moment. Guess I need to eat.'

'Right.' Ronan put one arm round Merry's waist; her legs felt too unsteady for her to object. 'Let's get you some sugar.'

Food helped, a little. But it didn't get rid of the fear rolling around Merry's stomach like a loose cannonball, or prevent the exhaustion that smacked into her as soon as she sat down in the van. Ronan was soon pulling up outside Merry's house. He turned the engine off and Merry picked up her bag, stuffing the remaining half of the chocolate bar inside.

She knew she should get out. Go in and see how Mum and Leo were doing. But she couldn't quite make herself take hold of the door handle, swing herself down from the seat. And she knew it was because she didn't want to.

Because if I stay here, in this moment, I can almost pretend that none of this has happened.

'You sure you're all right? You seem distracted.' Ronan was looking at the house. Thinking about Leo, perhaps.

'Oh – yeah. Stuff on my mind, I guess.' She glanced out of the window at the scarlet poppies, flowering despite the drought. 'Sometimes, it's hard to believe how terrible people are. If I could do this my way; if I was in control…'

'Things would be different? Better?'

'They might be.' Merry shrugged. 'But it's irrelevant, anyway.'

'You know, I never really understood why witches tie themselves in knots with oaths and suchlike. All that power, and they reduce themselves to nothing more than nursemaids. Running round after any plebs that have the wit to ask for their help.'

There was something in Ronan's voice, a note of… craving, perhaps? Merry glanced at his face, but his expression was hard to read in the dark interior of the van. She remembered the wolf-dog she'd created the other day and shivered.

'Sorry.' Ronan rubbed a hand over his face. 'I don't mean to be disrespectful. I envy you, in truth. Like I said, my training was incomplete; practically non-existent. I've had to scrabble around, picking up what I could here and there. A coven could have helped me. Supported me.'

Supported. Or suffocated.

'Yeah. Perhaps. Listen, thanks for the coffee. I'd better…'
She nodded towards the house.

'Sure.' Ronan leant over and placed a hand on the bare
skin of Merry's arm. 'Hope everything works out OK.
Let me know if there's anything I can do.'

Merry nodded and climbed out of the van, stifling a
yawn as yet another wave of exhaustion sucked at her.

Ronan had driven away before she made it to the front
door.

Two days passed. Mum just sat on the sofa most of the
time, staring into space, not talking, not sleeping. Leo had
a really tough time trying to persuade her to eat.
Occasionally, other witches from the coven dropped by,
giving Mum updates on their attempts to trace Gran:
different spells, contacting other covens, that kind of thing.
But so far they didn't seem to be any closer to finding
her, or to working out who had destroyed so much of
her stuff. Gran had arrived in Salisbury, but she'd only
stayed one night there. Roshni was the most frequent
visitor, though Merry couldn't help feeling that the main
reason for her popping in was to keep tabs on them: check
that she and Mum were obeying her 'suggestion' that they

didn't leave the house unless absolutely necessary. Allegedly, this was so they would get any new information as quickly as possible, but it seemed pretty lame as far as excuses went. Merry paced up and down her room for hours on end, feeling useless, until the temptation to smash something against the unresponsive walls was almost overwhelming.

So she tried a few things on her own. She cast the spell she'd used to spy on Leo, but the basin of water remained stubbornly black, and Merry ended up with a nausea-inducing headache. She also tried her favourite finding charm, attempting to locate Gran's wedding ring – which she always wore. But no image of the ring or Gran would come to mind. Finally, she'd borrowed a set of rune stones from Flo, but casting runes was not much use if you couldn't interpret the results, and none of the coven seemed inclined to teach her right now. The witches she asked muttered about not having any time, but Merry could sense their agitation. They didn't really want to have anything to do with her, whatever they claimed. They didn't trust her. Instead, she borrowed a book from Flo and tried to teach herself. By Friday evening, she'd only managed to get through the first chapter. She just about stopped herself from hurling the rune stones and the book out of her bedroom window.

★

When Saturday morning came, Merry decided she needed exercise and a change of scenery – whatever Roshni's opinion was – and ran to the gym. There was a fancy new treadmill that played videos of different landscapes; she jumped on it and selected New Zealand. But not even waterfalls and glaciers managed to distract her for long. She tried nudging the speed up a couple of notches.

The coven know I'm powerful. I could definitely help, maybe even find ways of searching for Gran that they haven't thought of. They're risking Gran's life because they're jealous.

She increased the incline, focusing on her feet striking the deck of the treadmill, her heart thumping in her chest, her lungs filling and emptying.

Well, maybe, another part of her brain said. *Or maybe they just remember how you nearly destroyed someone's leg at the last coven meeting. You can hardly blame them if they've decided you're too dangerous. After all, Gran isn't here to clean up after you.*

The sudden swell of grief almost choked her. She hit the emergency stop button.

Use your brain, Merry. You have to do something. All the power that built up in you because of Meredith and the oath, that means you can do things the other witches can't. You know things that they don't know.

Her breathing slowed gradually.

But what do I know that would help?

What do I know about that they don't?

The folder. The one she'd seen that evening when she'd told Gran that Ellie Mills was dead. The one that had been magically concealed inside the microwave.

Merry ran to the locker room, trying desperately to recall whether the microwave had been intact when she and Leo had walked into the frozen kitchen three days ago. She thought so, but whether she'd be able to work out how Gran had programmed the microwave to make the contents reappear... She'd just have to figure it out when she got there. After grabbing her stuff she hesitated, trying to decide whether to call Leo and ask him to drive her to Gran's house. But it wouldn't be much quicker by the time he got to the gym, and she didn't want Mum left alone. She swung her bag on to her shoulders and set off at a jog.

Merry came to a halt outside Gran's house, pausing to catch her breath. It looked completely unchanged from the outside. Like she could walk in and everything would be normal. She pressed the heels of her hands to her eyes. Gran could be super-annoying sometimes, but the idea of her being gone forever was just...

Hell. This year is turning out to really suck.

Merry blew her nose and walked up to the front door. The coven had added new warding spells to Gran's house, though she couldn't really see the point – whoever got in before hadn't been stopped by Gran's security precautions. It wasn't likely they were going to come back, anyway, was it? She pressed her hands against the door, preparing to murmur the charm to lower the defences.

But again, something was wrong. She could feel it as soon as her skin made contact with the wood. The defensive runes protecting Gran's house had already been overridden.

Someone was already inside the house.

Merry remembered Ronan's words in the woods. She'd gone to her grandmother's house, just like Red Riding Hood. Grandma wasn't there. But what if the big bad wolf was?

It's got to be him. Or her. Whoever took Gran.

She stood paralysed on the doorstep, trying to decide whether she should call Leo or the coven for backup. But if she delayed, whoever was inside the house might escape. It was too much of a risk.

She had to catch this monster. Now.

ELEVEN

MERRY CLENCHED HER hands, digging her nails into her palms. What was the best spell to use? Something to incapacitate, but not damage – not too much, at any rate. She wouldn't get any answers if the intruder ended up dead. Pushing the front door open as quietly and carefully as she could, she stepped into the hall, catching her breath, listening. There was nothing but silence, and then…

A muffled tapping sound. Only faint, but unmistakably there. The sound came from the sitting room. Merry crept further into the hall and peered round the corner where it lengthened into a corridor. There was no one in sight, but the tapping started up again, louder than before. Merry edged forward, until she could just peek round the half-open sitting-room door.

There were two people – a boy who looked like he was in his mid-teens, and a slightly older boy – stuck to the ceiling. Literally stuck. Spread-eagled, as if they'd been doing star jumps and had somehow ended up frozen in position, glued there like Spider-Man's less elegant cousins. The noise she'd heard was coming from the twitching foot of the younger boy knocking against the coving. He seemed to be unconscious. The older one, though, was very much awake. When he spotted Merry he widened his eyes and his lips moved fractionally, but no sound came out.

Some kind of binding charm. But who would have—

Roshni. She was an expert on binding charms. She'd clearly put a hex on the house, left a trap in case Gran's abductor returned. It would never occur to her that she actually ought to tell Merry or Bronwen about it.

Pretty impressive, though.

Merry had a hard time imagining that these two were responsible for whatever had happened to Gran. *Still...* She thought for a moment. The words to counter a binding charm mentioned the release of the body, so perhaps if she changed the wording a little?

She pointed up at the older boy's face and sang a short phrase. His head, no longer stuck to the ceiling, fell forward and he grunted with pain.

'You could've broken my neck, you airhead! What kind of idiot sets a binding hex in the middle of a sitting room?'

Merry was so shocked she didn't know how to react. She'd expected threats or possibly a plea for mercy, not this. She put one hand on her hip and pointed the other at him.

'Tell me what you've done with my grandmother right now or I'll do a lot worse than put a binding charm on you.'

The boy stopped groaning and looked at Merry. He frowned.

'What?'

'Where – is – my – grandmother?'

'Do you mean Mrs Foley? How should I know? We just got here.'

Merry shook her head in disbelief.

'Who are you? And what, exactly, are you doing in my grandmother's house?'

The boy closed his eyes for a moment and swore under his breath.

'Mrs Foley invited us to meet her here today. If you don't believe me, I've got an email on my phone to prove it.' He winced. 'For heaven's sake, will you please let us down? My neck really hurts.'

Merry hesitated, thinking back to when the King of Hearts — pretending to be Jack — had nearly killed her. Appearances couldn't be trusted. These two might have nothing to do with Gran's disappearance. Or they might have her stashed in the boot of a car somewhere. On the other hand, having a conversation with someone pinned to the ceiling was making *her* neck ache.

'OK. Brace yourself.'

She sang almost the same phrase that she'd used earlier.

The older boy dropped to the floor. For a few seconds he lay on the carpet, stunned, before pushing himself to his feet. He tried to walk towards her — but couldn't. His feet were glued to the carpet just like he'd been glued to the ceiling a moment before. A flicker of surprise crossed his face.

'What have you done?'

'A partial binding charm.' Merry kept her hands raised, ready to cast a shielding spell if necessary. 'Now, let me see this email.'

He pulled a phone out of his pocket, touched the screen

a few times, then floated the phone over to Merry. So he was a wizard, then. She plucked the phone out of the air to read the message on display. It certainly *looked* like an email from Gran, addressed to someone called – 'Finn? Is that you?'

The boy nodded.

'Yes.' He gestured towards the other figure still on the ceiling. 'That's my cousin, Ciarán. And I suppose you must be Meredith, right?' He glanced up at his cousin again. 'Could you let him go? He hit his head when the hex struck. He might be injured.'

'It's Merry. Not Meredith. And I'm not letting him down until you explain to me why you broke in.'

'We didn't. Or at least, we didn't plan to. Like I said, we arranged to meet Mrs Foley today. But when we arrived there was no answer and no warding spells in place.' He shrugged. 'We thought Mrs Foley might need some help. That she might have been injured. But then we walked in here and got smacked with a damn binding hex!' He took a deep breath, as anger flashed in his eyes. 'I get that you're annoyed we let ourselves in, but it seemed like a good idea. At the time.'

'I bet.' Merry bit her lip. What he was telling her might be the truth. Anybody magical would expect a witch's house to be warded if the house was empty. But if Gran had arranged for the two boys to visit, wouldn't she have mentioned it? Something about this story didn't feel quite right. Giving up the only bit of leverage she had might not be such a great idea.

'How about this: we leave your cousin here, and you come with me to visit another witch. She's taking care of things while Gran's… away.'

Finn shook his head.

'No. I'm not leaving him like this. Why don't we all go and see this other witch? Or just tell her our names – Finn Lombard and Ciarán Hyland. My father is Edward Lombard. She will have heard of us.'

Geez, this guy was really winding her up. Merry opened her mouth to tell him so when she heard the front door open and slam shut again. Roshni ran into the room, hands raised, but stopped short when she saw Merry.

'What are you doing here?'

'I came to… to check on something. And when I got here I found these two up on the ceiling.'

Roshni's gaze took in the two boys. Her eyes narrowed.

'Finn Lombard. Would you care to explain why you broke into our coven leader's house?'

★

187

Half an hour later, Merry had been banished to the kitchen with Finn while Roshni fixed Ciarán's concussion.

The microwave was still there, undamaged as far as she could see. Merry made herself a cup of herbal tea, got Finn a glass of water and sat down at the kitchen table.

'Thanks,' Finn said as she pushed the glass across to him. He smirked at her. 'Told you she'd know who I was.'

Merry scowled back at him.

'Sorry. Must have missed the issue of *Celebrity Wizard* with your face on the cover.'

Ciarán slouched in.

'That witch says we're to stay in here until the rest of them turn up.' He sat down next to his cousin.

'Feeling OK?' Finn asked.

'No thanks to these idiots.' Ciarán nodded towards Merry, causing her to raise her eyebrows. 'Seriously, I think the other one nearly broke my arm when she let me down.'

'Ciarán,' Finn frowned and inspected his cousin's arm briefly, 'you're fine. Stop whining.'

'But Finn—'

'Enough!'

The younger boy subsided, but he threw an angry glance at Merry. She decided to ignore him, on the basis that he was too immature and irritating to be bothered with. Instead, she got her phone out and began texting Leo and Mum, filling them in on what had happened. She explained that Roshni had recognised the two intruders, but Leo was still suspicious. Mum seemed more upset about Roshni setting a hex in Gran's sitting room without telling her. By the end of the text exchange Mum and Leo had decided to drive over.

Merry looked up and found Finn watching her.

'What?'

He leant forward, elbows on table.

'I feel like I probably owe you an apology. And that we might have got off on the wrong foot. Do you think we can start again?'

Merry almost choked on her tea.

'You *think* you owe us an apology? What do you want?'

'A coffee and a sandwich, ideally.' He held up a hand. 'I'm joking. Well, mostly. The only thing I actually want is for you to stop looking at me like you want to kill me.' His voice was serious, but there was humour in his eyes. They were an unusual colour: grey, like the sea on a cloudy day. He sat back in his chair again, running one hand through his tousled red hair. 'You'd really like me, if you gave me a chance.'

'I doubt it. Besides, you're unlikely to be here long enough for either of us to find out. With any luck.'

Finn scowled and opened his mouth to say something else when one of the other witches came into the kitchen.

'The coven meeting is about to start. Your presence is requested.'

Finn stood up, kicked Ciarán in the ankle so that he stood up too, then both of them bowed to the other witch, who nodded and walked out of the kitchen. Merry sighed quietly; as well as all her other missing knowledge, there was obviously some witch/wizard etiquette book that she'd have to locate and read at some point.

'Shall we?' Finn asked, gesturing to show that she should go first.

'You go ahead. I'm just going to wash these up.'

'OK. But in case I don't get the chance later…' He held his hand out to her. 'No tricks, honestly.' Merry extended her hand carefully and Finn took it. 'May wisdom be in your heart, and magic always at your fingertips, Merry Cooper.' Then he lifted her hand and kissed it.

The touch of his lips against her skin surprised her. For a moment she stood, her hand still in Finn's, uncertain how she should react. But a glance at Ciarán showed the younger wizard rolling his eyes; obviously, this was a move he'd seen his cousin make before. Merry snatched her hand away.

'Yeah, well.' She nodded towards the door. 'You'd better go through. They'll be waiting for you.'

As soon as they were out of the kitchen she shut the door behind them, put the cup and glass in the dishwasher and went to examine the microwave. It was empty, as she'd expected. She had no idea what setting Gran had used, but the machine only had two dials: there were a limited number of possibilities. Merry pulled a chair up to sit in front of the microwave and started to experiment.

Three and a half minutes on 'Defrost' turned out to be the charm. But she didn't have time to read the folder now. Instead, she wedged it down at the bottom of her bag and hurried to the coven meeting.

The gathering reminded Merry of when she'd had to go to Mrs Knox's house back in March, so Gran and the coven could assess her skills. But this time it was Finn and Ciarán sitting on chairs facing the group of witches, with the addition of Mum and Leo, who had arrived as she was leaving the kitchen. Merry thought that Finn should have looked a lot more uncomfortable than he did.

Roshni had used a spell to project the email message from Gran to Finn on to the wall. She turned to Finn, who seemed to be doing all of the talking.

'And the *problem* that Elinor refers to here…' She waved a hand at the glowing letters. 'Why were you requesting help? Why not your parents?'

'Well, my father is a very… proud man—' Finn began.

'Unbearably arrogant is my recollection!' Mrs Knox commented in an extremely loud whisper.

'So you may not know that my twin brother, Cillian, had an accident. Just over a year ago.' Finn dropped his gaze. 'He's, um, he's been in a coma since it happened.'

'I'm assuming it was magical, this accident?' Roshni asked.

Finn looked up at her, nodding. 'We've tried everything: approached all the wizards we know, the local covens. But nothing's worked. About six months ago my father just… stopped talking about it. But I remembered our aunt saying something about Mrs Foley. That she was the most skilled healer in Europe. So I emailed her.' He shrugged. 'Dad's given up on Cillian, but I haven't.'

Ciarán stopped studying the carpet and glanced up. 'And I just wanted to help my cousin, honest.'

Standing between Merry and Leo, Mum muttered

something that sounded suspiciously like 'the poor darlings'. Merry looked at her brother – he was obviously just as surprised as she was.

It'll be a bit much if Mum decides to get all super-maternal over a couple of teenage boys she's never met before.

Roshni was studying the email again.

'And Elinor invited you to visit her, and to stay here, I see…' Her tone was incredulous.

Finn nodded.

'Yes. That's why we came. And then, when we realised the wards were down, we thought Mrs Foley might be in here and in need of assistance. But it was very wrong of us to break in. And it's my fault, not Ciarán's. I'm extremely sorry.'

He didn't actually look extremely sorry, as far as Merry was concerned. 'I still don't understand. Gran doesn't even like wizards. How would your family know her?' She turned to Roshni. 'How do we know this email isn't faked, that he hasn't hacked into Gran's email account to give himself an excuse to be here?'

Roshni raised an eyebrow.

'Merry, haven't you read your grandmother's book yet? The Lombards are one of the oldest of the Kin Houses. Everybody knows them.'

'Your gran's been to stay with them quite a few times over the years,' Mum added. 'I went with her once.'

Ciarán sniggered. He tried to disguise it as a cough, but it was definitely a snigger. Merry felt the blood rush into her cheeks. And Finn just looked… smug.

Stuck-up git.

Her embarrassment flared into anger.

Finn tumbled on to the floor as the front legs of the chair he was sitting on snapped. The witches looked at each other, but apart from Leo, they all very carefully avoided looking at Merry. Obviously, showing her up because she hadn't read a book was one thing; revealing her unusual magical tendencies to outsiders was something else.

'Sorry about that,' Mrs Knox offered. 'Kept telling Elinor she needed to replace those chairs.'

'No problem.' Finn's voice was carefully controlled as he brushed himself off. 'So,' he asked, 'is Ciarán free to go?'

'You may both leave.' Roshni inclined her head. 'Please give our greetings to your parents.'

'Actually, Ciarán has to go home, but I'm planning to stay on.'

'And why is that?' asked Roshni. The question was phrased politely, but there was an edge to her voice.

Finn waved a hand at the still-to-be-mended bits of furniture stacked haphazardly around the room.

'Because whoever did this, whoever took Mrs Foley, was clearly an extremely powerful individual. A wizard, most likely. And I'm hardly about to leave a bunch of leaderless women to fend for themselves. It wouldn't be right.'

The room fell silent. It was so quiet, in fact, that Merry was sure she would have been able to hear a strand of hair float to the floor, let alone a pin. She peeked around and saw twenty pairs of eyes, all glaring at Finn. Leo, on the other hand, was staring steadfastly at the floor, his lips pressed firmly together, shoulders shaking slightly, trying not to laugh.

Roshni stood and beckoned Finn over.

'I can assure you, boy, that this coven is perfectly capable of looking after its own. You may have heard that, only a few months ago, Mrs Foley's own granddaughter defeated a wizard of immense power singlehandedly.'

Merry felt a needle of resentment coming from somewhere – Leo? – almost lost in an intoxicating wave of pride from Mum and the other witches.

'Elinor will be recovered unharmed,' Roshni continued, 'and we will deal with whomever is responsible for her disappearance. Your assistance is not required. Nor will any interference from you be tolerated.' She took a step towards him. 'Are we clear?'

Finn, for once, looked flustered.

'I apologise, Mrs Arora. I didn't mean to be disrespectful, to you or to the coven. My father – both my parents – have always spoken very highly of Mrs Foley.' He looked around at the other witches. 'That's one of the reasons I came here. My father would be –' he shook his head, glancing up at the ceiling – 'absolutely furious if he found out I had left without offering what limited assistance I could. But he's going to be even more mortified to learn that I've offended you. So please, let me redeem myself. I know some of the southern wizards; they might be more cooperative if I get in touch with them directly. It's possible one of them may have some useful information. Will you let me try?'

Merry could barely stop herself from groaning out loud. Did Finn really expect any of them to fall for his *misunderstood-but-heroic* act?

Mum cleared her throat and went to stand next to Roshni.

'I think, in the circumstances, we should accept any help offered. Even if the manner in which it was offered was… distasteful.'

For the second time in less than a minute, Merry wanted to wail in disbelief. She glanced over at her brother and saw his expression mirroring her own reaction.

There were murmurs from the other witches, but Mum ploughed on.

'If my mother trusts the Lombards, I think we should too. Don't you agree, Rosh?'

'It is not a matter of trust, Bronwen. I simply don't believe we will need help from a juvenile wizard. But, as you wish.' She turned back towards Finn. 'You may remain in our territory, as long as you stay with a member of the coven. Do you accept this restriction?'

Finn nodded.

'Why don't you come and stay with us?' Mum offered. 'We have a spare room and I'm sure Merry and Leo would appreciate having some company of their own age.'

Merry could hear Leo murmuring, 'Mum, for crying out loud, no!' Ciarán started to whisper something to his cousin, but Finn cut him off with a jerk of his hand.

'Honestly,' Mum added, 'I could do with a distraction right now.'

'Then I would be happy to accept your invitation.'

Finn smiled, though there still seemed to be a flicker of something in his eyes. Was it doubt? Or relief?

This is ridiculous. Why has the coven bought this clown's story so easily? I don't care who his parents are, how do we know he can be trusted?

Merry glared at her unwanted new house guest. But for now, there wasn't much else she could do.

They were outside, baking in the midday heat; the house had been magically sealed up again and Mrs Knox had agreed to take care of Gran's cat. Mum had brought out some of Gran's personal possessions – a hairbrush, a pair of earrings, a favourite photo – that the coven were hoping to use to trace her.

Merry felt a tap on her shoulder. Roshni was standing next to her.

'Before I leave, I'd be interested to know why you came here on your own today. Were you looking for something in particular?'

'Oh…' Merry wished her sunglasses covered more of her face. 'Not really. Gran said she'd been doing some research about the dead witches. But I don't actually know what to look for, and then those two were here…'

Roshni frowned.

'You know about the deaths?'

'Yes, Gran told me.'

The older witch shook her head.

'Merry, there is no reason to think what happened to those witches has anything to do with Elinor's disappearance. Or that the deaths of those individuals were even related. I know your grandmother thought they were linked somehow, but the last time I spoke to her about it, she'd found no evidence to back her theories up.'

No evidence yet, Merry thought. But Gran had been looking for it when she went missing.

'So what is going on, Roshni?'

'The coven will work it out. But the first, most important thing is to rescue your grandmother. I wish Elinor hadn't mentioned the deaths to you.'

'I *am* in the coven.'

'Yes. As a trainee.' Roshni paused, squeezing Merry's shoulder briefly. 'Let's focus on getting Elinor back. I'll let you know how the tracking spells go.' She turned away.

'But – what shall I do? Can I come to the coven meeting and help with the tracking?'

'I don't think you should. Sometimes an object can retain an... impression of its owner. We'll be attempting to summon such an impression of Elinor from the past, and use it to locate Elinor in the present, but it's a difficult task.'

'I'm sure I could—'

'No. It's a spell that requires a number of witches to work very carefully together, and there is enough scope for error as it is, without...'

'Without me being involved?'

Roshni sighed.

'What I need you to do is concentrate on looking after your mother. And keep an eye on him.' She nodded towards Finn, standing on the pavement a few metres away. He had one hand on Ciarán's shoulder and looked as if he was giving the younger boy instructions. Ciarán didn't look that happy about whatever it was.

'Things will be back to normal soon enough,' Roshni continued. 'I'll be in touch.'

And that was it. All the witches dispersed, leaving Merry alone with her family and the two interlopers.

'Merry, come on.' Leo had already started the car; he beckoned to her, his face stony. 'Mum and I are going to take this one –' he jerked his head to indicate Ciarán – 'to the station; he has to get back to London, apparently. So you have to go with the other one. Have you got keys?'

'Yes, but—'

'OK. We won't be long.' Merry watched the car disappear up the road. She turned to find Finn standing next to a small two-seater car parked a little further on. It looked shiny and expensive and very fast.

Ah. Now I understand why Leo was looking so put out.

Finn grinned and opened the passenger door.

'Your carriage awaits, my lady.'

Merry rolled her eyes. The best response was probably a dignified silence. She slid into the low seat, relieved she was wearing shorts and not a skirt. Finn got into the driver's seat and turned the key in the ignition. The engine started with a roar.

There's a surprise. Maybe I should ask him what he's compensating for.

Merry cleared her throat.

'OK. Take a right at the end of the road, then another right at the traffic lights.'

At least it wasn't a long drive home.

TWELVE

'**D**OES MUM THINK we're entertaining royalty?' Leo murmured in Merry's ear. 'D'you think she's confused Finn with Prince Charming? Maybe we should shove a bag of frozen peas under his mattress and see if he notices.'

Merry half stifled a giggle and Mum frowned at them both.

'Have you finished setting the table? And did you use the proper china?'

'Yes, Mum.' Merry exchanged glances with her brother. The proper china was reserved for special occasions. As was the dining-room table, which functioned as Mum's desk most of the year, since she preferred this room to her tiny, dingy study. But for some reason she had decided to push the boat out. Merry watched her mother pouring herself another glass of wine, fussing around the table. Maybe if she was busy cooking and looking after Finn, she couldn't be one hundred per cent focused on what had happened to Gran.

'Merry!' Mum had her hands on her hips. 'Can you stop standing there like a spare part and check the potatoes? Poor Finn will be starving.'

This time it was Finn's turn to snigger. Merry glared at him and hurried into the kitchen.

Finally, dinner was over. Finn took himself off to bed and Merry escaped upstairs. She slid the folder out of her bag, anxiety and excitement mingling in the pit of her stomach. Perhaps she was about to get some answers. What if Gran had expected an attack and had left a list of potential threats? What if there was an actual address?

She took a deep breath. Opening the folder, she began to examine its contents.

There was a list of names. But scribbled right at the bottom in Gran's handwriting was *Ellie Mills*. A list of dead witches, then. No indication of how they had died or who might have killed them. Behind the list, attached to it with a paper clip, were some photographs. Merry began to flick through them.

'Oh my God!'

She hurled the photos face down on the bed and wiped her hands along her jeans.

Corpses.

Photographs of mangled, bloodied corpses. Taken by the police, presumably – on the reverse of one of them, someone had stamped LANCASHIRE CONSTABULARY, with a name and a date. She grimaced and gathered the gory photos back into a pile – being careful not to look at them – and put them back with the list of names.

The next item in the folder was a map of the UK, marked with numbered crosses. The numbers snaked their way down the country, from one in Scotland to seven in north London: the locations of the deaths. Gran had written, 'MONUMENTS? CIRCLES?' in one corner of the map. But there didn't seem to be any pattern to the locations that Merry could discern, no way of using them to predict where the next death might occur. She folded the map up again.

Next was a separate plastic wallet containing several handwritten letters. Gran seemed to have underlined certain phrases, but since none of the letters were in English (three were in German, one in Italian, one in French and one in a language Merry didn't recognise), that wasn't particularly helpful. Also in the wallet was a small booklet with a long title: *A Treatise on the Historical Treatment of Male Witches and the Development of Ancestral/Cultural Archetypes*. Presumably it was similar to Gran's book on wizards; Merry made a mental note to call Finn a 'male witch' and see how he reacted.

There was a knock on her door. Merry grabbed her pillow and put it on top of the folder.

'Yeah?'

Mum opened the door.

'I'm going to bed, sweetie. I was hoping Roshni would call with some news but...' She shook her head.

A tremor of sorrow shot through Merry's core.

'Don't worry, Mum. I'm sure we'll hear something tomorrow.'

'Well...' In the lamplight Mum's eyes were flat and full of doubt. 'Don't stay up too late, OK?' For a moment Merry thought her mother was going to say something else, but she didn't; just blew her a kiss and shut the door again.

Merry stared at the painted wood for a few moments.

What was she going to do? The coven didn't seem to be getting anywhere, and the folder…

Pushing the pillow away, she glanced over the stuff spread out on the bed. She'd really thought there would be some obvious clue. Instead, she had a bunch of random items that just didn't seem to lead anywhere.

What did you expect? An essay from Gran, starting, 'If I'm abducted, please do the following…'?

It would have been handy. Merry rolled her shoulders back, trying to get rid of the tension in her spine, then began putting the folder back together. Letters, map, photographs and list, book. As she grabbed the book by its front cover something fluttered out from between the pages.

More paper, folded into quarters. It seemed to be a page torn out of another, larger book. The page had an illustration on it, a black-and-white woodcut-style print. It was a picture of a man wearing an old-fashioned costume – seventeenth century, Merry guessed, judging by the jacket and breeches thing he had going on. He was holding a young woman in his arms. It looked like he was about to kiss her, although… She held the picture up to the bedside lamp, squinting. And her blood ran cold.

This wasn't a kiss.

The man, his features fixed in a hideous grimace, held the woman's face between his hands, fingers curled, nails digging in. The woman's eyes and mouth were wide with pain. The artist had carved what looked like little bolts of lightning flying from the woman's head into the man's.

Fear prickled the skin between Merry's shoulder blades. And then she noticed the inscription in heavy Gothic lettering at the bottom of the page: *Der Zauberzieher.*

Der Zauberzieher? What on earth was *Der Zauberzieher?*

Merry took a deep breath and closed her eyes. She really wasn't sure she wanted to find out.

It was dusk. One of the in-between times, neither night nor day. But here, in the depths of the forest, the darkness was almost complete, drowning the undergrowth in impenetrable shadow. Water dripped from the canopy, pooling into faintly luminous puddles along the path below. She wrapped her red shawl more tightly about her shoulders and followed the trail further into the wood.

Eventually, it ran out into a clearing. And in the middle of the clearing sat a man, the hood of a cloak pulled low on his face, concealing his features. The man was sitting behind a spinning wheel and he seemed to be spinning. At least, his fingers looked as if they were pulling on something, and his feet were moving the treadle of the wheel. But there was no thread or wool that she could see. She drew closer and the man spoke.

'What are you doing here, little girl? Are you lost? Or are you on your way to Grandmother's house?'

She looked around the clearing: she knew this place, somehow. 'Neither, I think.'

'Then what do you want from me?'

What did she want?

'I want my grandmother back. I want my brother to be happy. And…' she paused, trying to remember the rules. 'I want to be free to choose my own path.'

'Really? Three wishes?' The man laughed – a low, sneering sound. 'Well, I can help you, for a price.'

'What is your price?'

'Three gifts for three wishes. You must give me one strand of hair that I may add to my spinning. One heartbeat that I may add to my power. And one night that I may add to my life.' He tilted his head. 'Afraid, little girl?'

'No.' She undid her plait and hastily yanked out a single hair to prove she spoke the truth. 'Here. How – how will you take the other gifts? Will it hurt?'

The man didn't answer, but he stretched out his hand towards her. And then she saw that instead of nails he had long silver talons growing from the ends of his fingers, just like black holly *thorns. She tried to back away, but an invisible force held her fast, as the talons came closer and closer to her chest…*

'Bloody hell!'

Merry shook her head to clear away the fog of the nightmare. One of the cats was sitting on her chest and staring at her.

Just a cat…

She pushed herself up on to her elbows – causing the cat to yowl and leap off her – and gulped down the water on her bedside table.

Geez. I am so sick of nightmares.

It was still early, not quite six o'clock. Merry shooed the cat out on to the landing, wedged a pile of books against the door in case it tried to get back in, and went back to bed.

She was woken by her phone buzzing. A text from Mum.

Taken Leo shopping, please look after Finn. No update from Roshni.

There was one from Leo too.

Taken Mum out to distract her, back in a few hours,

**she says you're to entertain him. Don't do anything I
wouldn't.** ☺

'Him' was obviously Finn.

Yeah, really funny Leo.

What was she supposed to do to *entertain* their unwanted
visitor – card tricks? Tour of their palatial accommodation?
Make him watch the extended versions of her favourite
sci-fi and fantasy films back to back?

That wasn't actually a bad idea. Maybe it would persuade
him to leave.

Merry rubbed the sleep out of her eyes, then texted
Leo back.

Whatever. Don't forget to buy me a birthday present.

She blinked at the screen. The idea of turning over and
going back to sleep was seriously tempting. But it was
already 10.45. Instead, she compromised by staying in
bed but retrieving her journey book from under the
bed. It was nearly three weeks since she'd last written
in it. Guilt swirled in her stomach: she hadn't practised
any more of the spells Gran had set her, either. She
decided she ought to make more of an effort. Gran
would want her to.

And I want Gran to be proud of me, if she comes back…

Catching her breath, Merry squeezed her eyes shut to get rid of the tears.

When she comes back. When.

Writing up her nightmare, as horrible as it had been, didn't take that long. A peek out of the window revealed Finn's car still in the driveway. But she didn't feel like hanging out in her room any more. After showering she got dressed and was about to head downstairs when she saw Gran's book – the one she'd actually written – still lying unread and accusing on her desk. Merry picked it up and flicked to the index. And there he was, or his family at least: *Lombard – p178. See also Dynastic Wizards and the Kin Houses, Chapter 10.*

She turned back to the relevant page.

LOMBARD. One of the oldest of the Kin Houses. Anglo-Irish. At time of publication head of the senior branch of the family is Edward Lombard. Married to Marie-Louise Williams. Children: Finn and Cillian.

It was like an entry in some musty old genealogy book. No wonder Finn was so full of himself. No mention of Ciarán or the Hylands, though; they obviously weren't 'senior' enough.

Merry sighed and dropped the book back on the

desk. Time to go downstairs and deal with Wonder Wizard.

Finn was sitting at the kitchen table, a map spread out in front of him and a laptop open next to him. When Merry walked in he hastily shut the laptop down, folded the map up and shoved it into a bag on the floor next to him.

'Planning where to go next?' Merry asked, walking over to the fridge to get some juice.

'Just thinking about some sightseeing.' Finn stood up. 'Would you like some coffee? I was going to make some more.'

'Sure.' Merry kept an eye on him. Just to make sure he didn't try to poison her or anything. And when she saw what he was doing, she stared, mouth open.

Finn waved his hand at the cafetière, and then – well, it basically emptied itself out and washed itself up. It was like watching some invisible servant doing all the work.

'What's the matter?' He raised one eyebrow. 'Never seen magic before?'

'Never seen it used for that before.' Merry pointed at the cafetière, now being dried by a bewitched tea towel. 'Can't you wash up yourself?'

Finn frowned at her for a moment, then shrugged and threw his hands in the air.

'Actually, I'm not that great at it.' He grabbed the cafetière and started spooning in the coffee. 'Mum got fed up and made me learn how to do it magically.' He smiled at Merry. She couldn't help smiling back.

Then she saw the photo of Gran that Mum had stuck to the fridge, and stopped smiling. She put some bread in the toaster and sat down opposite Finn.

'I've never tried to do anything like that. Witches tend to be quite serious about their magic.' *Too serious, to be honest.* There were a lot of domestic spells left over from the days when there were fewer household appliances, but nowadays it was sort of… frowned upon. Merry tried to imagine walking into Roshni's house and seeing a mop whizzing around the kitchen floor without being attached to a human. But she couldn't. Using magic like that was considered frivolous, and Merry had a hard time picturing Roshni being frivolous. On the other hand, Mrs Galantini tended to use magic as much as possible, so perhaps it wasn't the hard and fast rule she'd been led to believe.

'I don't blame you for staring – I am pretty damn gorgeous.' There was a mug of coffee in front of her, and

Merry realised she'd been gazing absent-mindedly at Finn all this time. She felt her face get hot.

'Um… I was wondering whether you and Ciarán are first or second cousins. I thought yesterday you looked pretty similar.' That was true. They had similar-shaped faces and colouring. But Finn was taller, more muscular, more chiselled. Just more, really.

Finn pursed his lips, considering.

'I guess there's a family resemblance. Ciarán is one of my first cousins. He's a wizard too, but he's only just turned sixteen and he's a bit crap. I'll be nineteen in December.'

'Leo's nineteen. He's off to study medicine in a couple of months. Are you going to uni?'

'No.' Finn sat back in his chair, and a look of petulance flashed across his face; the same kind of expression Merry had noticed yesterday. 'I'm not.'

She waited, but Finn was now staring moodily down at his coffee. She got up to put some jam on her toast.

This is way too awkward. Frankly, she had better things to do.

'So, has Mum given you some keys? The train station is right in the centre of town, if you want to go to London. Or there's the castle, or the river.'

'Trying to get rid of me?' Finn asked. But he smiled at her again. 'Don't blame you. I'm going for a walk, in any case.' He started chipping a spot of wax off the table with his fingernail. 'I'd love for you to come and show me around.'

The tone of his voice suggested that was the last thing he wanted.

'No, thanks. I've got some training to do.'

'Training?' Finn glanced up at her curiously. 'Still?' He made a noise that sounded suspiciously like a snort. 'Huh. I thought Dad must have been exaggerating. The idea of an untrained witch defeating a wizard—'

'Listen – whatever your dad knows, or thinks he knows, I don't care. The truth is that you know *absolutely nothing* about me.'

Merry turned away and started slamming dirty crockery into the dishwasher.

If he doesn't leave, I might kill him.

She flexed her fingers, trying to feel whether magic was about to explode out of her.

I might literally kill him.

Perhaps Finn read her mind; she heard a chair scrape against the floor and then he was next to her, handing over the last couple of plates and mugs.

'Sorry,' he muttered. 'That wasn't very polite.'

'Not especially.'

He started washing up the cafetière by hand.

'It must have been terrifying. I understand why you don't want to talk about it.'

Merry studied his face, looking for sarcasm or calculation. But his expression was carefully neutral and difficult to read.

He was right, though: she didn't want to talk about it. Because talking about it would mean thinking about Jack, picking away at a scab that seemed to be getting thicker with each passing day.

She ran her fingers across her left palm, where the King of Hearts' cursed sword had burnt her.

I should – I need – to let him go…

'Something wrong?' Finn was drying his hands, watching her.

'I'm fine. Enjoy your walk.' She went up to her room and didn't come down again until she'd seen their visitor leave the house.

Leo and Mum got back mid-afternoon. They both said they'd had fun, buying stuff for Leo to take away to uni, but Mum's eyes were red-rimmed and puffy, and Leo seemed to have permanent frown lines between his eyebrows. Roshni had called, apparently. But the coven still hadn't completed the tracking enchantments they were trying to do.

'I can't stand all this waiting around.' Mum picked up her car keys again. 'I'm going to Sophia's house to see how they're getting on. Do you want to come with me?'

Merry thought about what Roshni had said to her yesterday, and shook her head.

'I've been practising shifting spells for two hours now; think I need some exercise.'

'You can come for a walk with me, then,' Leo said in passing, his arms full of new bed linen. 'Just let me finish unpacking the car.'

Twenty minutes later Merry was following Leo out of the driveway.

'Where are we going?'

'To visit Ronan.' Leo paused. 'That OK? I know he's hanging out near the lake, but…' He shrugged. 'It's just a lake now, right?'

'Course. Let's go.'

They talked about Gran and Mum for a while. Leo still reckoned Ciarán and Finn were something to do with

Gran's disappearance; he'd tried to persuade Mum to send Finn home, but she refused to listen to him.

'She's convinced he's as innocent as he's making out.' He kicked a piece of old wood into the long grass at the edge of the path. 'I'm not. How do we know that he didn't disarm the wards? And remember what Gran said about wizards?'

'Yeah.' Merry hesitated. 'But on the other hand, Ronan's a wizard. And he's super-helpful and friendly.'

'I know. But that's different. He's different.'

Merry looked at her brother's profile and wondered whether – if – he was ever going to tell her what was actually going on between him and Ronan. So far she hadn't wanted to bring it up with him. Leo was smiling slightly, like he was thinking about something that made him happy.

'So, you and Ronan…' She left the comment hanging, waiting.

They walked a few metres further.

'We're sort of… together. I guess.' Leo rubbed the back of his neck and sighed. 'I don't know exactly. It's very early days. Nothing's really happened yet. But when I'm near him, I feel… I mean, I really…' He blushed and stuffed his hands in his pockets. 'You know.'

Merry did know, because that was how she'd come to

feel about Jack. Like there was a magnetic charge connecting them, drawing them together, tugging on her so hard that not being with him, not touching him, had made her insides ache. And then, when they finally kissed—

Enough, for heaven's sake! You're just torturing yourself.

She glanced at Leo; he was staring absently at a patch of nettles.

'That's great, Leo. Sounds like it's going the right way.'

'Hopefully.' He smiled at her. 'I'm sorry I didn't say anything to you before. I'm not deliberately keeping secrets. It's just this is sort of… uncharted territory for me, I guess. I don't know how long he's going to stick around, or how this is going to turn out.'

'You don't have to tell me stuff if you don't feel like it. Obviously, I'd rather know all the details, because I'm nosy and because I love you. But I can live without them.'

'Really?'

'Really. And as for Ronan, if he makes you happy, then I reckon you should go for it. Don't worry about what might happen next. I didn't get to spend much time with Jack, but I'm still glad we had the time that we did.'

'Even though it hurt you so much, losing him?'

Merry nodded.

'Even though.'

Leo held her gaze for a moment.

'OK. I understand. Although, I—'

He broke off as a faint, drawn-out shriek sliced through the ordinary summer sounds of the woods. They both froze, looking around, but the noise was too indistinct for them to be able to pinpoint the direction it came from.

'What the hell was that?' Merry shuddered. Had it been animal or human? 'Sometimes, I think these woods are—'

But Leo wasn't listening to her. He was staring up at the trees, his face grey.

'Hey.' Merry nudged her brother. 'You OK? You look like you've…'

Seen a ghost.

That's what she'd been about to say. But then she recalled their conversation about Dan's death, about what Leo thought he'd seen in the garden the other evening.

'Leo? It was just an animal. Come on.' She slipped her hand into his. 'Let's keep moving.'

Leo let her tug him further along the path. They walked for a while in silence. There was a large black bird hopping from branch to branch along the edge of the path, keeping pace with them; it almost looked as if it was following them.

Is that a raven? Or a crow? Or a – what's the other one? – a rook?

She picked up a pine cone and threw it at the bird, which squawked and flew further into the wood. Beneath the dense canopy of the trees, the afternoon heat was stifling. It was hard to breathe, almost. Mobile signal was really patchy here.

What if there's some news about Gran? And now we're getting near the lake, I…

She turned to Leo, about to suggest they should go home, or that she should return alone if he really wanted to see Ronan, but her brother had stopped walking.

'Merry – do you believe in ghosts? I never asked you the other evening.'

She thought for a while, brushing her fingertips over the bark of a nearby birch tree. The smooth surface was pitted here and there with old scars.

'I don't know. I think… I think maybe the ghosts are inside us. Places and times we remember. People we loved that we don't want to let go of.' She found herself tracing the pattern of the Algiz rune across the bark. 'Like Jack. And Dan. Why?'

Leo opened his mouth, but he didn't get to answer. Another long wail split the air, sending birds fluttering up from the treetops – very close by this time. And definitely human.

Either in pain or terror, someone had screamed.

THIRTEEN

LEO STARTED RUNNING in the direction from
which the scream had come.

'Leo, wait!'

He shouted at her over his shoulder. 'Hurry up! It could
be Ronan. I have to help him.'

Merry began running too. She quickly caught up with
her brother.

'How far?'

'Few minutes… left path…' Leo pointed, and Merry
pulled ahead, sprinting in the direction he had indicated,
through the trees, ducking branches and jumping over
roots, until she burst into a large clearing – and there was

Ronan, standing nearby. Further off a boy was lying on the ground, not moving. Right in front of Ronan, kneeling on the grass at his feet, was another boy who was sobbing and writing with terror, had actually wet himself—

It was Simon.

Merry came to a halt just in front of Ronan.

'What the hell are you doing?'

Ronan looked confused.

'What?'

'What are you doing to him?' Merry crouched down next to Simon, but he didn't seem to be aware of her. He was staring ahead at something that wasn't there, flinching, begging for mercy from some invisible threat. As she watched he threw his hands up in front of his face and screamed again.

'*Stop it!*' Merry flung her outstretched fingers towards Ronan and he stumbled backwards, tripping and falling on to the grass. For a moment she thought he was going to retaliate: he brought one hand up, red sparks playing across his palm.

But then he smiled slightly and lowered his hand. Simon put his hands down too, but his eyes were still wide with terror and he stayed on his knees, breathing raggedly.

Leo jogged up and stopped next to Merry.

'What's going on? Ronan?'

Ronan stood up and brushed himself off.

'Your sister and I obviously disagree on how we should be treating poisonous jerks like this one.' He waved a hand and Simon gasped with pain.

'You can't go round torturing people!' Merry yelled. 'Even if they are horrible. It's just not—'

'No, *you* can't,' Ronan interrupted. 'But I don't have to follow any rules. You know what he did. And you know he deserves to be punished. Who else was going to do it?'

'I...'

'You knew?' Leo's voice was shaky. 'You knew it was Simon who attacked me, and you did nothing?'

For a minute, Merry couldn't think of anything to say. Leo and Ronan were both just looking at her.

'I – you...' She took a deep breath. 'Yes, I knew. And I went round to his house the next morning. I messed up his car—'

'So you... scratched his paintwork? And that made up for what he did to me?'

'No, that's not what I'm saying! But – but you told me not to get involved.'

'Yeah, right. And since when has that ever stopped you,

224

Merry? Maybe you're just angry with Ronan because he's the one actually doing something. Because he's actually been sticking up for me!'

'Sticking up for you?' She pointed to Simon, whimpering and shaking on the grass between them. 'Is this what you want? Is this what you would have asked me to do? Does this make you even now?'

Leo glared at Simon, and the strength of his emotions buffeted Merry like a storm-force wind. Anger, loathing, revulsion and also… pity; his confusion was dizzying. He turned away and strode into the trees, stopping to slam his fist against the bark of a nearby oak.

'Come on now, Merry,' Ronan said under his breath.

She tore her gaze away from her brother.

Ronan was shaking his head, as though he didn't quite believe her. 'Just admit it. Deep down, you wanted this too. You wanted to make those scumbags pay for what they did to your brother. For what they're still doing to him.'

She took a step away from Simon, clutching her hands behind her back. Because Ronan was right, wasn't he? She *had* wanted to make Simon pay. Every time she'd thought about him for weeks, she'd wanted to make him suffer. But seeing him now, grovelling in the dirt…

'Yes. It's what I thought I wanted. But this…' She waved a hand towards Simon. 'It isn't right.'

Ronan didn't answer. Just stared at her, his expression unreadable, for what felt like an age.

'Have it your own way.' He waved his hand again. Simon slumped sideways, eyes closed, mouth slack, like he'd suddenly fallen asleep. Merry knelt down to check his pulse and see if there were any obvious injuries she could attempt to fix.

'They followed me here from town, you know.' Ronan came to stand next to her. 'Must have recognised me from the other night, when I stopped them attacking Leo. They told me, in fairly graphic detail, how they were going to teach me a lesson. What else was I supposed to do?'

Merry stood up again.

'You're a wizard. I'm sure you could have thought of an alternative to torture.'

Ronan rolled his eyes.

'You're making far too much of this. It was all in his head. I didn't physically damage him, much as I wanted to.'

'So he'll be OK?' Leo walked up and stood next to Ronan. 'Him and Adam?' He jerked his head in the direction of the second guy, still unconscious on the grass.

'They'll both be fine.' Ronan brushed one hand against Leo's arm. 'I'm sorry if I went too far. I can make them forget the whole thing, if you like. It would be as if it'd never happened.'

'Please.' Leo entwined his fingers in Ronan's, blushing as he did so. 'I know you've got my back. And I appreciate what you tried to do, but...'

'But never do it again?' Ronan asked.

'I'd rather you didn't, on balance.' Leo shrugged. 'Despite what I said earlier, I don't really want to hurt him.'

'OK.' Ronan disengaged himself from Leo and walked over to kneel beside Adam, placing one hand on his head; Ronan's lips moved like he was murmuring words to himself. He returned to Simon and repeated the process. 'It's done.'

Simon opened his eyes; both he and Adam got up and started walking away from them.

'They're going back to their car, and when they get there, they'll get in and wake up and will simply feel confused as to why they drove all the way out here.' Ronan extended his hand towards Leo. 'Am I forgiven?'

'Sure.'

'Great.' Ronan pulled Leo into a hug. Merry dropped her gaze. It seemed too private a moment for an audience.

But then a surge of emotion made her glance up again. Relief, mingled with desire – and an undercurrent of something else. Before she could understand what she was sensing, the impression faded and disappeared.

Ronan released Leo and turned to her.

'Merry, sometimes I get things wrong. That's what comes of not having a family to keep me on the straight and narrow.' He held out a hand and Merry took it, expecting that he was going to shake it and then let go. But instead, he kissed it –

What is it with wizards and hand-kissing?

– then twirled her round so that he ended up with his other arm clasping her waist.

'What are you doing?'

'We're going to dance, to celebrate you two still being friends with me.'

'But I don't do this kind of dancing!'

Ronan ignored her. He pulled her tight against him and started humming while waltzing round in a circle. Possibly waltzing – Merry had no idea. She just kept trying to step in vaguely the right direction; it was either that or fall over. Leo was laughing. Faster and faster Ronan turned, his hand warm against her back, holding her so close she could feel his heartbeat and smell the aftershave he was wearing. For a brief moment she risked looking up, and found him staring at her intently, his dark eyes burning. Faster and faster they whirled, until she started to feel dizzy, sleepy…

'Stop – I have to stop.'

Ronan slowed down, spun her one last time and lowered her into a deckchair set up next to his tent.

Merry yawned. From here she could see a climbing rose, straggling up the oak tree nearby and drooping its tendrils across the outside of the tent. It looked like one of the roses that had been growing near that injured puppy she'd found – the wine-red flowers had the same heady aroma. Which was weird, because she didn't think that kind of rose grew near the lake, though she was feeling so drowsy it was hard to be sure of anything.

'It's just… too hot.' She blinked at Leo, suddenly so tired she could barely string a sentence together. 'I think I need a nap. Wake me up in half an hour.' She gave in to the weight of her eyelids without even waiting for his response.

It was twilight when Merry awoke. She felt sick and shaky; not surprising, given the dreams that had raged inside her head. A wolf wearing Gran's favourite necklace, and a giant black bird with a cruel, thorn-like beak, had chased her through a forest until she tumbled into a pit and was slowly buried alive, crushed beneath a pile of straw spun out of pure gold.

There were no texts from Mum on her phone.

No news on Gran, then, I guess. Still, Leo shouldn't have let me sleep for so long.

She tried to conjure a ball of witch fire; frowned when it didn't work – *What is wrong with me today?* – and tried again. This time a sparkling violet globe appeared in her hand. She stood up, shook some of the pins and needles away from her left leg and limped off to look for her brother.

He and Ronan weren't in the clearing. Instead, she spotted them in the distance, sitting down by the edge of the lake. Despite the sticky heat of the air, Merry shivered. She hadn't been back here since the day of Dan's funeral. Not in real life, at any rate. Her phone was still in her other hand. She tapped the edge of it against her leg, wondering whether it would be too pathetic to text Leo and avoid the lake altogether.

Yes. It is too pathetic.

Like Leo said, the lake was just a lake now. To believe anything else, to give in to fear, would somehow be handing Gwydion power over her. She took a deep breath, held her head up and walked forward.

The darkening sky had made the distance appear further than it was. But by the time Merry had been walking for five minutes she was quite close to the lake. Close enough to see that it had changed. The surface level had dropped and the air smelt of stagnant water and rotting plants. It reminded her so much of the dream she'd had, she wondered whether the dream had actually been a vision. Closer still, she saw that Ronan had his arm draped round Leo's shoulder. They were facing away from her, gazing out over the lake, but as she approached, Leo turned and smiled at her. He looked happier than she'd seen him for ages.

S'pose I can't blame him for not waking me.

'Hey. It's kind of late. D'you think we should be heading back? See whether the coven have made any progress?'

'Oh –' Leo's eyes widened, like he'd forgotten that Gran was missing – 'of course.' He glanced at his phone. 'No messages. I'll, um… I'll just be a minute.'

'Sure. OK.'

Merry wandered further along the side of the lake, not stopping until she felt certain she wouldn't overhear anything Leo and Ronan were saying to each other. It was almost dark now. The evening star hung bright in the eastern sky, while in the west, the sunset had faded to a faint glow on the horizon. She moved nearer to the water's edge, remembering all the evenings she had spent here with Jack. If she looked down into the depths, she could almost imagine the swirling vortex was opening up again, that Jack was suddenly going to appear on the grass beside her—

There was a shadow beneath the water. Merry dropped to her hands and knees, peering over the edge of the bank. She could see her reflection, but underneath that... There was definitely someone down there. And the figure was growing, getting closer. Alarm crept up the back of her neck. She wanted to get away from the water, but she couldn't resist leaning forward even further – like some force was drawing her downwards. Was Jack trying to come back to her? To come back *for* her? Unwillingly, but unable to stop, she stretched out her arm, reaching down to the surface of the lake, closer and closer...

'Hey, watch out!' Somebody grabbed her, pulled her back on to the bank. Merry rolled over: Leo was standing above her. 'What on earth were you doing? You nearly fell in.' He craned his neck to see into the water.

Merry pushed herself on to her knees and glanced back

at the lake. There was nothing there. Just her and Leo and the reflection of the stars above them.

'I thought I saw something, but whatever it was has vanished.' Or was never there in the first place.

'What was it? An eel?'

'Something like that.' She held out her hand so Leo could pull her to her feet. 'You ready to go home?'

'Yeah. Ronan's going to drive us back. But there's something he needs to tell you first.'

Merry's stomach rumbled.

'Will it take long?'

'No. He just needs to fill you in on our house guest.'

'Huh?'

'Finn.' Leo grinned like he was really pleased about something. 'Turns out he's got form.'

A few minutes later Merry was nibbling a biscuit and sipping tea from a tin mug, while Ronan told her what he knew.

'Finn was born in Ireland, but brought up in England until about three years ago. Then the family moved back to Ireland – to Donegal – and that's where I ran into them. Finn, and his twin brother, Cillian. A decent bloke, Cillian was. Is, I mean. Not like that arrogant…' He pulled a face. 'See, the Lombards don't like to talk about it, they've tried to keep it secret, but Cillian is –' he cast a quick glance at Leo – 'non-magical. Ordinary. That's why he didn't end up full of his own importance. We became friends.' Ronan took a swig from the bottle of beer he'd opened. 'How much do you know about the Kin Houses?'

'Er… not much.' A vision of Gran's still largely unread book rippled uncomfortably through Merry's mind.

'Well, wizards aren't like witches. Most of them don't pass on magic to their kids. But some do. On to their sons, at least.'

Merry remembered the chapter title.

'Dynastic wizards?'

'Yeah. The magic usually runs out after a hundred years or so, but in a few families, it just keeps going. They call themselves the Kin Houses. And the Lombards have been magical for bloody ever, practically.'

Merry grimaced.

'They must think they're pretty special.'

'Too right. So having a son who's not a wizard… it just doesn't look good. Makes the other dynastic wizards wonder whether the Lombard line is starting to fail.' Ronan sipped some more beer. 'It would have been far better if he'd been born a girl. The Kin House daughters are never magical, but at least they're valuable for alliances. They can be married off to someone from another Kin House in return for power, magical artefacts, whatever.'

Merry nearly choked on her tea.

'I can't believe it! That's just… *medieval.*'

Ronan shrugged.

'It's the way they've always done things. But Cillian… that wasn't an option for him. And his parents were embarrassed. Wanted him to stay quietly at home, not cause a fuss. But he wanted more than that. He asked me to try to teach him some magic, to see if I could, I dunno, wake up his latent power. I didn't think it was likely to work, but I couldn't see the harm in helping him try. His father didn't agree.'

'You're not going to tell me that he put his own son into a coma?'

'As good as. When their dad found out what was happening, he and Finn followed Cillian to where I was staying. We got into a fight, and…' Ronan rubbed a hand over his face. 'They took him back home, locked him up somewhere, but Cillian – he'd had enough. He managed to get hold of a potion of some sort and overdosed on it.' Ronan rolled the beer bottle between his fingers. 'I don't want to know what he was trying to do. But they've never been able to wake him up.'

It was like something out of a fairy tale. If Merry hadn't found Finn and his cousin in Gran's house, if she hadn't seen Finn's flashes of arrogance, she would never have thought them capable of being so... callous.

His own brother. To treat him like some kind of criminal, just because he's an ordinary person. Just so the family can keep pretending to be some kind of damn wizard aristocracy.

'We have to tell Mum.'

'No – please don't,' Ronan said. 'If he knows I'm here, he'll come after me, try to run me off. Finn's not much of a brother, but I don't think he's involved in what's happened to your gran.'

'But he must be!' Leo burst out. 'I bet... I bet Gran found out what they'd done and was going to tell someone, and he decided he had to silence her.'

Merry threw Ronan a questioning glance – Leo's theory certainly sounded plausible – but the wizard was shaking his head.

'Who would your gran tell? There's no... wizard police force. Unless other local wizards or witches choose to get involved – which they won't – there's no one to stop any of these guys doing exactly what they want. And none of the other Kin Houses would think they'd done anything wrong.' He nudged Leo gently. 'Finn has no reason to attack a witch. Especially one who's been a guest in their house. I wanted you to know the truth, but, please – keep this completely to yourselves.'

For a moment Merry thought Leo was going to carry on arguing, but he just exhaled loudly and settled for looking unconvinced.

'OK. I promise. We should go, though – I don't like the idea of that guy home alone with Mum.'

Twenty minutes later Ronan was pulling up outside their house. Leo and Ronan had chatted during the drive, but Merry was too busy thinking: about Ronan, what he'd done to Simon, what he told them about Finn. She jumped down from the van and turned to say goodbye.

'Thanks for the lift. See you soon.'

'No worries. You two watch yourselves. Especially you.' He pointed at her. 'Remember what happens at the end of almost every fairy tale you've ever read.'

'What?'

'The handsome prince? Doesn't he always have his own agenda?'

Ronan drove away before Merry had a chance to ask what the hell he was on about. She looked at Leo, eyebrows raised; her brother just shrugged and trudged towards the house. He seemed kind of... deflated, now Ronan had gone. Merry hurried to catch up with him.

'Hey – you OK?'

'Yeah. Why wouldn't I be?'

'Well, it was pretty horrible. That thing earlier, with Simon. I still can't believe Ronan thought it was all right.'

Leo frowned.

'What thing with Simon?'

'Er... the thing where we found Ronan torturing him?'

Leo still looked confused. Then his face cleared.

'Oh, that. It was nothing, really. No harm done.' He yawned. 'Lord, I'm starving... Um, what were we just talking about?'

Seriously?

There was no way he could have forgotten already. Unless, she supposed, he wanted to forget.

'Nothing. Let's go in.'

FOURTEEN

'I'M PRETTY SURE that wasn't meant to happen.' It was Friday morning, nearly a week after Finn's unorthodox arrival. Merry looked up from the shattered remnants of Gran's teapot spread across the centre of her bedroom carpet, to meet Flo's gaze. 'Did you get anything?'

'Other than a cut from the flying china? I'm not sure. Images. But too many of them.'

Merry sighed.

'Same. Five or six different places, as far as I could tell.'

In theory, the words they had sung should have given a single, clear image of Gran's location. But according to

Flo, the coven – using Gran's hairbrush – had got exactly the same result, and some of the witches were now searching a number of different towns and villages across the country. Something or somebody was interfering with the spell. So much for following the rules and doing things the right way.

Flo began singing a cleaning spell to get rid of the evidence. At least they knew Gran was definitely still alive; being part of a coven (even as a trainee) bound witches together in such a way that if the coven leader died, all would feel it. Gran was like… the central point of a web: the coven's collective threads of knowledge and experience ran through her. But these ties also told Merry that Gran was getting weaker every day, burning more and more dimly, like a fire running out of fuel.

Flo stopped singing and flopped down on the beanbag.

'D'you think we should tell Roshni that the same thing happened to us?'

'Definitely not. You're supposed to be keeping me on the straight and narrow, practising –' Merry glanced at the schedule she had stuck to her dressing-table mirror – 'basic transformation spells. If we tell her what we've really been doing, you'll get into trouble. I'll get into even more trouble.' Earlier this week she'd asked Roshni again whether she could help the coven in their efforts to locate Gran, and again Roshni had brushed her off. Oh, she pretended it was for Merry's own good, said she was worried that whoever attacked Gran might come after Merry too. But the truth was, the coven didn't trust her. 'Is your mum sticking to the new rules Roshni's been making, Flo?'

'Not really. Your gran was always—' She broke off, her face flushed. 'I mean, she *is* a good leader. Strong. But she never interferes in our personal lives. All this stuff about travelling in pairs and not going out at night…' Flo pulled a face: she obviously didn't think much of Roshni's precautions. 'I wouldn't mind so much if she would tell us what she was so worried about.'

Merry's gaze drifted over to where Gran's folder was hidden under her bed.

'How's it going with Finn, by the way?' Flo leant forward, eyes wide with curiosity.

Merry thought about the wizard currently occupying the spare room. Over the last few days he'd spent a lot of time in his room, mostly appearing for meals. When he did emerge he was super-polite. Helpful, even: he'd cooked dinner one evening and had been contacting other wizards to ask for help in tracking Gran. But Merry had seen him a few times from her bedroom window, standing in the front garden and talking on his mobile, shooting furtive glances back at the house, sometimes gesticulating like he was angry. It was a bit…

'Weird. I think he's weird, to be honest.'

'Oh.' Flo screwed up her eyes as if she was trying to picture Finn. 'He's quite fit, though.'

Merry laughed. 'Do you want to date him, then?'

'Are you kidding? Mum would literally skin me alive. Witches and wizards don't hook up. Never have done, never will. How can you not know that?'

'Dunno.' Merry shrugged. 'Never came up, I guess.' Yet another gap in her magical education. 'Well, even if he is fit, he's still really annoying. Sticking around like a piece of old chewing gum. And I don't trust him.'

'He's a wizard. Why would you?' Flo stood up and stretched. 'Right. I promised I'd take the dog for a walk before work this afternoon. You fancy coming with me?'

'I would, but I'm supposed to be giving Mum a hand.' Their mother was dealing with her frustrations by trying to sort through fifteen years of accumulated stuff. 'We're starting on the attic today. But I'll see you at the cafe later.'

After Flo left, Merry lay on her bed for a bit. Crawling

around among the dusty boxes up in the attic wasn't honestly that appealing. Plus, she still hadn't made any progress with Gran's folder. She grabbed it and spread the contents across the duvet cover.

List and photos – she wasn't going to look at those. Map. Letters she couldn't read. Boring book. Horrible illustration.

Opening the map, she laid it out in front of her. What had Gran meant by 'circles'?

Witches dancing in a circle?

Crop circles?

The photograph of Gran with Ellie Mills and a group of other witches flashed into her mind.

Stone circles.

If—

'Merry? Where are you?' It was Mum, walking along the landing. Hastily she refolded the map and shoved everything back into the folder. Clearly, the attic couldn't be avoided any longer.

Merry had the job of closing up the cafe today. She checked her phone, waiting for the display to change.

Five thirty. Right – home time.

She and Flo had already emptied the till and put the

money in the (magically warded) safe, and replaced everything that needed to be kept cold in the (magically refrigerated) fridge. Now they just had to close the blinds, pull the shutters down and lock the front door – while surreptitiously chanting the protective spell that was the real security. There was also a line of runes carved into the wall above the cafe, for those with the knowledge to see such things.

Leaving the (magically air-conditioned) shop was like entering an oven. Even in the late afternoon, the heat shimmered off the pavements in town, hazing the horizon. Flo was going shopping, but Merry didn't feel like it. She sat at the shady bus stop, then endured the fifteen minutes standing on the furnace-like bus as well as she could.

The house was quiet when she got in. Mum was spending the evening with Mrs Knox, and Leo was... wherever Ronan was, probably. Finn's car was in the driveway, and he wasn't standing outside the house talking on his phone, so Merry assumed he was upstairs in his room. It was a bit of a surprise when she walked into the garden and found him lying on the grass, wearing a pair of cut-off jeans and nothing much else. It looked like he was asleep. Merry took a step back, about to retreat indoors.

But why should I? It's my garden. He's just a guest.

She looked more closely.

A guest with pretty amazing abs… but still.

She coughed loudly and went to sit in one of the ancient deckchairs on the patio.

Finn scrambled up, raising his hands as though he was expecting an attack.

'Oh. It's you. Sorry.' He grabbed his top and pulled it on quickly. 'I must've fallen asleep.'

''S OK. I've just opened some lemonade, if you want some. It's in the fridge.'

Finn disappeared into the house, but returned a few moments later with a glass. He sat down in the deckchair next to her; Merry groaned inwardly.

'Good day?' he asked.

'It was all right. Working this afternoon. And this morning I was training. Practising transformation spells.'

'No news on your grandmother, I'm guessing?'

Merry shook her head. She hoped that if she stayed silent Finn would take the hint and go away. But he just sat there. Out of the corner of her eye she could see him watching her. Eventually it got too much.

'What?'

'I'm just wondering why you still dislike me so much.'

'Apart from the fact that you're an arrogant show-off

who thinks he's some kind of – of – I don't know, wizarding god?'

Finn laughed.

'Fair point.' The smile faded from his face. 'I just want to help my brother, Merry. I miss him. I know I didn't make the best first impression, but can we really not start again?'

Merry squinted at him, trying to read his face. He looked honest enough; there was that hint of humour again in his grey eyes, but the only emotion she could sense was sadness.

Maybe Ronan isn't telling us the whole story. Maybe he had something going on with Cillian that he doesn't want Leo to know about. Or maybe Finn was forced into stuff by his dad…

The weight of family expectations. She knew something about that.

'Fine. Whatever. We can start again.'

Finn grinned.

'Great. My name's Finn and I'm a dynastic wizard. I'm good at tracking spells, and I enjoy cooking.'

Merry smiled despite herself.

'OK. My name's Merry and I'm a witch. I love sport. And in April I killed a fifteen-hundred-year-old Anglo-Saxon wizard, so don't get any ideas.'

'Useful to know.' He settled back in the deckchair, stretching out his legs and clasping his hands behind his head. 'But not a lot of detail. Pretend I'm your best friend. Tell me something… exciting.'

'I don't think so. You're nothing like my best friend,' Merry countered. 'Besides, your own description wasn't exactly in-depth.'

Finn gazed at her for a moment like he was weighing something up. Then he dropped the relaxed posture and leant forward.

'OK. You asked about university the other morning. The truth is…' He paused and ran a hand through his hair. 'I can't go to university because my dad won't let me. He reckons my job is maintaining our position in society, and I don't need to go to uni to do that. If anything, he thinks it would be a distraction. A pointless waste of time.' He picked up his lemonade and started swirling the liquid around the inside of the glass.

'Oh.' Merry wasn't sure what she'd been expecting him to say, but it wasn't that. 'By society, I'm guessing you mean Kin House society?'

Finn gave a wry smile.

'The only type that counts. My father has suggested various methods for me to rescue the family fortunes, none of which I find particularly appealing.' He shrugged. 'Your turn.'

Merry played for time by gulping down her lemonade.

'Well, my magic… it's not normal. Or maybe I'm not normal.'

'Really? How?'

'I have trouble doing stuff the way a witch is supposed to. Sometimes because I find it hard, sometimes because – because it's just too much! All the singing and endless rote learning, when there are things I can do simply by thinking about them. Without even thinking about them half the time, which is what the coven don't like.' Merry remembered how she'd knocked Ronan flying last Sunday. There should have been a sequence of words to express exactly what she wanted to do, a sequence of notes to help her learn the words and increase their power. There should definitely have been something that she could write down and teach to other witches. Instead, there had just been a flash of inspiration, and a release of power. 'At my stage, I'm supposed to do things the way they've always been done.'

'Interesting. It sounds like our system is somewhere in between what you have to do and what ordinary wizards do. We have casting books full of family spells we have to learn. But nothing like the amount you have to deal with,

I'm guessing.' He tipped his glass up and drained the rest of his lemonade. 'Have you ever thought about chucking it in? Just doing stuff your own way?'

'I tried that when I was younger. It didn't exactly end well.' The idea of being completely on her own again, without any sort of network, was a little bit scary. 'But to be honest, I'm more and more tempted to tell the coven to get stuffed. And maybe I will, when Gran comes back.'

'I'm sorry. It's no fun feeling like you're being... forced into stuff.' Finn leant back in the deckchair again. 'But I guess I shouldn't be encouraging you to go rogue. I'm not exactly popular around here as it is.' He looked out across the garden. 'What's that over there?'

He was pointing towards a tarpaulin-covered mound next to the garage.

Confession time was clearly over.

'That's my car. Or it will be, if it ever gets fixed. I'm turning seventeen next week and I'm supposed to start learning how to drive, but at the moment it's in pieces.'

'Can't you fix it with magic?'

'I suppose I could try. But if it went wrong and I drove into somebody... Leo will get round to it one day.'

'Yeah.' Finn started fiddling with the strap on his watch.

'And what are you doing for your birthday? Going somewhere nice with your boyfriend?'

Merry couldn't help rolling her eyes.

'No.'

Finn waited, one eyebrow raised.

'Fine, don't tell me. I'm just being nosy, that's all. No ulterior motive.' He shook his head and looked glum. 'The girls I like never seem to like me in the same way. It's tough.'

Yeah, right.

'I bet it is tough.' She smiled at him. 'Although, being forever alone will give you so much more free time.'

Annoyance flashed across Finn's face. But the next moment he laughed.

'I'm clearly a lost cause.' He picked a dandelion clock from the lawn, held it out in front of him and waved his hand. The seeds spiralled upwards into the sky in a delicate double helix, leaving him holding the bare stem.

'Pretty,' Merry commented. Though she couldn't entirely suppress a twinge of jealousy.

I bet no one tells him his method is wrong.

Finn stood up and stretched.

'I thought I'd cook again tonight – fancy giving me a hand?'

'Sure. But can I ask you something first?'

'Go ahead.'

'Your brother... what really happened to him?'

Finn frowned at her.

'Why?'

'I just – I'd like to know.'

He picked at the edge of one fingernail for a few seconds.

'Like I said... he had an accident. I wasn't there, but it seemed as though he'd tried out a potion on himself.' His voice was expressionless, but his face... He looked so different from the boy she'd been joking with a few moments ago. Tired. Older. Much more serious. 'Magic is dangerous. You know that.'

Merry hesitated. She wanted to ask, *Do you know a wizard called Ronan? Cos he's got a different version of what happened.* But she didn't. 'You're right. It is dangerous.'

Finn nodded.

'Especially if you're anywhere near Ciarán when he's been at my uncle's whiskey collection and decides to start magically redecorating whatever room he's in. Turned one of his friends tartan a few months back.' He winked and smiled at her, and the serious young man Merry had glimpsed disappeared again. 'Come on. Let's go chop stuff up.'

Merry stood and followed Finn into the kitchen.

He's either an extremely good liar, or he's telling the truth. I wish I knew which.

Finn had gone out by the time Merry got up on Saturday morning, so she, Mum and Leo had the house to themselves. During a late breakfast Merry filled them in on her rather bizarre evening with their visitor. For the most part Finn had been almost excessively charming, offering to teach her family spells and entertaining her with stories about the things he and his twin brother used to get up to as children. But every so often he would say something patronising or sexist, or both. Whatever he said about his dad, he clearly believed that there was a hierarchy in magical society: the Lombards were at the top, followed by the other Kin Houses, then regular wizards. Witches were most definitely at the bottom of the pile.

Mum chuckled – the first time Merry had seen her look even remotely happy for days.

'So how did Finn think that criticising witches was going to help him get into your good books?'

'No idea. He'd make some really ridiculous comment about a magical disaster caused because the people involved were "only witches" and then he'd go back to…' She paused. 'I don't know. If the circumstances were different, I'd say he was flirting.' *Like it was an Olympic sport, and this was his last chance to win gold.*

Leo looked puzzled.

'What do you mean, "if circumstances were different"?'

'Well, my gran's missing and his brother is in a coma. Surely he wouldn't be trying to flirt with me now?'

'He's a bloke. We're good at compartmentalising.' Leo frowned at his cornflakes. 'And he's a git, if you need more evidence. I think I should teach him a lesson, then throw him out.'

Mum tutted.

'Do stop being so... melodramatic, Leo. Your sister can take care of herself. Finn may be a bit full of it, but he's harmless enough. And he certainly is a very good-looking young man. Just like his father at the same age.' A sort of dreamy look came into Mum's eyes, and Merry and Leo grimaced at each other. 'But he was genuinely charming, and so gentle and compassionate.'

'Mum, please...' Merry began.

Mum laughed. 'Fine. But he *was* lovely. It sounds as though he's changed now, of course; it must be at least twenty years since I last saw him – and that woman he married.' She pulled a face like she'd bitten into an under-ripe plum. 'Not a good influence on him, I should think.'

'Huh.' Leo grunted. 'Must be where Finn gets it from.'

'Forget about him,' Mum said. 'How's it going with Ronan?'

The sulkiness disappeared from Leo's face like someone had waved a wand. He grinned at them both.

'Well, he's great. Really great.' Leo went off into a long, involved description of how perfect Ronan was. He was mostly talking to Mum, so after a couple of minutes Merry let her attention wander and stared out across the sun-bitten garden. The cracked earth and desiccated flower beds were so different from how they had looked in March.

Trouble is, if I keep comparing everyone I meet to Jack, I'll never trust anybody.

Finn seemed to be more or less on the level. And Ronan seemed to be good for her brother. Leo was definitely in love and for all she knew, Ronan loved him back. It was still difficult to excuse what he'd done to Simon the other day. But love made you do strange things sometimes – things you wouldn't do in normal circumstances.

She of all people knew that.

★

Merry was woken at seven the next morning by the grandfather clock on the landing; Finn had helpfully found the key and wound the damn thing up again. It was going to be another hot day. Sunbeams were already blazing round the edges of her curtains, gilding the slowly tumbling dust motes. She watched them through half-closed eyes and thought about her dream.

She'd been at the lake with Jack again. This time they were dancing in the moonlight – old-fashioned dancing like Ronan had made her do the other day. Jack hadn't spoken to her, hadn't even really looked at her. Then halfway through a turn, he'd stopped being Jack and had become Finn. And she'd been glad because Finn held her close and smiled at her and she could feel the warmth of him. And even when he started telling her how he'd killed his brother, she didn't really care…

Guilt nagged at the back of her mind, and she forced herself to get up and open the curtains. There was a slightly odd smell in this part of the room – sort of smoky. She opened the window to let in some fresh air.

'Oh…'

The rune on the windowsill, the one she'd carved the other day, had turned black round the edges. She ran her finger across it. A smudge of soot came away on her skin.

Had someone tried to break through the protection of the rune? Or was it breaking down because of something she'd done? Some fault in the way she'd made the mark?

There was a knock at her bedroom door. Mum came in, her eyes red-rimmed like she'd been crying again. Merry hurried towards her.

'Gran?'

She held her breath, but Mum shook her head.

'No. Still no news on Gran. I've just had Flo's mum on the phone, and something... something's not right.'

'What?'

'Apparently, Flo said she was going out yesterday afternoon to meet up with some boy she's become friendly with.'

'Oh yeah. She's mentioned him. I think she met him at a party a few weeks back.'

'Well... she didn't come home last night. She isn't answering her phone. And no one knows where she is...'

FIFTEEN

'**DENISE HASN'T SEEN** her since yesterday morning. But it's possible she planned to leave. There's a…' Mum paused, pinching the bridge of her nose. 'A rucksack missing and some of her clothes.'

'We talked a while back about going to the festival in Godalming,' Merry said.

'Oh, really?' Hope leapt in Mum's eyes.

'Yeah, I thought she'd kind of lost interest. Maybe she changed her mind.' Though why would she go without telling anyone? Merry's stomach cramped. Running off in secret didn't seem like Flo's kind of thing. 'We should help look for her.'

'No.' Mum held up a hand. 'I have offered, but Roshni wants us to stay here. She's asked some of the others to go with Denise.'

Merry groaned.

'Why won't she let me help with anything? I'm going to go anyway.'

'Absolutely not!' For a moment, Merry was reminded of how stubborn her mother had been before Merry nearly died in Northumberland; perhaps Mum was reminded of the same thing. She continued in a softer voice. 'If there is someone going round targeting witches...' Mum took a deep breath, exhaling slowly. 'I might have lost my mother already. I can't risk losing you too. I'm not *telling* you, but I'm *asking* you: please stay at home. For my sake.'

There was no way Merry could argue with that.

The next couple of days were an unpleasant mixture of boredom and tension. The coven, based at Mrs Knox's house, were trying everything they could to trace Gran and Flo. Favours had been called in from other covens, and teams of witches were scouring the country, magically and physically. Even though the tracking spells still seemed to be malfunctioning, they were following up each and every lead. But there was no news. Merry spent pretty much the whole time cooped up inside the house, trying – and failing – to make sense out of Gran's folder. She wasn't *not* allowed out, but she knew Mum would worry unless she went with her or Finn. It was sort of an informal house arrest.

Leo was allowed to carry on as normal, so she didn't see that much of him. Whenever he was at home, he seemed oddly detached. Like all he could think about was Ronan. It made Merry a little nervous. But she reminded herself that the coven would definitely have checked Ronan out – they were hardly likely not to investigate a wizard who had arrived in Tillingham only a couple of weeks before Gran disappeared. And if Ronan was keeping Gran hostage, why on earth would he simultaneously be dating Leo? So Merry decided not to worry about it any more. Ronan made Leo happy. And if Leo was happy, then she was happy too.

Now it was Wednesday morning, exactly two weeks since Gran went missing. Merry went down to the kitchen; Mum was there, finishing a piece of toast and staring absently into the air, but there was no sign of Leo or Finn.

'Hey, sweetheart.' Mum smiled automatically. 'You're up early. What have you got planned today?'

'Oh, not much. Some practice, I guess. Update my journey book. I might drop into the fencing club.' Duelling with somebody would probably be quite therapeutic. 'What about you?'

'I'm going to visit Belinda. Hopefully I'll bring back some cake.' Belinda was a slightly older witch. Merry didn't know her very well, but she had a reputation for motherliness and awesome cooking. 'I'll probably be home late afternoon, but I've checked with Finn and he said he can stay here all day. If you do want to go out, ask him to drive you.'

Merry gritted her teeth.

'I wish you wouldn't ask Finn, like he has to babysit me or something. I don't mind if he's here, but—'

'Just humour me, darling.' Mum tilted her head and studied Merry's face. 'Besides, I get the impression he wants to be here.'

Merry didn't reply.

Whatever game Mum is playing right now, I am not joining in.

'OK, then.' Mum got up and emptied the dregs of her coffee into the sink. 'If you decide to go out, text me.'

Merry didn't ask Finn to drive her anywhere. She didn't want to feel like she owed him anything, especially if Mum was putting pressure on him to stick around. Instead, she went up to her room and got the map out of the folder and began studying the seven locations again, looking them up on the internet, checking for nearby stone circles or for something else that might be described as a monument. Which turned out to be almost anything. Single stones, barrows, cairns and countless other structures. After a couple of hours she had a list in her journey book, but it needed serious narrowing down. The trouble was she didn't know enough about what she was actually looking for. How big the 'points of intersection' were, whether they were permanent, whether they were caused by stone circles or other monuments, or whether the monuments were built to mark them.

Gran must have had a book about it. A book that was probably destroyed by whoever took her.

Merry swore and threw the map across the room, wincing as the muscles in her neck and shoulders complained.

This is hopeless.

Her fingernails hurt. She started shaking her hands, trying to get rid of the excess energy coursing through her body, but as she did so she caught her forefinger on the splintered edge of her desk and sliced it open –

'Ouch!'

Three drops of blood fell on to the pages of her journey book, spreading across the paper, soaking into her list of potentially magical places, and a memory stored in her subconscious exploded...

Blood magic.

She'd seen a book on it once, at Gran's house. A very old book. Gran had snatched it out of her hands when she'd caught Merry reading it.

Dangerous magic. Or not natural, for a witch.

But for a wizard?

Two minutes later, Merry was knocking on the door of the spare room. She still didn't particularly trust Finn, but there was no one else to ask. The murmur of a conversation stopped, and Finn opened the door, mobile in hand. He looked like he'd just woken up – his hair was rumpled and he was only wearing a pair of boxers. Merry could feel herself blushing.

Though I don't know why I should be embarrassed. I'm not the one standing half-naked in someone else's house.

She cleared her throat.

'Do you know anything about blood magic?'

Finn frowned.

'I know that it's risky. Why?'

'I want to try to use it, to find Gran. But I don't know how. Can you help me?'

'Not sure. I only have a... theoretical knowledge. Why aren't you suggesting this to the coven?'

'Cos I'm pretty sure they won't do it. Not until they've tried everything else. And by then it might be too late.' Merry swallowed, forcing back the sudden swell of sorrow that had risen in her throat. 'Please? You said you wanted to help.'

'OK. Give me ten minutes. I'll come to your room.'

Merry went back to her room, sat on her bed and texted Flo again.

> I hope you pick this message up. I'm going to try something. Hope it will lead me to Gran. Hope it will lead me to you too, eventually. Please be OK. Text me back if you can. Xx

Finn knocked on her door a few moments later. Merry let him in, threw him a beanbag to sit on and put a privacy spell on the door.

'OK. So what do I need to do?'

★

Half an hour later, Merry was starting to understand why Gran had snatched the book out of her hands. Blood magic, even at the 'reasonably respectable' end of the scale, was definitely creepy. As Finn shared his knowledge, Merry realised that she'd already participated in a blood-magic ritual: back in March, when Gran had cut Merry's hand open and had used her blood in creating the protective rune on the back of her hand, just before she went to face Gwydion. She'd also seen it used in a vision: Gwydion himself, feeding the puppet hearts he'd created with his own blood. The risk of using blood magic, especially in such dark spells, was that it tended to attract the evil energy of the shadow realm, and that was not the kind of attention anybody in their right mind wanted.

Finn was regarding her thoughtfully.

'Are you sure you want to do this?'

Was she? The established spells weren't working, and the information Gran had left was too sketchy to provide any quick answers. She didn't really have any other options. But that wasn't all. The idea of doing something not in one of the official knowledge books, something *not* tried and tested by a hundred other witches – it was liberating. Exhilarating. Like she was breathing freely for the first time in weeks. The power flowing within her hummed in response, making her skin tingle.

'Yes. I'm sure.'

'Good.'

Merry raised her eyebrows.

'They think they have all the answers,' Finn scowled down at his hands. 'My dad. Your coven. But they don't.' He gestured at the stack of books on Merry's desk. 'And neither do they. You should go for it. We just have to figure out what exactly you might do.'

For a while they both thought silently, Finn now sprawled in the wicker chair in the corner, Merry pacing up and down the room. She kept going back to what she knew Gran had done.

Finn sat up.

'There was something I read once, about magic blades being used as compasses. Do you think you could get hold of a set of knives?'

Knives?

Bloody hell, I'm an idiot.

In two strides Merry was on her knees in front of the wardrobe, pulling out the box hidden in the bottom. Finn came to look over her shoulder.

'What have you got there?'

'This.' She held Gran's knife up. 'Obsidian blade.' The handle felt warm in her hand, almost like it was reacting to the power under her skin. 'It's the knife Gran used on me in the spring. I bet she used it on herself at some point.' She screwed her eyes up, trying to remember. 'And there was something in the book she had, something about blood having a memory...'

'That might work.' Finn was nodding. 'You're related, so your gran's blood is in you already, in a way.'

Merry went to perch on the windowsill, looking out across the hedge and the road and the fields beyond.

A book with a proper spell, properly written out, would be kind of useful right now.

But as far as she knew, there was no such spell. She smiled to herself a little.

I'm going to do this my way.

They'd closed the curtains, and Merry was lighting candles that she'd arranged in a wide circle around the room. It probably wasn't necessary, but they created the right sort of atmosphere. More... witchy.

She set the last candle in place and glanced across at Finn. 'Ready?'

'Not quite.' He waved a hand at the nearest candle,

extinguishing then relighting it. 'I think we need to strike a bargain. You want me to help you with this, and I want something in return.'

Merry narrowed her eyes.

'What exactly do you want?'

'A kiss.' He smiled slightly. 'It's not much to ask.'

A kiss? What kind of game was he playing? *Being a typical arrogant wizard, presumably. Or maybe just a typical teenage boy.* Merry shook her head.

'No. No way.' She arranged a pile of old tea towels on the floor in front of her, and put Gran's knife on top of them. Finn didn't seem to be in any hurry to storm out of the room. When she looked back up at him he was frowning at her, chewing on his bottom lip.

'Well? Are you going to help me or not?'

His eyes hardened. 'I'll help you. But –' he reached over and caught hold of her wrist – 'if I do, and if it works, then you have to kiss me. Otherwise I won't help you again.' He let go of her. 'Deal?'

Merry stared at the knife in front of her. From what Finn had said, blood magic was unreliable as well as dangerous. Even with his assistance, the most likely outcome was that absolutely nothing would happen. And if it did work…

I could tell him to get stuffed, because I probably won't need his help again.

Or I could kiss him.

The sudden spark of desire in her belly startled her. She rested her fingertips on the cold solidity of the black blade.

It's been a long time since I've kissed anyone. And Jack... Jack isn't coming back.

'Fine.' She spoke to the knife, not looking at Finn. 'We have a deal.'

Picking up her own knife, she held it firmly in her left hand. 'OK. I really have no idea what I'm doing, but I want you to use any spells you know for memory: strengthening it, calling it back, that sort of thing.'

'There's a spell we call *Reminisci*. My dad made me learn it by heart a few years back. What are you going to do?'

'I'm going to force the knife to talk to me. To help me find Gran.' That was the general idea. 'Ready?'

Finn nodded and held his hands above Gran's knife. He began... not exactly singing, but definitely chanting. Strands of pale blue light started to snake from his fingers, swirling across the space between them. Merry took a deep breath, held her right hand out and pushed the point of her knife into the soft skin of her palm. The blood began to drip on to the obsidian blade below, and as it did so, she spoke to it.

Remember me? You've tasted my blood before, a few months ago…

She imagined herself back in the circle of witches, Gran holding the obsidian knife, drawing it across her hand – the bitter sting of the cut; the blade gleaming in the firelight; the blood running across its black surface.

Remember…

Some other force grabbed her mind, and images began to race across her vision. Images from Gran's life, not hers: watching Merry walk away through the woods to face Gwydion; the unbearable waiting; the relief when Merry and Leo returned alive; training Merry; running coven meetings…

The images sped up, blurring together: healing Leo's eye, Ilaria's leg breaking, taking the train to Salisbury – faster and faster, until Merry was crying out for it to *slow down, wait* – shock and magic and anger and pain and exhaustion, overwhelming her, dragging her towards nothingness…

'Merry? Are you all right?' Merry felt an arm round her shoulders, supporting her head. Another hand was on her neck, cool fingertips resting against her skin, checking her pulse.

Leo?

She opened her eyes. Not Leo, but Finn, brows drawn together, his face full of concern.

'Yes,' she murmured, 'I think so.'

Merry gazed up at him, watching the candlelight flicker across his features, bringing out the red of his lips and the hints of steel blue amidst the grey of his eyes. Her pulse started to race beneath his touch. Finn moved his hand from her neck to her face, curving his fingers round her cheek, bending closer, and she began to tilt her mouth up to meet his…

He drew back, letting her down gently on to the floor and sliding his arm out from underneath her neck.

'I'll, um—' He stopped and cleared his throat. 'I'll get you some water.' Merry heard the bedroom door open and close. She rolled on to her side and sat up.

What had just happened?

And why would he act like he wanted to kiss me, and then…

Was he playing her? Or had she completely misread his actions?

This is ridiculous.

I don't even like the guy.

Bloody wizard.

I just… I really thought he was going to kiss me.

She got up and opened the curtains and leant out of the window. The next moment Finn was beside her, holding out a glass.

'Here you are.'

His fingers brushed against hers. They both flinched, spilling half the water across the windowsill. Both tried to apologise at once. Both paused.

'After you,' Merry prompted.

'Um… Do you know if it worked? The blood magic?'

Merry drank what was left of the water and put the glass down.

'Well, something happened. We should check.' She went to fetch the obsidian knife, but Finn caught hold of her arm.

'Hold on – your hand.'

Merry looked down. Blood was smeared across her palm, and was still oozing from the cut she'd made.

'It's fine. I'll sort it out.'

'No, it's not. Injuries from magical blades take longer to heal, you know that. And you can't put a bandage on with one hand.' He picked up the first-aid kit that was lying on Merry's bed and tore open an antiseptic wipe.

There didn't seem any point in arguing. She held her hand out while Finn cleaned the wound, spread some of Gran's healing salve on the skin and covered it with a dressing.

'There.' He started to repack the kit. His voice was steady, but Merry could see he was blushing. She muttered her thanks and turned away to get the knife, taking it to the window so she could look at it in the light, wondering whether Finn had noticed the scarlet in her cheeks too.

'Oh...'

'What?'

'The blood's gone. And I'm pretty sure these runes are new.' The blade, smooth and polished before the blood magic, was now covered in lines of runic writing. Merry couldn't read the whole thing, and the runes were so small she had to screw up her eyes to see them clearly, but she recognised some words: *river, valley, darkness*. The description of a place? 'Can you read this?'

Finn came to stand next to her and she passed him the knife, carefully not touching his hand this time. For a while he stood, peering at the blade, running a fingertip across the runes.

'How the hell did you do this? I mean, it's obsidian. Magically hardened volcanic glass. How did it suddenly get... engraved?'

'I don't know. I just... wanted some information.' Exactly the kind of magic the coven didn't like: she couldn't explain what she'd done, and she couldn't teach anyone else to do the same thing. Finn was still turning the knife over in his fingers.

'It's seriously impressive. You're more powerful than I thought.'

'Thanks a lot. But do you know what it means?'

He shook his head.

'Sorry. I'm not good with runes.'

'Damn.' She pressed her fingers to her temples.

The one thing I really, really don't want to do.

But it looked like she had no choice. 'I'll have to talk to the coven.' She held out her hand for the knife.

Finn didn't give it to her.

'I think...' He paused, biting his bottom lip again, like he was making a difficult decision. 'I think I should come with you.'

'What? No!' She didn't want to owe Finn for any more favours. Or irritate the coven more than she was already going to by turning up with a wizard in tow. 'I can take care of myself.'

'I know that. But I can drive you.'

'I'd rather walk.'

'Then let me walk with you. Please?'

Merry stared into his eyes, trying to figure out what on earth his deal was.

First he wants to kiss me, then he doesn't, and now he's desperate to go on a walk with me. Is he deliberately being irritating, or can he just not help himself?

But Gran was only hanging on by a spider's thread; Merry didn't have time right now to get into a fight with Finn.

'Fine.' She took the knife out of his hand, ignoring the lurch in her stomach when she touched his skin. 'Let's go.'

The coven was currently using Mrs Knox's house as a base, so it wasn't that far. Finn spent the whole time basically explaining to Merry how wealthy his family was. That's how it came across, at any rate. Every topic of conversation somehow led on to a description of the house where he'd grown up (in the poshest part of London, naturally), or the place where he lived now (five acres of land in Donegal, set on the edge of a sea lough), or what kind of car his dad drove (a Bentley). When a mention of Leo somehow turned into a discussion of Finn's grandfather's brilliant medical career, Merry tuned out.

She wondered briefly why Finn was telling her all this stuff, but she was too preoccupied with how she was going to explain the blood magic to the coven to give his bragging much brain space.

If I give the knife to Roshni on her own, perhaps she won't tell the others what I did. Surely she won't want to make my reputation for crazy, non-witch behaviour any worse?

'So what do you think?'

Merry blinked. 'Um…'

Finn gave a huff of exasperation.

'You weren't listening to me.'

'Yes, I was. Donegal, London, Bentley… I only missed that last question. I've got a lot on my mind.'

'I s'pose. What I said was, we've rented a villa in Tuscany for the last week of August. Would you like to come with us?'

Random. And thoughtless, in the circumstances.

'Finn, my grandmother is missing. And now one of my best friends has vanished too. And even if everything was totally normal, tagging along on your family holiday would be weird.' Finn flushed. He looked upset – with himself or her, she couldn't tell. Merry sighed. 'Thanks for asking me, though. I guess.' Mrs Knox's house came into view round the bend of the road. 'Oh, look, we're here.'

She was aware of Finn sticking close behind her as she walked through Mrs Knox's front garden. He was obviously more nervous of the coven than he let on. Merry rang the doorbell and within a few moments Mrs Knox had opened the door. She smiled at Merry, but frowned when she spotted Finn.

'Had a feeling we might see you today, Merry. Come in.' Merry stepped forward, and so did Finn – but Mrs Knox stuck out her arm to block his way. 'Not you. You can wait out here.'

That sulky glower Merry recognised marred Finn's features, but he didn't reply. Just slouched over to the nearby garden bench. Mrs Knox waited till he'd sat down before leading Merry inside. She began striding back down the long corridor that lead to the old ballroom and Merry had to hurry to keep up.

There were only seven other witches in the large room; Mum had told her that most of the coven were still out investigating the various locations indicated by the tracking spells, and others were now searching for Flo. Merry could see evidence of the work that had been going on: a large glowing map of the country magically projected on to the back wall, with more detailed maps on the other walls; stacks of books everywhere; long tables cluttered with rune stones, knives, bowls, bunches of herbs and bottles of variously coloured liquids. The air was scented – woodsmoke, pine needles, incense, among other things – and she noticed that the flames of the candles dotted about the room seemed to be edged with a kaleidoscope of different shades.

Roshni walked over.

'Merry. What are you doing here? Did you leave the house unaccompanied?'

'The wizard came with her.' Mrs Knox's voice was neutral, but Roshni's frown deepened.

'I had to come. I need to show you something.' She reached into her bag and brought out Gran's knife. 'Can we go somewhere private?'

But Roshni didn't seem to be listening to her. She was staring at the knife.

'Where did you get that?' Her eyes widened and she plucked the knife from Merry's hands. 'And *what* have you done to it?'

'I found it on the day Gran went missing.' Anger flared in Merry's chest. 'It's my grandmother's knife. Why shouldn't I have it?' The other witches were moving closer, drawn by the raised voices. Merry tried to ignore them. 'I wanted to do something to help. And I think I have. These runes are directions of some sort. If you can—'

'Blood magic.' Roshni finally looked up from the blade of the knife, cutting across Merry's explanation. 'You did blood magic, on your own and without any training. Have you any idea how dangerous this is?'

'I know, but nothing else seems to be working.' Merry paused, then she couldn't help herself. 'Sticking to the rules and doing what we've always done isn't going to bring Gran back.'

Roshni's fury hit Merry like a hammer blow, filling her mind with such a storm of anger that it forced Merry backwards.

'So you're trying to prove that the way you do magic is better? That centuries of tradition and learning are worthless?'

'No, that's not what—'

'Did it ever occur to you that the rules you seem so intent on disregarding are there for the protection of *all of us*, not just you? That your reckless behaviour is risking the lives of every one of your coven sisters? That your arrogance might have injured your grandmother further, or led Flo into some terrible danger?' Roshni shook her head, like there weren't enough words to describe Merry's stupidity. 'Was Flo mixed up in this? Or that young wizard?'

The thought of telling Roshni that she'd involved Finn in the blood magic made her feel sick.

'No. And Flo didn't do anything wrong.' The other witches were completely silent. Merry felt the tears filling her eyes, overspilling on to her cheeks, and dashed them away uselessly. 'But what about the knife?'

Roshni glanced at the blade again.

'The coven will examine it, and then we will make a decision.' She passed the knife to Mrs Knox. 'We have work to do, Merry. Go home.'

The coven. Not including her. Merry felt like the anger, frustration and humiliation swelling in her throat was about to choke her. As Roshni turned away, Merry stepped forward and grabbed her by the arm.

'But you wouldn't let me help! You just kept excluding me. What was I supposed to do?'

Roshni shook her hand away.

'While Elinor is missing, I am responsible for the welfare and protection of this coven.' Her voice was like a whip. 'You were supposed to do as you were told.'

SIXTEEN

MERRY PRACTICALLY SPRINTED out of the ballroom. As she hurtled through the front door, Finn jumped up and raced after her. 'Hey, what's wrong?'

'We're leaving. Don't talk to me.'

She didn't want to tell him what had happened. Didn't want to explain that Roshni had publically humiliated her. That the coven had rejected her help – again. That she was being sent to wait at home like a naughty child, while the *real* witches got on with trying to rescue her grandmother. But by the time they'd walked halfway back to the house, the silence was unbearable. She turned on Finn.

'Just say it, why don't you?'

He frowned at her.

'What?'

'Say what you're really thinking: that there's something wrong with me. That's why none of the others trust me, why they keep excluding me—'

'Hey! I wasn't thinking that at all. I was thinking about lunch, actually.' He took a step towards her. 'Maybe you'll feel better if you eat something. You might be able to, you know, put things in perspective...'

Merry struggled to think of a response.

'*Perspective?* Are you an actual idiot? I don't need perspective. And I don't need a lecture on meal times. What I need is to find my grandmother!' Her fingernails started to ache. Worse than they had done for weeks. 'Oh no.' She began running away from Finn, into the woods, but she could hear him following her, calling out for her to stop.

She tried to speed up, to lose him. But the agony in her nails was growing, spreading through her hands and up her arms until it was so bad she stumbled and fell to her knees, moaned with the pain of it, couldn't hold it back any more—

Magic blazed out of her fingers, a torrent of white

sparks swarming over the huge yew tree directly in front of her, somehow bleeding it of colour…

'What the hell are you doing?'

Finn was not far off now, staring at the tree. As the sparks faded and Merry slumped backwards, he started to walk towards her.

'Get away from me.'

'No. I need to take you home.'

Merry brought her hands up. They were shaking and there was blood oozing from the edges of her nails, streaking her fingers. She remembered what she'd done to Ronan, how she'd sent him flying.

Finn fell backwards like someone had shoved him. His eyes widened in surprise.

'I'm warning you,' Merry called out to him. 'Go away!'

He shook his head and got back up.

'No.'

She gritted her teeth and sent another spell towards Finn – a stinging hex. But he was ready for her this time and blocked most of it with a shielding spell. He winced, but he didn't stumble.

Oh, for…

'Leave me alone!' Merry screamed at him, hurling spell after spell in his direction, not thinking, barely breathing, the rage and grief boiling out of her. Still Finn kept coming, until he was standing barely a metre in front of her. Abandoning magic, she leapt at him, trying to hit him, to hurt him. For a moment they struggled.

Sounds floated across the air, breaking through Merry's fury: voices, laughter, high-pitched squealing. A family out for a walk. She froze. Finn pushed her to the ground and clapped a hand over her mouth.

'Stay still.' He closed his eyes, murmuring something under his breath. The voices got closer and closer.

Merry panicked. She kicked Finn, trying to shove him away so she could run, but he tightened his grip, holding her still, hissing in her ear 'Wait! Just – wait…'

The voices began to recede. The family had obviously changed their minds about walking in that direction. Or they'd had their minds changed for them.

Finn let go of her and rolled away. Merry lay where she was, staring up at the chinks of blue sky between the trees. There was a plane flying somewhere nearby. Birdsong. Everything was normal.

Maybe nothing from the last ten minutes had really happened. Or maybe she could pretend they hadn't. Maybe, if she lay here long enough, the whole of the last month might somehow be erased…

Finn grunted with pain and the illusion slipped away. Merry pushed herself up to see what she'd done, and nearly stopped breathing.

He'd taken his T-shirt off and was prodding at a large red bruise across his right side. His arms were covered in scratches and burns and there was a smear of blood on his neck.

'Finn?'

He didn't look up. Why would he? Any minute now he was going to walk away. He'd pack up his stuff and go back home and she'd never see him again, and there would be no one left to help her, no one.

She turned away from Finn and curled into a ball on the forest floor as the sobbing erupted, forcing itself up through her chest and throat, wracking her whole body, making her shake.

Finn's arms were round her, pulling her up so her head was resting on his chest.

'It's OK, Merry. It's going to be OK.'

Eventually, the tears ran dry. Merry didn't want to move. It was comfortable, having Finn hold her, listening to his heartbeat in the darkness behind her eyelids. But Gran was still missing, and so was Flo. She disentangled herself and sat up.

'I'm really sorry. I didn't want to hurt you. That's why I ran away.'

'Don't worry about it: I'll live.' Finn pushed himself to his feet, wincing slightly, and went to retrieve his T-shirt. 'When we get home, I'll use some of that potion you've got. It won't take long to…' He frowned at something behind her, folded his arms and let out a low whistle. 'Never seen that before.'

He was looking at the yew tree that had borne the brunt of Merry's outpouring of magic. At least – it still had the same shape as a yew tree. Merry stood and walked up to it. She could see the individual needles, the berries beginning to develop. But everything was colourless, transparent.

Ice?

She reached out to skim her fingers across one of the branches…

It shattered beneath her touch, dissolving into a crystalline powder that glittered against her skin.

Glass.

'I… I just don't…'

'No.' Finn carefully tapped a fingernail against one of the sparkling branches; it chimed. 'Me neither.' He started walking round the tree while Merry brushed the glass powder off her hand. She couldn't even figure out what kind of spell she must have used. The tree was undeniably beautiful. But there was no point to it.

It's even less useful than a glass slipper....

A shout of horror from Finn jerked her out of her preoccupation. Finn was crouching down, looking at something, but as she ran towards him he staggered up and held his arms wide.

'Merry, wait!'

There was somebody lying on the ground, half hidden by the undergrowth.

Finn was talking, but Merry couldn't hear him; the thumping of her heart was too loud. Pushing past him, she sank to her knees and swept aside the curtaining ferns.

The neck and arms were bruised and streaked with dark, dried blood. And the face – the face was covered with deep scratches. And – and holes on each side, where the flesh had been gouged out, leaving everything swollen and disfigured. But not disfigured enough to stop Merry recognising the features of her friend.

Oh God, Flo. What happened to you?

The coven arrived quickly. Finn – after both he and Merry had thrown up – had taken her mobile and called Mum and Roshni. Within a few minutes there were a dozen or more witches in the woods. Lots of them were crying.

Now, Merry and Finn were sitting by themselves, waiting in silence. Some of the witches were caring for Flo's body. Some were examining the site, casting reveal spells and taking samples of the earth. Some were staring at the glass tree.

Then came the moment Merry had been dreading: Flo's mum, Denise, arrived. She was supported by Mrs Galantini and another witch whose name Merry couldn't remember. But when she saw Flo's body, she broke away from the other women, ran to her daughter and gathered her up in her arms, screaming her name over and over.

It seemed to go on forever. Merry wanted to cover her ears, to block out the shrieking and the crying. But she forced herself to listen until, finally, Denise ran out of energy. She might have fainted; from where Merry was sitting, she couldn't tell.

Roshni came over and crouched down in front of Merry. Her face was as expressionless as a marble slab, but her voice was gentle.

'Flo died at least two days ago. We know this isn't your fault. But you need to tell me what you were doing here, and how you found the body. And what that is.' She jabbed a finger towards the glass tree.

'Well,' Finn began, but Roshni held up a hand to silence him, waiting for Merry to speak.

'I was angry, after what you said to me. Finn and I got into a fight and then...' Merry looked down at her fingers; some of her nails were starting to turn black. 'It was like what happened earlier in the year. But much worse. Like the magic suddenly built up inside me, and the pain of trying to hold it back was...' She shrugged. 'I couldn't stop it. I wasn't thinking about making it happen. I wasn't thinking about anything. And then afterwards, Finn walked round the tree and – and he found her.'

Roshni gazed at Merry for a moment. Then she grabbed one of Finn's arms and studied the burns and cuts across his skin.

'Hmm.' She stood up again, and Merry and Finn stood up too. 'You should go home and fix yourselves up. I think that—'

'You!' Denise seemed to notice Merry for the first time. She began to hurry towards her. 'This is all your fault!'

Finn shifted so he was slightly in front of Merry, glancing at Roshni. 'You'd better stop her.'

Denise was shaking, half sobbing as she spoke.

'You're a freak, Meredith Cooper. I don't care what

the others say, you killed my Flo.' She raised trembling hands as though she was preparing to attack. 'You killed her!'

'Denise, that's enough!' Roshni signalled to two other witches.

The air in front of Denise began to shimmer faintly, and Denise yelped and stumbled backwards. She stared at Roshni for a moment, open-mouthed, before dissolving into tears again. 'My Flo, my baby...'

Merry started forward. 'I'm sorry. I really I am.'

But the shimmering shield was still in place. Roshni put an arm round Merry and steered her away. 'Finn, please take her home. Bronwen will be there by now.'

Fifteen minutes later, they were back at the house. Mum hugged her tightly – hugged both of them – before getting out the various healing salves and dealing with their injuries. But as soon as she could, Merry went upstairs to her bedroom. She locked her door, closed her curtains, threw herself on her bed and cried herself to sleep.

She woke a few hours later, with a dull ache in the centre of her chest. Opening her curtains, squinting against the early evening sunlight, she saw Mum and Leo sitting at the splintery old table in the garden. Mum looked wrecked: like she'd been weeping continuously for the whole afternoon. Merry went down to join them.

'You OK, Mum?'

She nodded.

'I keep thinking – it could have been you lying there…' Her voice broke and Leo passed her another tissue. 'Sorry. I don't seem to be able to stop crying.'

Merry and Leo glanced at each other.

'Mum,' Merry began, 'I know you don't like taking medicine. Even our sort of medicine, but… maybe you should try those drops that Mrs Galantini left for you? So you can get some rest?'

To her surprise, Mum nodded.

'You're right. I'll make myself some tea, then I'll go up to bed, I think. Will you be OK?'

They both said yes, and watched their mum walk into the house. Merry examined her fingernails; her hands shook a little, but the bruising was starting to fade. Another few hours and she'd be completely healed. On the outside, at least.

'I guess –' She swallowed, then took a deep breath and tried again – 'I guess you know what happened, right?'

'Yeah. I'm so sorry, Merry.' Leo reached over and gripped

her shoulder briefly. 'I wish… I wish you hadn't been the one to find her.'

'At least we did find her. Where's Finn?'

'Upstairs in his room.' Leo's face flushed darker. 'If you hadn't got into a row with him you'd never have been in the woods, and then—'

'He isn't to blame, honestly. I was…' Merry ran her fingers across the rough grey surface of the table. 'He helped me, earlier. He looked after me.'

Leo grunted and sat back in his chair, gazing across the garden. After a few minutes he cleared his throat.

'I dreamt about him again last night. You know who I mean, right? And I was thinking about what you said: that we carry our ghosts inside us. Something like that.' He shifted in his seat, glancing over his shoulder. 'Do you think we'll ever be free? Of what happened in the spring?'

Merry looked at Leo. Really looked at him. He didn't outwardly seem very different to how he'd been six months ago. His hair was a little bit longer. But inside…

'I don't know. We can't just wipe out our memories. Well, we could try, but…' She paused, rubbing a spot on her hand where the glass had cut her, earlier. 'The only way to forget about Dan's death would be to forget about Dan. And I know you don't want that. So I guess you need to find a way to live with what happened. To… to let go of Dan, even though you're holding on to his memory.'

Like I'm going to have to let go of Flo…

A fresh wave of shock and horror washed through her as the image of Flo's body, her mutilated face, forced itself into her mind.

'Merry?'

'I'm OK. It's just… horrible. Seeing Flo lying there.' She sighed. 'I don't want that memory in my head. But if I don't remember, I'll lose her completely.' Leo was frowning at the table. 'Does that make any sense?'

'Yeah. Sort of. It's not right, though, is it?' He glanced up at her. 'People are supposed to die when they're old. We shouldn't be having to deal with this. We shouldn't be having to go to funerals of other teenagers—' He broke off, dashing a tear away from his cheek. 'It's not right.'

'No. It isn't right.' Merry watched her brother for a couple of minutes, running her fingers through her hair, pulling out the tangles. At least one of them could be happy. It would be better than nothing. 'Leo, why don't you go and hang out with Ronan for the rest of the evening?'

'I can't do that. I can't leave you after what happened

today. I should stay here and look after you and Mum.'

'She's probably already asleep. And…and I don't want to talk any more this evening. I'm too tired.' Leo still seemed doubtful. 'You could ask Ronan if he saw anyone in the woods in the last couple of days. He might have noticed something important.'

'I suppose. Will you really be OK on your own, though?'

'Yes. Besides, Finn's here.'

Leo rolled his eyes. But Merry could tell he was wavering. 'Seriously, you should go. And you should go to work tomorrow too. I really want something around here to be normal.'

'All right, all right.' Leo stood up. 'But text me if you need me, and I'll come straight back.' He dropped a kiss on to the top of her head. 'Love you.'

'Love you too.'

After Leo left, Merry sat in the garden for a while longer, watching the sky get darker and the stars come out. Eventually she went inside, picked up a slice of leftover pizza from the kitchen, wandered into the living room and switched on the TV. Mum had pressed pause in the middle of some drama series and it started playing, and Merry found herself watching episode after episode, even though she was nodding off over the remote control. But the idea of going upstairs to bed made her shudder. A line from *Hamlet* kept running through her head: *...to sleep, perchance to dream...*

Though I'm pretty sure he was talking about death.

One of the cats leapt in through the open window, making her jump. She got up, switched the TV off and moved towards the window to shut it, but... there was that sensation again. The same feeling she'd had before when looking out into the garden at night: a prickling across her nerve endings like something was out there in the darkness, watching her. It was even closer this time. She remembered her conversation with Leo earlier, talking about memories and ghosts.

What if the ghosts are the ones who can't let go?

She closed her eyes and saw Jack reaching up through the water, coming back for her—

'What are you doing?'

Merry gasped and spun round.

'Oh. It's you. I was... I was just going to shut the window.'

Finn shot her a sceptical look, walked past her and shut it himself.

'You do know that you're safe here, don't you? Your mum told me about all the runes around the house.'

Merry nodded. But deep down, she wasn't sure she trusted the runes any more. So many things she used to believe in – that Tillingham would always be safe, that Gran was indestructible – no longer seemed true. Finn was waiting for her, his hand on the light switch.

'You coming?'

'Yeah.'

She followed him up the stairs.

On the landing, Finn turned towards the spare room. 'Night, then.'

Merry moved towards her own room, hoping she would be able to open the door, to force herself to go inside.

'Merry…' Finn was walking back along the landing.

And without even really thinking about it, Merry blurted out: 'Don't leave me. I mean…' She dropped her gaze. 'I don't want to be alone in my room. Not tonight.' Peeking up, she saw an emotion she couldn't identify flit across Finn's face.

But all he said was: 'Of course. Why don't you get ready for bed?'

Merry got her pyjamas and went to the bathroom. When she came out, she found Finn had moved the mattress from the spare room on to the floor of her room. He went to brush his teeth, then got into bed, and Merry turned the light out without either of them saying another word. She lay there in the darkness for a while, listening to the sound of Finn breathing, before eventually falling asleep.

SEVENTEEN

MERRY OPENED HER eyes and saw sunlight dappling the ceiling above her. One of the cats was on the landing, mewing and scratching at her door. It was morning, presumably, but—

Her memory kicked in. The blood magic. Roshni telling her to go home. Fighting with Finn. And Flo… Closing her eyes made it worse: all she could see was Flo's body lying amid the ferns.

She swung her legs out of bed, wincing at the pain in her head. Then she noticed the empty mattress next to her, remembered begging Finn not to leave her.

But her whole world seemed to be falling apart; what he thought about her was hardly important.

Mum was on her own in the kitchen. She checked Merry's hands to make sure they'd healed properly, made her some breakfast, asked her how she was feeling. When she realised that Merry didn't want to discuss what had happened, she switched to talking about other topics, trivial things that were in the news. Hoping to distract them both. Merry understood. She could sense the distress that Mum was trying to keep hidden, almost like a physical shadow around her. Having to experience someone else's pain as well as her own was exhausting.

Finally Mum wandered off, muttering something about catching up on work, and Merry was left alone. After getting showered and dressed, she rifled through the stack of cards Mum kept in the sideboard and found one labelled 'In Sympathy'. She tried to write something to Denise, something comforting and sorrowful and respectful all at the same time. After an hour, all she'd got was: *Dear Denise, I'm so sorry Flo is gone. She'd become one of my best friends over the last few months…* It made her cry so much the card got wrecked.

Almost as bad was talking to Ruby, telling her some of what had happened. Ruby was shocked, upset… and frightened too. She offered to drive over, or to take Merry out somewhere, but Merry told her that she wanted to stay at home, to have some time on her own.

She couldn't quite shake the feeling that Ruby was relieved. Though she might have imagined it. She hoped she had.

By mid-afternoon she was tired again and went out to the garden to sink into a deckchair. There was too much anguish in the air. It was tainting everything. And there was nothing she could do about it.

Merry closed her eyes and listened to the sounds of the garden: birds chirping nearby; cars zooming along the road in front of the house; one of the neighbours mowing their lawn; somebody playing music in the distance. Eventually, she dozed off.

When she awoke, Finn was standing in front of her.

'Hey. How are you feeling?'

'All right.' Merry put her sunglasses on. Finn came and sat next to her, just like he had the other day.

'Do you want to talk about it? I mean, not about Flo, unless you want to. I was thinking more about what happened yesterday, before—'

'Not especially.' She turned her head away, but she could feel him staring at her. Could sense his pity.

'You shouldn't be sitting so close. I might hurt you again.'

Finn didn't move.

'I'm not frightened of you, Merry. I would hardly have slept in your room last night if I was. And I don't blame you for what you did, either. The coven are nuts, excluding you like this.'

'No, they're not. I can't control myself. You saw how bad it was. How dangerous. That's why no one will work with me any more.'

'So don't work with them. Other people are overrated in my experience. We in the Kin Houses—'

Oh, spare me. Merry interrupted. 'Well, I'm not in one of the Kin Houses. And I'm supposed to be normal by now. More or less.'

'Normal?' He sounded like he was almost laughing.

'Normal for a witch.' Merry scowled at him from behind her sunglasses. 'You know what I mean.'

'What if I was to tell you that I could help? Wizards generally have to get by with a lot less support than witches. There are techniques that have been developed, ways of controlling one's power without actually using it. I could teach you.'

'Really?'

'Sure. For example,' he leant forward and lifted Merry's hand away from the arm of the deckchair, holding it in his, 'you feel your power here, right?'

Merry nodded.

'But if you can learn to feel it earlier, when it's here,' he brushed his fingers briefly against her breastbone, 'then it's much easier to channel or disperse before it gets unbearable. Does that make sense?'

'I suppose so.'

Finn's phone beeped; he let go of Merry's hand and stood up to get it out of his pocket. Whatever the message was, it obviously wasn't welcome. The humour in his face was replaced by the sullen expression he'd worn yesterday when Mrs Knox wouldn't let him into her house.

'What's wrong?'

'Nothing. Just my dad.' There was the sound of a car in the driveway. 'I guess Leo's back from work.' Without another word, Finn stomped away across the garden and towards the house.

Merry watched him go, thinking about the three wizards she'd known so far: Gwydion, a psychopath; Ronan, a rootless wanderer; and Finn. Who was just... completely inexplicable. There was a line in *The Lord of the Rings* about not messing around with wizards. Merry decided she was going to look it up and get it tattooed somewhere on her body, so she wouldn't ever forget.

Leo came and sat down in the now-vacant deckchair.

'What was he doing? Flirting with you again?'

Merry gritted her teeth.

'He was just talking to me. He wanted to see if I was OK, after yesterday.'

Leo hunched his shoulders.

'Sorry. But he really irritates the crap out of me.'

'Well, he bugs me too. But he's not that bad.'

'You sure? I've been thinking about the wards on Gran's house. How they were down both times. What if Finn was the wizard who visited Gran the day after I got attacked? She'd have let him in if she knew him. And then—'

'But Ronan was the one who visited her. Wasn't he?' That was what they'd both assumed. 'Have you asked him?'

'Not yet. But he's never mentioned it. And you remember what he told us about Finn. And what happened with Jack...'

'That was completely different. Finn's not controlled by an ancient Anglo-Saxon curse, and he's not been buried alive under a lake for fifteen hundred years.' She glanced up at the window of the spare room. Finn was definitely more complicated than Jack. But he was also funny, and cute, and he didn't come across as someone who would hurt his own brother. Or torture somebody in cold blood. She studied Leo's face. 'Look… I know Ronan saved you from Simon, but are we absolutely sure that he's completely… on the level?'

Leo drew back.

'Don't spoil this, Merry. Ronan's done so much for me. More than anyone else ever has.'

That really hurt. But Leo didn't notice.

'And he's trying to help me…' Leo paused, looking momentarily flustered. 'He's trying to help me deal with stuff. I told him what you said yesterday, about me needing to find a way to live with what happened.'

'But — if he hurts you…'

'He's not going to hurt me!' Leo's face flushed. 'I think I love him, Merry. And I think he loves me too.'

So don't make me choose…?

'All right.' There was nothing much else Merry could say.

'Hey,' Leo nudged her arm, 'did Mum tell you?'

'Tell me what?'

'The coven have got some new information. Something to do with Gran's knife. They think they're zeroing in on where she might be.'

'What?' Suddenly, there didn't seem to be quite enough air in the garden. Leo was still talking.

'…So the coven will bring her back. Any day now. You don't need to worry any more.'

Even her brother seemed to have decided that Merry wasn't really part of the coven. And he obviously didn't know she was the one who thought of using the knife to reveal Gran's location. Did Mum? Or had Roshni concealed the truth completely?

I worked out how to do the blood magic. I caused the runes to appear on the blade of the knife. I took the risk.

All the coven had done was take the knife. And now they weren't even acknowledging her.

She glanced back at her brother; he was playing with a twisted metal bangle on his wrist. Merry hadn't seen it before, and wondered if Ronan had given it to him. The dull headache she'd had all day was spreading; muscles in her shoulders and neck were stiff and sore. She stood up.

'I need some exercise. I'm going to ask Mum to drive me to the fencing club.'

'What? Oh, sure. Have fun.' Leo smiled at her, but Merry knew he wasn't really listening.

★

The fencing helped. She'd started learning how to fight with a sabre instead of a foil: her experience with the King of Hearts under the lake had taught her the importance of being able to switch techniques. It was fast and exhausting, and she had to concentrate too hard to think about anything else. When she got back home she went straight to bed and slept long and dreamlessly.

Overslept, in fact; it was late morning by the time she made it downstairs. Mum had left a note on the kitchen table.

Leo's gone to work, Finn still in bed. Lasagne in freezer if you want it. I'm going to see Roshni and find out what the coven's plan is. xxx

Going to see Roshni? Sure, she hadn't told Mum exactly what Roshni had said to her. But Mum knew they'd had an argument. That the coven had basically turned on Merry. And she was still going to hang out with them.

Merry tore the note into tiny pieces, threw it in the bin and marched back upstairs to her room. They could try to exclude her if they wanted. But she had the photos she'd taken of the runes on Gran's knife. And there were things in Gran's folder that she hadn't yet examined properly. She tipped out the contents again. Map. Letters. Illustration…

The illustration. She picked up the picture of the woodcut. There was the poor, terrified woman. There was the evil-looking man, digging his fingers into the side of the woman's face, ripping holes in her flesh.

Flo's face.

She reread the name written underneath the vile image. *Zauberzieher.*

The paper slipped from Merry's fingers. She scrambled over to the pile of books next to her desk and unearthed the other book Gran had given her, the one with the dark fairy tale in it. But instead of turning to the story, she started reading the introduction.

There is no exact word in English to describe the creatures that in German are called Zauberzieher. *The nearest translation is enchantment-extractor. When a* Zauberzieher *comes of age, his magic is initially extremely powerful. They are traditionally very gifted at transformation spells, but their power is short-lived. Temporary. To keep practising magic, they constantly have to steal power from other witches and wizards. They became creatures of horror and hence of legend, remembered only in the type of story I have recorded in this book. But I have met a* Zauberzieher, *and they are real…*

Merry closed the book. There was only one way to be sure. Hands shaking, she took the police photos of the dead witches out of the folder and forced herself to look at each one.

A body.

A body.

A body.

A face – the close-up of a face. The features were distorted and the blood was less obvious in black and white. But the marks were there: ten irregular holes, four on each side of the face, one under each eye. The same as Flo.

Merry's glance fell on the discarded illustration.

That thing is real. And it's got Gran…

It took Merry half an hour of pacing to even begin to calm down. Her first instinct was to run out of the house and start searching for Gran. But since she had literally no idea where her grandmother was, that wasn't exactly feasible. There was no point going to the coven: Roshni would probably just yell at her again and dismiss it out of hand. So should she try to act completely alone – or should she trust Finn?

If the illustration from the folder was accurate, a

Zauberzieher would look like a normal person. He or she could be anywhere. Or anyone.

Merry needed some air. She grabbed the stuff from the folder, picked up as many relevant books as she could find, and went down to the garden.

It was another wiltingly hot day, with no sign of a break in the weather; the lawn was cracked, turning to dust as the grass died. She sat in the shade of a tree, got out the list of monuments she'd made the other day and started checking the indexes of the wisdom books Gran had given her – thankful, in that moment, for witches' tendency to be organised. In the third book, she found what she was looking for. There was a whole chapter on points of intersection: how certain places, both man-made and natural, had been used by those with the gift as a way of reaching other times and places. Other worlds and dimensions, even, if the ancient sources were to be believed. Then the writer gave some examples of such places, and how they had been marked in the landscape; as well as stone circles, she listed barrows, standing stones, waterfalls, springs, even individual trees.

If the runes on the knife referred specifically to a stone or a spring, she might be able to narrow her list down. But she still didn't know what the murderer might be using a point of intersection for. To get around? As a source of power? Or as somewhere to hide out?

Too many questions. She was still flicking through the wisdom book when Finn walked into the garden. He came and lay down on the remnants of the grass next to where she was sitting.

'What are you doing?'

'Gran left some information about whoever – or whatever – she believed had been going round killing witches. I've been trying to make sense of it, maybe get some clues.'

He picked up her journey book and started reading the jottings she'd made so far that day: local place names, map references.

'Aren't the coven meant to be sorting this out?'

'They're looking for Gran. I'm searching for the person who took her.'

Finn kept reading the notebook. She watched him, studying his profile, weighing up all the things he'd said and done, trying to come to a decision…

'Um, have you heard of a *Zauberzieher*?'

'A what?' Finn put down the notebook.

'A *Zauberzieher*. I'm not sure I'm saying it right.'

'I've heard of it. But it's just a story. The sort mothers

in the Kin Houses tell their children to make them behave.' Finn sat up straighter, shading his eyes against the sun.

'I'm not so sure. From what I've read, and from the way Flo and the other witches were killed… I think there's one here. Somewhere nearby.'

He laughed.

'Very funny. Fairy tales coming to life? What next, an actual gingerbread man?'

Merry didn't reply and the laughter faded from Finn's eyes.

'You're not joking?'

'I know all about fairy tales. Sometimes they don't stay in books.'

'A *Zauberzieher*?' He shook his head, picking at the fraying binding of one of the wisdom books lying nearby. 'Bloody hell. I hope you're wrong.'

'So do I.' She scrunched her eyes up; her eyeballs felt dry and scratchy. 'Anyway, I – I might need your help to deal with it. If I ever work out where to look.'

She picked up her phone and started studying the photographs of the knife blade, until Finn reached across and plucked it out of her hands.

'Hey!'

'Leave that for now. I want to show you something.'

Merry snatched the phone back.

'I don't have time. Gran doesn't have time. You can show me later.'

Finn grabbed the phone again.

'Seriously, it will take two minutes.'

Merry paused. She could keep arguing, but that would probably just take even longer. And then Finn held out his hand and said, 'Please? It's a surprise. I worked really hard on it...'

'Fine. Two minutes. What do you want to show me?'

Finn jumped up and jogged across to where the collection of motor parts that passed for Merry's car was hidden under a tarpaulin.

'So, I know your birthday isn't until Saturday, but... I decided I couldn't wait any longer.' He waved his hand and the tarpaulin flapped away across the garden, as though caught by a sudden gust of wind. 'Ta-daa!'

Where there had been junk, there was now a small car that, if not exactly shiny and new, was at least in one piece and driveable.

Merry realised her mouth was hanging open.

'But − you fixed it. That's just...' She walked round to the front of the car to admire it from another angle. 'How did you do it?'

'Friend of a friend. He owns a garage and he's made up all sorts of spells for fixing cars. I sent him some photos and he sent me back the right spell set. It was tricky,' Finn shrugged, 'but nothing I couldn't handle.'

Merry opened the driver's door, cast a spell to cool down the oven-like interior, and slid into the seat. The inside was so much... cleaner. Finn had even managed to get rid of the stains on the floor and the collection of old chewing gum welded to the underside of the dashboard. He got into the passenger seat.

'Do you want to go for a drive?'

'I'd love to. But currently, I have no licence and no ability.'

'I can fix that.' Finn raised his hand.

'No. I don't mind using magic to help me remember stuff, but to rely on it totally...' Merry shook her head. The memory of those times when she'd tried to use magic and it had let her down were still too vivid. 'But thanks, though. It's so kind of you to do this.'

Finn shifted in his seat, turning more towards her.

'Kind enough to earn a kiss?' He tilted his head, questioning.

'Sure.' She leant forward and kissed Finn quickly on the cheek. He looked... amused.

'Not quite what I had in mind. You smell really nice, though.'

'Thanks,' Merry muttered. She turned to get out of the car, but Finn caught hold of her hand.

'Wait a second. You still owe me another kiss.'

'What for?'

'Helping you with the blood magic on Wednesday. Did you think I'd forgotten? Or changed my mind?' His pupils were large in the dim interior of the car, the black almost swallowing up the grey.

'Well... yes.' Merry felt her face getting hot. But when Finn reached across and cupped her cheek gently in one hand, she shivered. And when he leant forward, stopping only when their faces were almost touching, she gave in to the moment and closed her eyes.

It was different from how it had been with Jack. Then, desire had roared through her veins like a fiery blast of superheated air. This was... slower. More measured. Surprise – that Finn was such a good kisser, that she was kissing him back – almost as much as yearning. She leant into the kiss, enjoying the cool firmness of his lips moving against hers, the pressure of his hand as it slid down to the small of her back, the tingling sensation in her stomach.

He tastes nice. Like he's just brushed his teeth...

Finn broke away, breathing hard.

'Shall we go somewhere more comfortable?' His voice was husky, and her insides fluttered.

Then the guilt came back, smacking her in the face like a bowlful of cold spaghetti. How could she allow herself to be happy, even for a moment, when Flo was... was...

'I can't. I just – I want to. I really want to. But...'

She heard him sigh.

'The timing's not great, is it?'

'No.' She slumped back against the seat. 'It's not.'

There was the sound of a car door slamming nearby; Mum was home again. Finn was tapping his fingers against the edge of the passenger seat, frowning. Merry watched him, until he nodded to himself – almost like he'd made a decision – and opened the car door. He got out and then stuck his head back into the car.

'I've got some stuff to do. I'll be back later, or maybe tomorrow morning. Just – don't forget, OK? That kissing me was fun. That we could be good together.' He stared at her for a second before he shut the car door and strode back to the house.

Two hours later Finn hadn't returned, as far as she knew. Driven out of the garden by the heat, Merry shut herself into her bedroom and set her phone to *Do not disturb*. She found a translation spell in one of her books, tried it out a couple of times on some basic French, and set it to work on the letters from Gran's folder. Then she dug out her headphones and lay on her bed, turning the music up as loud as she could stand. But despite the noise, her mind kept drifting back to Finn. The way they'd kissed, the way his lips had felt against hers...

A spike of guilt made her squirm. Guilt that she was thinking about kissing, when Gran had disappeared and Flo had just been murdered. Guilt that she was imagining kissing Finn and not Jack. Merry knew she was being stupid: it wasn't as though she and Jack had ever even dated. But she couldn't quite silence the soft voice whispering that it was too soon; that having any kind of a relationship with Finn would consign Jack even faster to oblivion.

She got up and checked on the letters. The translation had finished, but the handwriting – even in English – was pretty hard to read. She focused on the underlined phrases and one jumped out at her: *male witch*. She'd seen it before somewhere. Taking off the headphones she retrieved Gran's folder from the floor and pulled out the oddly-titled pamphlet.

But before she could do more than open it, her bedroom door was flung open. Mum, grinning and crying at the same time, ran into the room.

'Didn't you hear the noise downstairs? They've found her, and she's still alive!'

EIGHTEEN

THERE WAS NO denying it: Gran looked terrible. Awful. A pale, skeletal, shadow of herself. The shock of her appearance made Merry's stomach churn; numbed the joy she knew she should be feeling.

But at least she's back. She'll be better in no time.

Doubt turned her thought into a question. Merry yelled at herself to just shut up – as if even thinking the worst might somehow make it come true.

Gran was lying in Mum's bed now, still unconscious, her chest fluttering in shallow, gasping breaths. The other witches had done their best: washed her, combed her hair, healed all obvious injuries. But still…

It was after midnight. Merry crept out of the room. She closed the door behind her, but could still hear the low chanting of the two witches who were taking the night shift, singing spells of rest and recovery. Yawning, she made her way down to the kitchen, wondering whether she should drink some coffee to help her stay awake or some chamomile tea to help her sleep. Leo had already said goodnight and gone to bed, and Finn hadn't come back from wherever he'd disappeared to earlier. But Mum was sitting at the table, listening to Roshni.

'...and we'd been led down completely the wrong path. I still can't understand it. The only person I've ever met with that kind of skill in misdirection is Elinor herself.' Roshni paused as she noticed Merry hovering in the doorway. 'Good evening, Merry. Come in.' She gestured to the seat opposite her. Merry ignored the gesture and went to sit in a different seat, next to Mum. Roshni's eyes widened a little, but all she said was, 'How are you feeling?'

How did she feel? She was shaky. Her eyeballs hurt. Her brain hurt too, because she couldn't get it to shut up. Her feet kept twitching like some part of her had decided now was a good time to take up tap dancing. But what 'feeling' did that all add up to? Merry had no idea.

'I'm OK.' She shrugged and squeezed Mum's hand.

'You should go to bed. D'you want to sleep in my room?'

'No, you stay put. I've set a camp bed up in the study. When your grandmother is on the mend, I'll sleep in my room with her.'

'I assume you'll tell the wizard to leave now?' Roshni asked.

'He has a name, Rosh,' Mum replied. 'And he's just a boy.'

'I suppose so. But there's no reason for him to stay, is there?'

Mum glanced at Merry. Roshni noticed the glance and stared at Merry.

Merry crossed her arms. 'What? Why are you looking at me like that? And what's it to do with you whether Finn stays or not?'

'Merry!'

Mum was shocked. But Roshni – she just looked tired. Really tired.

'It's OK, Bronwen. Merry is upset with me, with some justification. The runes we used to find Elinor in the end...' Roshni flattened her hands on the table top, staring down at them. 'Merry performed the magic that revealed them.'

Mum pulled Merry into a hug.

'Clever girl. Why didn't you tell me, Rosh—'

'Because it was blood magic,' Merry interrupted. 'And I didn't follow the rules.'

'Blood magic?' Mum asked.

Merry nodded. Was this the point where her mother was going to side with Roshni? Tell her off?

'Well.' Mum turned to look at Roshni. 'I think my daughter has already done more than enough this year to prove herself. To prove that she deserves to be trusted. She's an amazing witch, whatever quirks her magic may have. But,' she glanced at Merry, 'witches are safer when we stick together.' She stood up. 'I'm going to bed. I'll leave you to talk.' Dropping a kiss on Merry's head, she left the kitchen and closed the door behind her.

Roshni sighed.

'Merry…'

'Am I out of the coven?'

'Of course not.' The older witch waved her hand at the kettle, murmuring something under her breath, and it switched itself on. Merry just about supressed an 'Oh' of surprise. Maybe witches – under certain conditions – weren't as different from wizards as they liked to think. 'And I'm sorry about the way I spoke to you the other day. I should have dealt with the situation differently. But,' she got up to put a tea bag into a mug, 'I stand by what I said. With any magic, you must consider the impact on the coven as a whole. Blood magic is far more dangerous than you realise. In the wrong hands, it can rip apart the fabric of reality.'

'But without the blood magic, and without the runes, you would never have found Gran.'

'We were working on other methods. We would have found her eventually.'

'You'd have found her too late.'

Roshni nodded.

'Perhaps. But would I have been justified in risking the rest of the coven for the life of one witch? Would your grandmother not have made the same choice?' She finished making the tea and sat down again, leaning forward across the table. 'The rules are there to protect the coven. Some of the rules are very old. And some in the coven are not comfortable with things changing. Or with people being different.'

'So what does that mean? For me?'

Roshni sighed and rubbed one hand across her face.

'It's been a long day, Merry. The coven has been injured terribly, and we still have to find out who did this. Who killed Flo.'

So let it go. Move on. That's what she's saying.

Well, maybe I should. Or put it to one side, at least.

Roshni was watching her over the rim of her mug.

'Do you want to know how we found her?'

'Sure.'

'OK.'

Roshni's explanation was as efficiently organised as she was herself. The witch most skilled in runes had examined the knife, and her interpretation pointed strongly to one particular location: an abandoned chalk quarry, about half an hour across the county border into Hampshire. The coven had waited another twenty-four hours to assemble maximum strength, then went to the site late in the afternoon. They found Gran in a cave, partially concealed by a stream that tumbled down the rocks by the entrance. But they'd found no trace of whoever had incarcerated her there. The spells used to bind her – like those Merry had discovered in Gran's house – had somehow been stripped of identity. Or they'd never had any in the first place.

Roshni closed her eyes for a few seconds, pressing her fingertips to her temples.

'There was one other body there as well.'

Merry tensed.

'Another witch?'

'No. We checked his identification: just an ordinary teenage boy, apparently. I've informed our contact in the local police force.'

That didn't make sense. There would be no reason for a *Zauberzieher* to kill a normal person. Perhaps Merry had leapt to the wrong conclusion. Perhaps the marks on Flo's face were just... coincidental?

'There's nothing much else to tell,' Roshni continued. Your grandmother is unconscious due to physical stress and exhaustion, not because she is under a spell. At least as far as we've been able to establish. She will wake up in time. Although...'

'What?'

'I don't know. Something is bothering me. But I'm too tired to think about it tonight.' Roshni pushed herself up from the table. 'I'll talk to the coven tomorrow.'

The coven again. Merry felt like sticking her hand in the air and waving and saying, *Yeah, I'm in the coven too. You could talk to me.* But Roshni was already at the front door.

'Goodnight then, Merry.'

'Goodnight. And – thank you for bringing her home.'

The older witch's dark eyes glittered in the dim light from the porch lamp.

'Elinor's my closest friend. This is the first night in more than two weeks that I'll sleep properly.'

Merry went to close the door, but Roshni paused on the front step and turned round.

'The wizard, Finn — it won't do to spend any more time with him than you have to, Merry.'

Merry frowned. 'But why not? Gran's stayed at his parents' house. And Mum.'

'Your grandmother, because of who she is, has… latitude. Your situation is different. Witches do not fraternise with wizards.'

'Let me guess — this is one of those rules you mentioned?'

'More of a guideline. But yes.'

'But why? Because all wizards are untrustworthy?'

Roshni let out a single, short laugh.

'No. Because in the past, they used to try to kill us. The distant past, I'll admit… but covens have long memories.'

Roshni got into her car and drove away. Merry went back into the kitchen to put the mugs into the dishwasher, then went up to bed. But she couldn't stop thinking about everything that had been said that evening. Roshni had apologised, sort of. But she couldn't undo what had happened. By now, all the other witches probably knew that Merry had practised unauthorised blood magic. Had risked the safety of the coven.

Is that the reason I'm now in a 'situation'?

She sighed and turned over, closing her eyes. Whatever was going on, there was nothing she could do about it tonight.

Gran was still unconscious when Merry checked on her the next morning. There was a different pair of witches flanking the bed – Mrs Knox and another, younger woman – but neither of them were singing. Mrs Knox escorted Merry back out of the room.

'Nothing to worry about – the spells are set and we're keeping her asleep now. She'll heal more quickly that way.'

'But – if she wakes up, she can tell us who did this.'

'That can wait. Two more days, maybe three.'

'Is there anything I can do?'

'Tea and biscuits, in about –,' Mrs Knox checked her watch, – 'forty-five minutes would be lovely. Other than that, don't worry.' She clapped Merry on the shoulder and marched back into the bedroom.

Downstairs, Leo was sitting at the kitchen table, a cafetière of coffee and a mug in front of him. He was dressed, but he looked heavy-eyed and rumpled, and he yawned enormously as Merry walked past him.

'Didn't sleep well?'

'Not especially.' He rubbed a hand over his face. 'At least I'm not working today.'

Merry got the milk and the juice out, and picked up a note Mum had left stuck to the fridge door.

I'll call later – gone back to the office. Please remind Leo he MUST go to supermarket today. His turn. xx

'I'll come shopping with you later, if you like. Have you seen Gran this morning? Mrs Knox reckons she'll wake up in a couple of days. That's good, isn't it.'

'Yeah.'

Merry glanced sideways at her brother. He was staring out of the window, twisting the bangle on his wrist absent-mindedly.

'Well,' Merry continued, hunting for her favourite cereal in the cupboard, 'it would be amazing if she wakes up on my birthday. Did you eat the rest of my chocolate granola?'

'What?' Leo scowled with irritation. 'I might've done. I'll get you some more later.'

Merry sighed, got out some oatflakes instead – they never seemed to run out of oatflakes – and sat down at the table.

'Are you sure you're OK? You've not... you've not been worrying about Dan again, have you? I mean – you've not seen anything?'

'No. And like I said, Ronan's helping me with that. It'll be fine.' Leo didn't really look like he thought it would be fine. Whatever *it* was. Merry was hit by a burst of uncertainty and discomfort, enough to make her draw back from her brother.

'What exactly is he doing to help you?'

'Just – don't worry about it. Please? Tell me what you want for your birthday, instead.'

Merry stirred her cereal, turning it to mush. He was telling her to butt out, basically. And maybe she should. Maybe he and Ronan had had some kind of... lovers' quarrel. Assuming their relationship had got that far.

This is so weird. Not knowing what's really in his mind, other than the fact that he's not nearly as happy as he was a couple of days ago.

'I don't know. Vouchers, I guess. Oh – one thing you don't have to worry about any more – Finn's fixed my car. Totally fixed it. It's almost like new.'

Leo's whole posture stiffened.

'He's done what?'

'He fixed the car… It's like, a good thing, Leo.'

Her brother stood up and stomped over to the sink, pouring the rest of his coffee away.

'He had no right to do that. *I* was going to fix it.'

'But you hadn't fixed it, so…' Merry threw her hands in the air. 'Why does it even matter?'

'Because… because…' Leo scowled and bit down on his lower lip. 'I really hate that guy.' Merry widened her eyes at the venom in his voice. 'You have to stay away from him, Merry. I mean it.' He started pacing up and down. 'In fact, I'm going to tell Mum tonight what Ronan said about him. Or maybe I should tell Roshni, get her to throw him out…'

Merry's insides seized up with agitation.

'No – don't do that. He's been really helpful, Leo. I would never have been able to do the blood magic without him. And—'

She caught her breath, remembering the way Finn had kissed her yesterday, hoping the blush she could feel blooming across her skin wouldn't give her away.

'And he was only able to fix the car because he used magic—'

328

Leo smacked his hand down on the table, making her jump, tipping up the box of oatflakes so they spilt across the floor.

'That's what it always comes down to, doesn't it? All of you, apart from Ronan – you all think you're so much better than the rest of us.'

'That's not true, Leo.'

'Yes, it is. The coven are upset because Flo was a witch. Do you think they'd care if – if you'd found Ruby lying in the woods murdered?'

'Of course they would!'

'No, they wouldn't. Look how they've treated you because you're not exactly like them. And as for Finn, spouting all that Kin House superiority crap, after what he did to his brother—'

'I think you ought to get your facts straight.' Finn was standing in the doorway, glaring at Leo. His voice was hard and flat. 'Otherwise you're going to say something you'll regret.'

Leo swung round, his fists clenched.

'Just shut up, you absolute scumbag. And get out of my home!'

The anger in Finn's eyes was subsumed into a look of disdain that Leo could hardly have missed.

'Or you'll do *what*, exactly?'

'What I should have done the moment I first laid eyes on you.' Leo lunged forward, bringing his right arm back, ready to throw a punch. At the same time Finn raised his hands, sparks already playing across his palms.

No bloody way –

Ice-cold anger tore through Merry's veins. She flung her arm out and silver filaments cascaded from her fingertips. Within seconds, a sparkling net hung in the air between Leo and Finn. She could hear the energy within it crackling.

'Stop it right now! You're acting like a couple of three-year-olds!'

For a moment neither of them took any notice of her. Then Finn retreated, holding his hands down behind his back.

'I'm sorry.'

Merry looked at Leo. His arms were hanging by his side now, but his hands were clenching and unclenching like he couldn't quite give up the idea of punching Finn in the face.

'Leo, come on.' Merry lowered her hand and the net faded into nothingness. 'We've got to stick together.'

He turned on her.

'*We?* So it's you and him now, is it?'

'No – that's not what I meant.'

'Just forget it. I can't even be around you any more.'

There was a chair blocking his path. He picked it up and hurled it to one side, smashing a vase of flowers and making Merry flinch, before running out of the kitchen.

'Leo – wait.'

Merry started forward, but Finn grabbed her arm.

'Leave him – he'll calm down eventually. Sometimes plebs get—'

Merry wrenched her arm out of his grasp.

'Don't you dare call him that!'

The front door slammed, and a moment later Merry heard the unmistakable sound of Leo's ancient Peugeot tearing out of the driveway.

NINETEEN

'YOU UTTER, UTTER imbecile. I could have stopped him if you hadn't got in the way!'

'But Merry…'

'No.' She took a deep breath, lips clamped together, fingernails safely curled within her fists. 'Don't talk to me. Just – clean up this mess. And make some tea and biscuits for the two witches looking after Gran.'

She turned to walk away. But Finn called after her.

'That net you threw between us – do you have any idea how much power it was carrying? If Leo had touched it, he'd be dead.'

Merry stopped, but she didn't turn to face him.

'You should let me help you, Merry.' She could sense him moving closer to her. 'Like we talked about on Wednesday.'

'I don't need...' She swallowed. 'I don't *want* your help, Finn. Leo's right. You should go home.'

Merry walked away.

She messaged Leo again –

I'm sorry. Please text me. Let me know you're ok.

– and dropped her phone back on to the bed next to her. She knew he was going to ignore her. He'd ignored all her texts, calls and messages for the last two hours. Her stomach growled, but if she went downstairs – Finn might still be there, sitting in the kitchen, being smug.

Or he might have left. He might be driving westwards, back to Ireland...

Merry pressed her hands to her stomach, wondering about the anxiety tying knots in her intestines. Which possibility was she actually most worried about?

The front door slammed. She glanced at the clock on the bedside table: half past twelve. Far too early for Mum to be home.

That was it, then; Finn had left. Merry sighed.

Unless…

There was a knock at her door. She jumped off the bed and opened it.

'Leo?'

But it was Finn, not her brother. He was carrying a pot plant of some sort.

'Can I come in?' He thrust the plant towards her. 'Please? I want to apologise.'

Merry shot him a scornful glance, but she took the plant and let him in. It was that or shut the door on his arm.

'Well?'

'I just want to say, I don't mean to be a muppet.'

'Why do you keep doing it, then?' Merry put the plant down on her desk. 'I don't get it, Finn. I start thinking you're actually a nice guy, then you go and threaten my brother and call him horrible names.'

'He was going to hit me!'

'Like you'd ever have actually allowed him to land a punch.' She sat on the edge of the bed and picked up her phone. But there were no messages from Leo. Finn sat next to her.

'I'm sorry. I wish I hadn't called him a pleb. But we

334

were never allowed to spend time with... normal kids. It's much easier to write off a whole group of people if you don't actually know any of them personally.'

He wasn't wrong. Perhaps that was the reason witches still mistrusted wizards; perhaps the covens should be encouraging fraternising, not outlawing it.

'Have you never been to school, then?' Merry asked.

Finn shook his head.

'Home-schooled. To protect us from any –' he pulled a face, like there was a bitter taste in his mouth – 'contamination.' My amazing social skills come from spending lots of holidays with other Kin House families, whether we liked them or not.' He ran one forefinger over a faint scar on the inside of his wrist; Merry hadn't noticed it before and wondered why whoever dealt with the injury had left the scar there. 'I really miss my brother.'

Merry opened her mouth, about to ask – *But why didn't your brother go to a normal school?* – when she remembered that Finn hadn't confirmed what Ronan had told them, hadn't acknowledged that his brother was... ordinary.

Instead she asked, 'So why is there not some kind of wizard school for all you guys to go to?'

Finn frowned at her.

'How many wizards do you think there are?'

Merry shrugged.

'Dunno. But surely a boarding school—'

'Think about it. There are, maybe, eighty or ninety Kin House children who are currently the right age for school. Of those, about a third are girls, who won't be learning magic. Not every family wants to send their kids away to school. Plus, we all have our own family spells and charms – stuff we wouldn't voluntarily share even with the other Kin Houses. It would never work.'

'But other wizards—'

'Usually don't find out they're magical until they're in their teens. And there're not really that many of us. Slightly more witches, my dad reckons. But you guys go down the kind of, hidden-in-plain-sight route. We have the power, but the—' Finn stopped, a slight flush across his cheekbones. 'The regular people, they have the numbers.'

It was like a glimpse through a window into a previously unvisited, unimagined room. Merry wondered whether she would have learnt this stuff if Mum had allowed her to be trained earlier, or whether young witches only ever learnt about... other witches. She thought about the knowledge and wisdom books she hadn't yet read, the weight of all that required learning dragging at her like a lead-lined cloak.

Finn nudged her.

'I am trying, you know. To be less of an… imbecile.'

'I guess. Just – don't make Leo feel bad. Be nice to him. What I did in April, the stuff with Gwydion and Jack –' she caught her breath for a moment, very aware that this was the first time she'd spoken his name to anyone apart from Leo for months – 'I couldn't have done any of that without him.'

'I understand. I know Leo's a good guy. And I know how important he is to you.' He picked a bit of fluff off the blanket at the end of Merry's bed. 'Tell me about Jack. He must have been pretty amazing for your ancestor to bind her whole bloodline to an oath to help him.'

She looked at Finn curiously, wondering why he was asking, what he already knew.

'The oath wasn't just about that. But yeah, he was kind of amazing. Sweet and gentle, and incredibly brave. He was certainly different from the boys I'm at school with…' Merry trailed off. Talking about Jack while sitting next to Finn made her uncomfortable. 'What about you? That line you fed me about not having much luck with girls. I mean, that was a line, right?'

'I'm flattered you think so. But the truth is, we – as in the Kin Houses – we don't have a lot of freedom in terms of relationships.' His shoulders sagged. 'We don't really have a lot of freedom full stop.'

He looked so sad.

'Well, I've already been told to stay away from you. Apparently witches don't 'fraternise' with wizards, in case you kill us. But… I guess I don't mind breaking the rules if you don't.' Finn was gazing at her with the same strange expression she'd noticed on Tuesday night. 'What?'

He smiled.

'Nothing. I'll explain it later.' He slid his hand across the space between them until the outside edge of his little finger was just brushing against hers. 'Am I forgiven?'

Merry felt the beginnings of that same fizzing excitement she'd experienced when they'd kissed yesterday. Like gravity was losing its grip, just a little.

'Yeah. I guess so.' She glanced across at the plant on her desk: smallish, pink, rose-like flowers with a mass of oval leaves. There was a scent like fresh apples that she hadn't noticed before. 'Thanks for the flowers.'

'It's sweet briar; it seemed appropriate. And I couldn't find an olive branch.' Finn moved his hand nearer still, lying it on top of hers. 'Is… is the timing better now? Now your gran's back?'

'But what about Leo?' She glanced at the still-blank screen of her phone. 'I think I should go after him.'

'Do you know where he is?'

'Probably.' She sighed. Leo seemed to think Ronan was the only one who cared about him now. The only one who mattered.

'Look – don't follow him yet. Give him time to calm down. Hopefully he'll realise that *I'm* the one he should be angry with. But if you haven't heard from him by this evening, I'll drive you to wherever he is. If you want me to. Promise.'

'Really?'

Finn shifted position so he was facing her on the bed, and leant forward to sweep her hair back off her shoulder, his fingertips grazing the side of her neck. 'Really.'

Merry couldn't fight it any more. She didn't want to fight it, whatever Roshni might say. She waved a hand at the door so that the key turned in the lock, swung her legs up on to the bed and moved across to make space. Finn was watching her, his lips slightly parted. She patted the duvet next to her.

'Much as I love my new car, I think this will be more comfortable.'

He grinned, pushed her down on to the bed and began

kissing her throat, her neck, her jawline, until his face was just above hers, close enough for her to see the tiny flecks of blue and green in the grey of his irises.

'Are you sure about this?' he murmured. 'Forbidden love and all that. Remember what happened to Romeo and Juliet…'

Merry slid her arms around Finn's body, pulling him closer.

'Just shut up and kiss me.'

★ ★ ★

Leo slammed the brakes on, oblivious to the churned-up gravel adding even more dents to the car's paintwork, got out and ran from the parking area into the woods. He burst through the trees and saw Ronan's tent, saw Ronan – alone, luckily, no sign of Ethan – and sprinted across the last stretch of open ground.

Ronan stopped what he was doing and jumped up.

'Whoa, Leo – what's going on?'

The running caught up with him. He bent over, hands on his knees, waiting for the stitch to fade.

'It's – it's Merry.' He paused, waiting for his breath to slow; straightened up. 'Not her, really. It's Finn, that arrogant—'

'Finn?' Ronan frowned. 'What's he done now?'

'He – I – we got into an argument. A fight, really. And Merry – she took his side.' He scrunched his hands into fists again, remembering the anger that had overtaken him. 'I lost my temper.'

Ronan moved closer.

'Calm down, Leo. Finn's an obnoxious git who would try the patience of a saint. I'm sure your sister wouldn't really side with him against you.'

'But she did. She said…' He thought back, trying to recall exactly what Merry had said, but everything seemed a bit… hazy. 'If she hadn't stopped me, I'd have tried to kill him, I reckon. How stupid is that: attacking a wizard?' Leo shook his head. 'I just – I don't know what I'm doing any more. I really don't.'

Ronan came to stand in front of him, placing his hands on Leo's shoulders.

'Look at me.'

Leo raised his head reluctantly.

'You know I want to help, don't you?'

Leo nodded.

'And you know I've told you what you need to do? How we can make the pain go away, together?'

Leo nodded again.

'I know you can do this,' Ronan said quietly. 'You can

have everything that you want. The question is, do you trust me?'

Leo stared into Ronan's dark brown eyes.

'Of course I trust you. But...'

'You still have doubts? I get that.' He pulled Leo gently towards him. 'Perhaps I can dispel them.'

'Wait.' Leo barely breathed the word. But Ronan paused, one eyebrow raised. Leo could feel the warmth of Ronan's body, only centimetres away; he could smell the aftershave Ronan was wearing, mingled with the scent of the roses growing around the tent. It made it almost impossible for him to concentrate, to figure out what he was feeling. Desire, yes; but also... nervousness. There'd been that brief moment of contact with Ronan nearly three weeks ago, but they'd never actually kissed. Leo had dreamt about kissing Dan lots of times, but – what if he did it wrong?

And then, almost as if he was reading his thoughts, Ronan said, 'Kissing is kissing, Leo. You're not going to turn into a frog.' He put one hand round the back of Leo's neck and swayed forward and then... and then Leo was kissing him, like an asteroid was about to destroy the planet and he was trying to make up for lost time, and he had his arms around Ronan's body and was pulling him tight against him and it just felt… right. So right, that he wanted to live in that moment and never, ever leave it.

They were sitting next to each other now, looking out over the lake again at the western sky, where the sun was just starting its descent towards the horizon. They'd kissed for ages, until Leo had lost all track of time, but then his stomach had rumbled and Ronan had pulled away, laughing, insisting they should stop and have something to eat. While he cooked some fish over the fire, he told Leo to text Merry, to let her know that she didn't need to worry about him. Leo did it without arguing; the exhilaration of what he'd experienced with Ronan was still coursing around his body like particles in a collider.

'And then, the eejit goes and mispronounces the last line of the charm, so instead of him disappearing, the boat he's standing in turns into matchsticks and dumps him in the lake. I've never seen a man look as surprised as he did in that split second he realised he was standing on water.'

Leo laughed and drank some more cider; Ronan was entertaining him with stories of various magical disasters he'd witnessed or heard about.

'So…' Ronan leant on one elbow, pulling the petals off a dandelion that was growing nearby. 'Have I banished your doubts now?'

Leo lay on his back, gazing up at the sky.

'I trust you, Ronan. I do. But… what you're suggesting… I guess I've seen enough magic to know how dangerously unpredictable it can be. Merry's the most powerful witch I know and even she doesn't seem able to control it.' He waited, but Ronan stayed silent. 'I want to get past what happened to Dan, and I believe what you've told me about – about why I keep dreaming of him. Why I keep seeing him.' He shivered, despite the warmth of the evening. 'I'm scared; that's the truth of it.'

'You know I'm only doing this for us, don't you?' There was an undertone to Ronan's voice, a sort of… barely controlled tension. Leo was sure he'd heard that tone before. But as much as he searched his memory, he couldn't remember when. He sat up.

'I know that, but—'

'I want you to be happy. And I thought… I thought you wanted me to be happy too.' Ronan was frowning at the ground, stabbing it with the end of a twig.

'I do, I—' Leo stopped, swallowed, took a deep breath. 'I'm in love with you, I think.'

Ronan threw the stick away and took Leo's hands in his.

'And I love you. I want us to be together forever. But we can't. Not while this… shadow is still between us.' He put one hand up to Leo's face, caressing his cheek. 'Think about it, Leo. You know I'm right. Dan is trapped out there, under the lake, and until we release him, he's never going to let you go. But I promise you: do what I'm asking you to do, and all the pain you're still feeling will just… evaporate. And you will become the most important thing in my life.'

He kissed Leo again — softly, this time — then drew back, waiting for an answer.

Leo shuddered.

'"You have witchcraft in your lips."'

Ronan's eyes narrowed.

'What?'

'It's a quote. From a play Merry made me watch once.'

'Oh. So is that a yes?'

Leo nodded.

'Yes. I'll do whatever you want.'

Ronan exhaled loudly, then smiled.

'Good. I have a few more preparations to make. But it won't take long; two or three days at most. And in the meantime, why don't you stay here? I really don't want you to leave me.'

Leo nodded, too choked with emotion to speak, and drew Ronan back down on to the grass.

TWENTY

'SO, YESTERDAY WAS my birthday.'

It was two days since Leo had stormed out. Merry was in Mum's bedroom, holding Gran's hand, watching the August sunshine moving across her grandmother's gaunt features. She'd got up early and had been sitting with her for a couple of hours (there was only one witch on duty at a time now), reading and checking out the trending hashtags on Twitter. But it felt wrong, not filling Gran in on what had been happening. So now Merry was chatting to her. Talking at her, really.

First thing that morning Mrs Galantini had lifted the

spells that had been keeping Gran unconscious, but so far Gran hadn't shown any sign of waking up. Merry watched her grandmother's face and wondered whether she could actually hear what was being said to her, whether she would remember it when she woke.

'It was a bit of a weird day, to be honest.' A Saturday, so Mum had been around, which was nice. Though the first thing they'd done together was drive to the woods so Merry could lay some flowers where Flo's body had been found. There was no other place to go yet, to remember her. And then Leo… Leo had texted her. But he hadn't come home, hadn't even called. Thinking about Flo and Leo made Merry's chest ache, like she was going to start crying.

'It was better later. Ruby and I went into Tillingham in the afternoon, and she bought me the electric-blue eyeliner that I'd wanted for a while. Mum gave me some money towards those new trainers that I've been saving up for. And Finn…' The sadness of a moment ago passed, replaced by fluttering excitement in the pit of her stomach. Merry took a deep breath. It was all happening so fast. Too fast, almost. It wasn't like Finn was pressuring her, but… 'There's something going on, if only I could figure it out. S'pose it might be to do with his brother; he probably feels guilty, hanging out with me when he only came here to get help for Cillian.'

Bizarrely, it had felt much more straightforward with Jack. Would Gran still remember who Jack was when she woke up? Roshni was worried that she might have some memory damage. 'I dreamt about him again last night. Jack, I mean.' Another nightmare from which she'd woken, gasping with fright. She'd been back in the forest clearing with the hooded man and the spinning wheel, but this time she hadn't been alone. Finn and Leo had been there too, and Jack, standing just behind them, holding the King of Hearts' sword. All three of them staring at her. And the hooded man had said to her: *Which one do you choose?* She'd argued and said she didn't want to choose, but he just kept repeating the question. So eventually, he'd said, *I'm sorry, Finn*, and pointed to Leo. And then – and then Jack killed her brother. Drove the sword into him from behind, so that the point burst through the front of Leo's chest. Merry swallowed; even the memory of it sickened her.

'I hope you can help Cillian when you wake up, Gran. It's been bad enough watching you like this for just a few days; I don't know what I'd do if it was Leo lying in bed the whole time for months on end, his life just...wasting away.'

The door opened and Mum came in to take over, a laptop and a stack of books in her arms. Merry got up, straightened the covers on the bed and kissed Gran's forehead. 'I'll see you later, Gran. Wake up soon.'

She went downstairs and made herself some toast. Finn wasn't around, and Ruby had left this morning to visit her family in St Lucia; there was no one around to distract her from going over and over everything that Flo had said to her in the last couple of weeks, searching for a clue she might have missed. And when she stopped doing that, she just switched to worrying about Gran and Leo. She thought briefly about going to the gym, or the fencing club, or hanging out with some of her other friends – Verity had sent her a photo on Snapchat, a drawing of a pizza with a question mark next to it – but everything in the *normal* world felt so distant. Disconnected. So she went back to obsessing about what her brother was doing, what he might be feeling.

By late morning, the temptation had become too strong to resist. Whether Leo liked it or not, she had to find out where he was. Make sure he was safe. Tossing the book she'd been pretending to read on to the sofa, Merry ran upstairs, grabbed her silver bracelet and the bag of polished stones from her room and locked herself into the bathroom.

This time, she wasn't going to take any chances. There were a couple of tealights on the windowsill; she lit those and pulled down the blind before running the water into the basin. She added the bracelet, aquamarine and amethyst, then hesitated, her hand stretched over the stones spread out on the bath mat, and finally selected a piece of red jasper, placing it in the bottom of the basin with the other items. Jasper gave additional protection from evil, at least according to her wisdom books. Finally she sang the incantation in full. Remembering what Gran had told her, about the words of the spell giving definition to a witch's will, and acting as a form of protection against anyone on the other side of the spell, she concentrated especially on the last line. 'Shield the seer from all who would harm her.' The water in the basin went through the transformation from clear liquid to a looking-glass to a black, unreflecting pool.

Show me my brother.

Leo appeared in the blackness. But not just Leo. Ronan was there too. They seemed to be standing outside Ronan's tent, talking; Merry could just discern the shadowy outline of his van in the background. As she watched, they put their arms around each other and started kissing intensely. Merry looked away. Shame made her insides squirm: she shouldn't be intruding on Leo's privacy. How would she feel if she found out he'd been watching her with Finn? Turning back to the basin, she stretched out her hand to dismiss the vision. But what she saw made her draw in her breath sharply. They'd stopped kissing, but they were still hugging. Leo had his back to her, his head resting on Ronan's shoulder. So far, so cute. But the expression on Ronan's face – it was wrong, somehow. His arms were tight around Leo's body, like he wanted them to be one person, instead of two. But what Merry saw in his eyes didn't look like love. Desire; greed; wolfish, ravenous hunger; but not love.

She yanked the plug out of the basin: the vision broke up and vanished. But she couldn't get Ronan's face out of her mind. The front door banged. Hopefully, it was Finn. Merry wanted some answers and he might be the only person who could provide them.

Finn was in the kitchen, unpacking some bags of shopping – *Sucking up to Mum again*, Merry thought – at the same time as having an angry-sounding conversation with someone on his mobile.

'I've told you already: it's going as well as can be expected, in the circumstances. How quickly do you really think I can go from—'

He noticed Merry standing in the doorway and broke off, looking self-conscious.

'Er – have to go. I'll get back to you later.' He put the phone in his pocket. 'Hey. I've been shopping. I thought I'd make a chicken salad for lunch.'

'Great. But I need to talk to you.'

'Sure. What's up?'

'This guy, the one Leo's hanging out with the whole time. He told us he knows you. Said that he was friends with your brother, before his... accident.'

Finn froze, one hand on the fridge door, the other holding a carton of juice. For a split second he tensed, the top of the carton bulging slightly in his grip – then he carried on with what he'd been doing, putting the rest of the chilled stuff away before turning back to Merry.

'What's his name?'

'Ronan. I'm worried, Finn. About Leo, I mean. This guy is a wizard and I'm not sure I trust him. I think he's got... something else going on.'

An echo of Ronan's warning about Finn came back to her: '*The handsome prince. Doesn't he always have his own agenda?*' She crossed her arms, watching Finn, waiting for his response.

'Ronan...' He sounded faintly surprised. 'Uh, yeah, I

remember him. Vaguely. He was only around for a few weeks. Cillian didn't spend that much time with him.'

'That's not how Ronan tells it. He says Cillian is ordinary – non-magical – and that when he tried to help him, you and your dad basically… ran him off.' Merry could see a muscle twitching in the side of Finn's face, as if he was grinding his teeth. But she pressed on. 'Ronan says Cillian took a potion of some sort because he was so miserable, because he was fed up with being locked away like some kind of freak.'

'That's not true! It's—' Finn stopped, got a glass out of the cupboard and filled it with water from the tap. He was moving carefully, but Merry was sure she could see his hand shaking slightly as he drank. 'It's much more complicated than that.' He sat down at the kitchen table; Merry sat opposite him. 'Cillian isn't a wizard. I never said he was. My parents tried to give him a normal life and he wasn't unhappy. But it's never been easy for him, surrounded almost entirely by people who have something he doesn't have, and can't ever have.' He looked down at the scar on the inside of his wrist again. 'You love your brother, Merry. Do you think I'd let mine suffer without doing everything I could to help him?'

'So Ronan was lying?'

'I would say… he was telling you only what he knew, or assumed he knew. I don't know what Cillian said to him, about life at home. Dad asked Ronan to leave, because he thought he was making Cillian more unhappy. In retrospect…' He paused and picked up his glass, swirling the water around the inside. 'In retrospect, that may not have been the best way to deal with the situation.'

'Is Ronan dangerous?'

'All wizards are dangerous, Merry. You know that.'

Merry stiffened.

'Is he going to do something bad to Leo?'

'What's he been doing to Leo so far?'

'Nothing, as far as I know.' She shrugged. 'Kissing him.'

'Oh.' Finn's eyebrows went up. 'Look, I really don't know the guy. I honestly don't know what he wants with Leo. Maybe he genuinely likes him.'

Merry stared at Finn. Was it her imagination, or was he looking a bit… shifty?

Finn put down his glass and took her hand.

'I'm assuming the coven know Ronan is in the area? And your mum?'

Merry nodded.

'And you don't have any actual evidence that Ronan might be hurting Leo?'

'No.' She pressed her fingertips to her eyelids, trying to work out whether her distrust of Ronan was no more than jealousy. 'Leo's in love with him. Says Ronan loves him too.'

'So maybe he's right. You should try not to worry about it. I'm sure Roshni would have acted if she thought there was any danger.'

'I suppose. You don't care that Ronan is telling lies about you?'

'People will always take the word of my family over that of a drifter like him.' He must have seen the distaste in Merry's eyes, because he flushed slightly. 'Sorry. But it's true.'

By 'people', he means wizards. Possibly, at a stretch, witches. I really don't think he can help it, but... poor Cillian. What a place to grow up.

Finn was checking his phone.

'Shall I show you some more of those techniques I mentioned, to help you keep control of your power?' The flush across his cheeks grew deeper.

'These techniques... I'm guessing your teaching method is going to be pretty hands-on?'

Finn shrugged with fake modesty.

'I find I get the best results that way.'

Merry smiled despite herself. 'OK.'

'Great.' He stood up. 'Let's go into the garden. You'll pick it up much more quickly if we're undisturbed.'

Finn disappeared after lunch, saying he had some more errands to take care of. Merry was desperate to go for a run, but Mum still didn't want her going out alone, and she didn't want to ask Mum to leave Gran and drive her to the gym. Instead, she paced up and down in her room, and thought about Leo and Ronan. Finn was right: she had no evidence that Ronan was doing anything wrong. No specific reason to suspect him. It was just an impression. Hardly enough for her to try to take away the only thing that was currently making her brother happy. Even contemplating causing Leo that much misery made a horrible mixture of guilt and sadness well up inside her. But whatever Finn said about Ronan being harmless, she just couldn't quite believe it. She went over in her head everything that Ronan had said about himself. She thought about the things she definitely knew he'd done. He'd been there to save Leo from Simon. He'd been there to save her from the wolf. But he'd exaggerated – at the very least – what had happened to Cillian Lombard. He'd tortured Simon.

She paced faster, trying to sort through all the other information she'd come across over the last few weeks. The marks on Flo's face. The points of intersection. The story about the *Zauberzieher*... Her glance fell on the letters from the folder that she'd translated yesterday, just before the coven brought Gran back. It seemed such a long time ago. And she still hadn't read them, just looked at that one underlined phrase about a male witch...

She froze.

That oddly-titled booklet: *The Historical Treatment of Male Witches*, or something similar. The one thing in Gran's folder that she hadn't yet examined. Pulling the booklet out of the folder, she went to sit by the window and began skimming the text. The pages were densely printed and the tension in her body made it hard to take in the detail. But some sentences leapt out at her.

A male witch, rarely spoken about in polite society, is of course the son of a witch who inherits her magical abilities...

...rare and powerful, yet often subject to various magical deformities, these unfortunates frequently demonstrate some degree of insanity by the time they reach puberty. In less enlightened times, the covens usually drove such children into exile, incarcerated them, executed them...

...such acts of cruelty that, whether driven by insanity or

desperation, lead us to conclude that male witches are the reality
that lies behind such mythical creatures as Der Zauberzieher.

Oh.

It was like one of the floodlights coming on in the
garden. Ellie Mills, Flo, Gran: they weren't the victims of
a fairy-tale character. The *Zauberzieher* was just a – a cloak.
A mask. And behind the mask was a murderously insane
male witch.

Merry hurried back downstairs. Mum was in the
kitchen.

'You just missed Leo.'

'What? Where is he?'

'Gone back to stay with Ronan for another night. He
just popped in to get something; said he'll be back
tomorrow.'

'But, Mum, I think we need to—'

The phone rang.

'Just a sec, Merry. Can you unload the dishwasher while
I get this?'

Merry gritted her teeth and started putting the cutlery
away. A horrible sense of urgency was growing in the
back of her mind; a feeling that if she didn't get Leo away
from Ronan soon, something terrible was going to happen.

Even if that's only Leo having his heart broken again.

Mum came back in. Her face was sombre.

'Who was it?'

'Oh, Dan's mother. She'd had some news about another of Leo's friends. You remember Simon, don't you?' Merry just nodded. 'Well, he's been taken to a psychiatric hospital. The poor boy's been having some kind of violent hallucinations: barricading himself in his room, too petrified to sleep, apparently.' She wrapped her arms round herself like she was cold. 'I don't know. Dan and Flo, and now Simon — it's just awful. And Leo's going to be so upset…'

Mum was still talking, but Merry couldn't hear her any more. She couldn't focus on anything apart from the fact that Ronan had lied. The damage he'd done to Simon had been permanent. And Finn had told her that Ronan was harmless — was that a lie too?

Mum put a hand on Merry's arm.

'Are you all right, love? You've gone white as a sheet.'

Merry opened her mouth, to say *No, I'm not all right, we've got to get Leo away from him right now!*

But before she could speak, Mrs Knox threw the kitchen door open.

'Bronwen, come quickly. Elinor is awake.'

★

Gran was sitting up, leaning against some pillows. She was still deathly pale, her eyes watery and grey. She turned her head a fraction towards Merry and Mum as they came in, but she didn't seem to recognise them.

'She's very groggy,' Mrs Knox whispered as quietly as she could, 'and she's not making a lot of sense. I'm going to call the others, and I'll mix up some sage and ginger tonic while I'm downstairs.'

Mum sat on the chair next to the bed and took one of Gran's hands.

'Mum? It's me, Bronwen. And Merry's here too. You're safe now.'

Gran looked towards her daughter, then past her, at Merry.

'It's gone. He stole it…' Gran's voice was weak and rasping, her eyes wide.

Merry's chest tightened. She'd never seen her grandmother look frightened before. And now, Gran was absolutely terrified. Merry could taste it.

Mum smoothed a strand of hair away from Gran's face. 'Just try to relax. You need to rest. We can talk later.'

But Gran pushed Mum's hand away, still talking to Merry. 'He's taken it. It's gone. All gone.'

Mum stood up.

'This is scaring me. Stay with her, Merry, I'm going to make sure Roshni's on her way.' She hurried out of the room and Merry slid into the empty chair.

'Taken what, Gran? What has he taken?'

Gran closed her eyes briefly.

'Nothing left. *Nothing…*' Her eyes filled with tears and she stretched out her hand to Merry. Clearly, she wanted to tell her more. But she was just too exhausted.

No one had yet taught Merry a proper spell that would let her see what was inside someone's mind. But right now…

'I have to know, Gran. I have to know if I'm right.' She just hoped her mental barriers would be porous enough. Squeezing Gran's hand tightly, she closed her eyes and thought: *Show me what happened.*

The world around her began to dissolve.

It was dark: she had a blindfold over her eyes. But the cold, and the hard surface she was lying on, and the drip-drip-drip *of water nearby, told her she was in a cave. Metal chains were bound tightly around her wrists and ankles, cutting into the flesh, and she was thirsty. More thirsty than she'd ever been in her life.*

There was the sound of footsteps, and a faint brightness just discernable through the blindfold and her eyelids. Voices.

'…In here, Master?' This voice was doubtful, scared.

'Yes, Ethan. Kneel there. This won't take long.'

Silence. And then a shriek, abruptly cut off, and a terrible gurgling, bubbling sound, gradually dying away.

Somebody sighed.

'Hardly worth the effort, poor pleb. Still, I don't like leaving loose ends and I'll be out of here shortly. Just one last delicious transfusion, I think.'

The speaker dragged her upright, then grasped her head in his hands, digging his nails in, burning her skin. She flinched and gasped and tried to pull away, but he wouldn't let go. The pressure in her skull began to build slowly until she felt weak to the bone, as if she were fading away, losing herself…

The man relaxed his hands, breathing heavily.

'I'm almost going to miss that. I've never had a witch as powerful as you before.' He let her drop back on to the floor of the cave. 'But the place I'm going next, I won't need witches. And not even Finn Lombard will be able to track me.' He leant close so she was breathing in the scent of his aftershave. 'Nice knowing you, Mrs Foley.'

Merry gasped, let go of Gran's hand and put her arms out to steady herself.

It was Ronan. All this time. He'd stolen Gran's power, and now…

What? What does he want with Leo?

And Finn *knew* about him.

Her magic ignited within her, sending a flare of pain up her arms, making her flinch.

'Gran, I—'

Gran nodded a little, and murmured 'Go.'

Merry ran out of the bedroom, started down the stairs – ran back up again and burst into the spare room. Finn was lying on the bed, but he jumped up when Merry came in.

'You bastard!' She crossed the room in two paces and slapped him hard on the face. 'You know what Ronan is! You knew all along and you didn't tell me!'

Finn's expression passed rapidly from shock to anger to guilt. His face was white, apart from the red patch where she'd struck him.

'I didn't know. Not for certain. Not until today.'

'You're lying.'

'No! He looks completely different, and he's using a different name... I was beginning to think he really was just a regular wizard who had fallen for Leo. Ever since Cillian got sick, I've been tracking him – I just couldn't risk losing him again.'

'What's he doing with my brother? Leo hasn't any power for him to steal.'

'I don't know, honestly. He's never stayed so long in any one place before. I kept thinking that he was going to come after you.'

Merry couldn't believe what she was hearing.

'So I'm the bait, am I?'

Finn flushed and narrowed his eyes, but he shook his head.

'Course not. I was hoping to – protect you.'

Merry dug her nails into her palms, to keep control of her magic and to stop herself slapping him again.

'I'm going after my brother. And you better hope he's OK, because if not...'

She turned to run from the room, but Finn called out, 'Wait!' and the bedroom door slammed shut in front of her.

'Wait – I can get you there, almost instantly.'

'How?'

'There's a spell I sort of know: *Intervolitare* – it's a form of transportation spell. I've never done it with another person before, and it can be dangerous, but...'

He was talking about the broomstick spell.

'I don't care. Just get me there. Now.'

'OK.' Finn held his hands up, palms out, pacifying. 'But we should go outside. It's safer.' He opened the door and Merry ran out, almost knocking Mum over on the landing.

'What's going on?' Mum looked from Merry to Finn and back again. 'Merry?'

'It was Ronan, Mum — Gran showed me.' Her mother staggered slightly, her face draining of colour; she put one hand on the wall for support. 'Leo?'

'We're going to get him. Right now.' Merry took Mum's free hand. 'I need you to tell the coven, to get them to come after us. Ronan's camping down by Black Lake.' Mum still looked stunned. 'D'you understand?'

'Yes.' She nodded. 'Go.'

Merry and Finn tore down the stairs and out into the front garden.

'What do we do?'

'We'll have to stand close together and…' He paused, frowning. 'Damn. Hold on — notebook.'

'You've got to be kidding me.' But Finn was already running back into the house. He reappeared a couple of minutes later with a black notebook in his hand, pulled her nearer to the street light and opened the book.

'Right.' He peered for a moment at the words on the page, struggling to hold it flat against the breeze. 'We'll have to put our arms around each other.'

Merry swore under her breath. Never had she felt less like giving Finn a hug. But she stepped forward and slid her arms around his body. He slipped one of his arms round her back and held her close.

'Good. Now, I'll say the spell. You just have to hold on. I think.'

Over Finn's shoulder Merry could see a narrow crescent moon floating low above the horizon, a few clouds scudding across the sky. For the first time since Gran had woken up, she realised she didn't really have a clue what she was doing. She had no idea how powerful Ronan was, or what he was doing with Leo. She didn't have her brother by her side. And this time, she didn't even have a magic manuscript to guide her. Despite the warmth of the night air and the heat of Finn's body, she shivered. Finn tightened his grip around her and started chanting the words of the spell.

'*Volo intervolitare astra…*'

And there was no longer any possibility of feeling scared, because there was just too much pain.

TWENTY-ONE

LEO SHIVERED, THOUGH the night was warm; sultry, even. His T-shirt was sticking to his back. Perhaps it was the atmosphere. A yellow curved moon hung in the sky like the leftover grin of the Cheshire Cat, casting a sickly light across the water. Or perhaps he was nervous. Despite all of Ronan's reassurances, what they were about to do was... scary. Especially here, standing by the lake where he'd twice seen his sister nearly die. Holding the sword with which he'd destroyed the puppet hearts.

Ronan was nearby, carving symbols into the ground with a knife. Runes of some sort, Leo guessed, like the ones the coven had put around the house after Jack got into Merry's room. Guilt stabbed at him; he should have gone home for Merry's birthday. Or at least called her. Now he thought about it, he couldn't quite remember why he hadn't. Ronan had told him not to, had explained why. *A good explanation*, Leo had thought at the time. Though now, he couldn't remember Ronan's reasons.

'OK, nearly done.' Ronan drew the back of his arm across his forehead and took off his top.

Leo stared at Ronan's muscled chest. He found it hard to think at all when Ronan was standing this close to him. 'Um... remind me what we have to do now?'

'You have to give me the sword, so that I can touch it safely. And then we have to reawaken it with our blood. Feed it, if you like.'

Leo frowned. He remembered someone else saying something once, about feeding a blade. Had it been... Merry? No, that wasn't right. It was that guy, the one who'd been at the lake with them...

It was Jack, wasn't it? Or...

Ronan said something and the thought slipped away.

'Sorry, what?'

'The sword, Leo. You have to give it to me, or I can't touch it.'

'Oh, sure.' He held the blade carefully, extending the hilt towards Ronan, trying to remember the words the wizard had taught him earlier. '"What was mine is now yours; I release it into your care." We will get it back again, right?'

'Of course.' Ronan took the sword and a smile spread slowly across his face. 'Yes. I can feel this is going to work. It'll be perfect.' He took Leo's hand and led him forward so they were both standing inside the circle of symbols Ronan had carved. At the centre of the circle a small fire was burning, on either side of which Ronan had placed two blocks of stone. Now he laid the sword across them so that the hilt was resting on one block, the tip of the blade on the other. Picking up the knife he'd been using earlier, he wiped the blade on a cloth, then passed it to Leo.

'Like we talked about, remember?' He held his left hand – quivering – out above the sword.

Leo examined the knife he was holding. The blade was some kind of dark metal, narrow and very pointed; almost like a needle. The hilt, made of the same material, was formed of two snakes intertwined around a globe. It looked ancient.

'Where's this from?'

'It's Roman; I picked it up somewhere along the way. Are you ready?'

Leo nodded. He took hold of Ronan's left wrist and placed the point of the knife against his palm. As Ronan started intoning a phrase – in Latin, Leo thought, though he wasn't certain – Leo drew the tip of the knife across Ronan's flesh, wincing as he did so. Ronan gasped slightly, but his voice didn't falter. When the incision was made Leo waited, still holding Ronan's wrist, until three fat drops of blood had splashed on to the sword blade below. A little of the blood ran off into the fire; the rest seemed to… vanish. Like the sword had absorbed it.

Ronan wound a bandage around his injured hand.

'OK. Good.' He was breathing heavily, whether from relief or excitement, Leo couldn't tell. 'Your turn.' Leo took a deep breath, gave the knife back to Ronan and held out his hand. Ronan took it and kissed the middle of Leo's palm. 'Try to relax. It'll be over soon.'

Leo nodded, not trusting himself to speak. He closed his eyes as Ronan pressed the point of the knife hard against his skin, biting his lip so as not to cry out, trying to concentrate on the words Ronan was saying rather than the pain radiating across his palm as the blade sliced downwards. He felt the knife stop moving, knew that his blood must be dripping on to the sword. Ronan released him and he opened his eyes again. The cut didn't look as bad as he had imagined, but it was bleeding freely.

'Here.' Ronan passed him an antiseptic wipe as well as a bandage. 'I need to keep you healthy.'

'Thanks.' Leo cleaned and wrapped his hand while Ronan stamped out the fire and picked up the sword, holding it so he could look along the blade. 'What's next?'

'We're almost ready to free him. But first… you'll need to lose the shirt.'

Leo felt his eyebrows shoot up.

'Why?'

'Because you're the link that's going to draw him out of the lake. I have to mark you.' As Leo hesitated, Ronan moved closer and kissed him gently. 'No more knives, I promise.'

'OK.' Leo pulled off his T-shirt and dropped it on to the floor. Ronan bent and scooped some ash out of the cooling fire. Dipping one finger into it, he drew something on Leo's chest. Leo didn't look down – he didn't want to see what it was. Then Ronan picked up the sword and held the hilt against the same spot he'd just drawn on. Leo frowned as he felt a tightening against his ribs, like some kind of invisible band had been looped around him.

'Don't panic – we're nearly done.' Ronan's voice was soothing. He pressed his fingertips to the skin just above Leo's heart, as if he was checking his heartbeat. 'Good. Let's go.' He took Leo's hand. Together, they walked to the lake, climbing up to the top of the small cliff from where Jack had jumped back into the water, stopping a little way from the edge.

There was a breeze coming off the water, chasing ragged clouds across the sky. Ronan plunged the sword into the ground so that nearly half the length of the blade was buried in the dried-up turf. Holding his arms wide, he began to sing in some language Leo didn't recognise at all, and Leo was suddenly reminded of the coven singing as they'd placed the runes around the house.

The surface of the lake began to tremble, the water rippling and folding in on itself like liquid origami. Leo – unwilling, yet somehow unable to resist – stepped past Ronan and moved closer to the edge of the cliff. It was so like that moment when Merry and he had followed the King of Hearts into the water, looking for a way into Gwydion's realm. But this time, he was waiting for something – for someone – to emerge.

He didn't have to wait long.

As Ronan continued his chanting, a faint figure began to form amid the foam and shadows. Just outlines and hints of washed-out colour to begin with. Leo inched closer again.

'Dan?'

The figure became gradually more opaque, hovering above the swirling waves.

Arms, legs, torso; definitely a male figure. But the hair, and the clothes...

It wasn't Dan.

The spectre turned round, and Leo saw Jack's face. But it wasn't Jack, either. The cold cruelty of the features could mean only one thing: it was the King of Hearts.

'No!'

He tried to back away, but Ronan was behind him, grabbing his arms, pinning him there as the ghostly figure rose from the water.

Leo struggled to free himself, but Ronan was too strong. As the King of Hearts drew nearer still, the mark on Leo's chest began to burn like acid, and he started to scream.

All the while Ronan was murmuring in his ear, 'Don't fight it, Leo. Just let it happen. Surrender to him and there will be no more pain, no more anxiety.' Ronan tightened his grip again, forcing Leo's head back. 'I promise you, this is best for both of us. He's going to take us with him, and we will both be free.' The apparition stretched out an arm and touched Leo's skin with the tip of one finger and the pain grew until his nerve endings were singing in agony and his vision failed and he was losing control, losing himself…

★   ★   ★

Finn's arms were still tight around Merry's waist and shoulders, holding her against him, holding her up; her legs were shaking and she would have fallen without his support. The effects of the broomstick spell had been nothing like Merry had imagined, or expected. There had been an agonisingly painful sensation of being stretched sideways, of being in two places at once. She'd actually been able to see the driveway outside the house and the woods at the same time. And now… now she felt so horribly sick.

Finn slid his hand under her T-shirt, pressing his fingers against the bare skin of her back. Warmth, comforting despite the heat of the night, radiated from where he touched her, and the nausea faded.

'Deep breaths. Sorry, I should have warned you.'

Merry obeyed, breathing slowly, eyes closed, head resting on Finn's shoulder. The shaking stopped.

'Finn – you can let go now.'

'Oh, OK.' He stepped away from her and she turned to look around, getting her bearings.

'I think I know where we are. The lake—'

A howl of pain carved through the rustling of the woods. Merry's heart began hammering against the inside of her chest.

Leo.

Finn grabbed her by the arm.

'Hold on, you can't just rush off. We need a plan—'

Merry didn't waste time arguing. She kneed him in the groin and started sprinting in the direction of the scream, ignoring Finn's pained calls for her to wait. Nothing mattered apart from getting to her brother, saving him. It was like running through treacle: every metre felt like a mile. But finally she broke through the edge of the woods, was speeding towards the lake, towards the two figures standing on the high ground off to one side, and she raised her aching, tingling hands, thinking, *I'm going to kill him if he's hurt Leo; I'm going to rip him to shreds and bury him at the bottom of that damn lake.*

Ronan was watching her, arms crossed. Leo was standing next to him, trembling, eyes wide, forehead glistening with sweat. A sword – Leo's sword – was hovering in empty space, its point pressed against the back of Leo's neck.

Merry stopped running.

'That's right, Merry. Nice and easy now. And keep your hands where I can see them. I'm the only thing keeping your brother alive.' Ronan's gaze flicked past her to where Finn was rapidly approaching. 'You'll need to deal with him.' She hesitated, wincing as she noticed a strange rune burnt into the skin of Leo's chest. Ronan waved his hand towards the sword and Leo gasped. 'Hurry.'

Merry began murmuring the opening words of a sleeping spell under her breath. Finn was staring at Ronan, and he didn't notice as she flung out one arm and hurled the spell in his direction. He crumpled on to the grass and lay there, unmoving.

'Let my brother go.' Her voice sounded weak. She swallowed and tried again. 'Let him go. He's not magical. You can't feed off him.'

Anger flashed across Ronan's face, but he controlled himself quickly.

'So you think you know what I am?' He forced a laugh. 'You know nothing. Trust me.'

'Then what do you want?'

'You're going to give me some of your blood. Three

drops. Then I'll release him and you can both go. If you want to. I promise.' He grinned at her, his teeth white and sharp in the faint moonlight.

'Why?'

The grin faded.

'No more questions.' Ronan picked something up off the ground and sent it floating towards her, just like Finn had once done with his phone. Merry glanced across at him, wishing he would wake up.

A small package arrived in front of her. She unwrapped it: a knife with a narrow blade, and a bowl.

'You know what to do.'

Merry plucked the knife out of the air. Its blade was already stained.

'Merry…' The throb of terror in Leo's voice caught at her heart like a trailing thorn. 'Please, hurry.'

There was no time. Holding her hand out she slashed downwards, waiting until there was a small pool of blood in the bottom of the bowl. The knife was tugged out of her hand as Ronan summoned the implements back to him.

'There now. It wasn't so hard, was it?' He walked behind Leo, not taking his eyes off Merry, and poured her blood over the blade of the sword. The whole thing began to vibrate slightly, and Leo moaned. Merry took a step closer.

'Let him go!'

Ronan shrugged.

'As you wish.' He grasped the hilt of the sword, pulled it away from Leo's neck and stabbed it into the turf. Leo fell on to his hands and knees on the grass, panting. 'I thank you for your cooperation. You're free to go.'

'Leo...' Merry stretched out her hand to her brother. 'It's going to be OK. Please, just walk away from him. Let me take you home.'

Leo looked up at her and smiled. But there was no relief in his expression, no humour. Horror settled on her like a shroud. 'Leo?'

Her brother pushed himself to his feet, pulled the sword out of the ground, then stood, both hands resting on the hilt. All expression had drained from his face; he was like an effigy on a tomb. And Merry remembered how Jack used to look, all those evenings at the lake, when he'd turned back into the King of Hearts and she had to speak the words from the manuscript, to send him back into the water...

Ronan laughed and caressed Leo's face lightly.

'Sorry, Merry, but it looks like Leo has made his choice. He belongs to me now.'

TWENTY-TWO

MERRY HURLED A spell at Ronan. She acted purely on instinct, her desire to punish Ronan, make him pay.

He threw his arms up, shouting the words of a shielding spell. As Merry's spell hit, he cried out and swayed backwards, but most of the force was deflected, sent into the ground where it incinerated the grass.

'Wait! You can't hurt me without hurting him,' Ronan yelled. 'Look.' He turned his face so she could see a cut that had opened up across his cheekbone. Merry glanced at Leo and saw the exact same injury on his face. Blood was running down on to his neck, though Leo seemed completely oblivious to it.

Merry lowered her hands.

'What have you done to him?'

'Have you not worked it out yet?' Ronan shook his head, dabbing at the side of his face with a bandage that was tied around his hand. 'Did you really think something this powerful,' he gestured at Leo, 'wouldn't attract attention? Dark magic from the shadow realm, and you...' he shook his head, 'you just left it lying around for any passing wizard to—'

'You're no wizard.' Merry spat the words at him. 'You're a – a *freak*.'

'Shut up!' Ronan screamed at her, the veins in his temples throbbing. 'I thought you'd be better, but you're just like the rest of them. You can't accept someone who's different, someone who doesn't follow the rules. You want to destroy what you don't understand—'

'I understand all right. I understand that you're a monster!' Merry cut across him.

'A monster, am I?' Ronan strode forward, away from Leo, and Merry wondered if this could be her chance. Somehow, she must try to separate Ronan from her brother. She surreptitiously aimed a stinging hex at Finn; he twitched a little, but that was all. Ronan was close to her now. She could feel the wild fury coming off him in waves. 'Do you know what other witches used to do to people like me? They used to put us in dungeons. If we were lucky. Can you imagine that: for a child to be taken from his family, locked in a cell, kept there until he died? That's why my mother ran. She had to leave her home, everything she'd known.' Ronan looked past Merry like he wasn't even really seeing her. She sent another hex towards Finn. 'Over the years, she came to resent me. She hated me, by the end. I didn't blame her, but it did make it easier for me to kill her…' He blinked, saw Merry and glared at her. 'Besides, I needed her power. But now,' he glanced back at Leo, 'now I have power of a different kind. More power than I could ever have imagined. Thanks to you.'

Merry shifted position, trying to get between Ronan and Leo.

'Maybe… maybe there's some way I can help you? I'm powerful. You know that.'

Ronan laughed.

'Are you going to be all self-sacrificing? Offer to take his place, perhaps?'

'Yes.' Merry tried to keep her voice from wavering, but her heart was racing. If she could just persuade Ronan to set Leo free. 'I'll go with you. Let you… let you take my power. I won't fight it, I promise. If you'll only release him, get rid of the evil you've put inside him.'

Ronan looked her up and down slowly. It made Merry's flesh crawl. She had to force herself to hold her gaze steady.

'Well, I won't say I'm not tempted.' He ran his tongue across his lips. 'I'm ravenous just thinking about it. But…' He held up his hands, palms out, and backed away a little. 'I have to be sensible. I'd use you up eventually, and then where would I be? But Leo… what's inside him now is going to provide me with enough magic to satisfy me forever, once I fix it there.'

'He trusted you. He thought you loved him.'

'I do love him. And we're going to be together. Just… not here.' Merry could see sparks of magic beginning to sizzle off Ronan's fingertips. 'Tell you what, I'll throw you a bone. Guess my real name before I kill you, and I'll let him go.' He paused, grinning. 'No idea? Then I think we're done talking. Leo and I have somewhere to be.' He raised his hands. 'Remember, if you hurt me, you hurt your brother, so I wouldn't fight back if I were you. Think of it more as… an execution.'

Merry brought her hands up.

'You're insane. Leo would rather die than be left like this.' She swallowed, forcing herself to think the worst, even though saying the words somehow might make them real. 'For all I know, he's dead already.'

Anger blazed from Ronan's eyes.

'My new servant has already given me more than enough knowledge to defeat you.' He muttered something under his breath, and Merry saw bright red light begin to flow from his fingertips. He moved his hands like he was writing in the air, and shapes appeared, glowing against the still-dark sky.

Fire runes. Merry hadn't seen this kind of magic since she'd fought Gwydion.

But I fought it then, and won. I can fight it now.

She began to sing: a spell for rain, to draw water down from the overburdened clouds that were gathering in the sky above. But before she could complete the first phrase, Ronan stumbled, his whole body sagging. He looked towards Leo.

'No… no…'

Merry followed his gaze: Leo was prostrate on the ground, the sword by his side.

Ronan groaned and collapsed.

Merry ran to her brother, and knelt beside him.

'Leo!'

She pulled him up into her arms, struggling with his weight. If she got Leo away, maybe distance would destroy whatever connection Ronan had forged.

'Merry…' Leo's voice was weak. Merry lowered him so she could see his face. 'You – have to go, before he comes back.'

The King of Hearts, that's who he meant.

'No. We're both leaving, now.' She stretched out her arms above his body. But Leo grabbed one of her hands.

'He's going to take us…'

'Take you where?' Leo's eyelids fluttered and Merry shook him. '*Where*, Leo?'

'Somewhere that Ronan…' His voice sank to a murmur beneath the strengthening breeze, forcing Merry to bend close. 'He wants to destroy…' Leo's body began convulsing, over and over again. At the same time Ronan groaned and started pushing himself on to his hands and knees, shaking his head.

Merry leapt up, thinking desperately.

The net –

She started spilling magical silver filaments from her fingers, trying to use the technique Finn had taught her to modulate her power, and the proper words to control and finesse the spell. As she wove a cage around her brother, she sang about protection and isolation, spinning the silver threads carefully so that Leo was safe but surrounded. Just in time: he sprang up and began hacking at the net with the sword. Merry watched, holding her breath, but his blows seemed to have no impact.

It's going to hold, it's—

The fire runes hit her from the side, searing across her skin and knocking her to the ground. She rolled, trying to ignore the pain, throwing up her hands to ward off another attack. Ronan was on his feet, striding towards her, snarling with anger.

'Release him!'

A quick glance confirmed that Finn was still lying inert on the grass and Merry wondered for a horrible moment if she'd killed him. She would have to deal with Ronan on her own, break the enchantment...

One of the first lessons in her wisdom books came back to her. *When a witch or wizard dies, their enchantments are usually dissolved; therefore, in theory, one can dissolve an enchantment by taking the life of the enchanter.* Whatever Ronan had done to Leo, whatever sorcery he'd used to summon the King of Hearts, this was her best chance to undo it. She would have to kill him.

Ronan struck at her again. But this time she deflected the fire runes back towards him, forcing him further away from her brother. Taking a deep breath, she tried to remember how it had felt when she'd turned the yew tree to glass; that unstoppable release of raw power. Merry stretched out her fingers, ignoring the wind that was whipping at her hair, bracing her hands against the combination of revulsion and fear that was making her tremble, and thought: *Please, let this not hurt Leo.*

The magic exploded from her nails and smashed into the fire runes that Ronan was conjuring. For a moment the runes hung there, glowing against the night sky, before evaporating in a sheet of blue flame. Ronan tried to back away again, tripped and fell, cradling his arm. Merry glanced across at Leo, but he was still trying to break out of the cage she'd constructed around him and showed no sign of injury. Excitement flashed through her. She could do this: she could kill Ronan, send the King of Hearts back to wherever he'd come from, put everything right.

She raised her hands, summoning her power again...

Finn swore loudly and staggered to his feet.

'Quickly, Finn,' Merry called, 'help me kill him!' She directed her power at Ronan, knocking him over again, pinning him to the ground. He was still trying to fight her, drawing fire runes in the air, but she could see his stolen magic was running out. The runes were fading almost as soon as he'd written them. She sang a few words of strength, increase – and Ronan began to scream. Merry closed her eyes, not wanting to see what she was doing to him, willing it to be over quickly—

Something slammed her to the ground, paralysed her, leaving her staring up at the wind-wracked sky. She couldn't think. There was just – pain. Too much pain in her head and spine from where she'd been hit.

A binding spell. Someone had hit her with a binding spell.

Finn appeared in her vision.

'You can't kill him. I need him alive. I have to find out about the potion he gave to Cillian.' Shock turned her stomach. 'Now, I'm going to let you up. But—'

Finn cried out and dropped to his knees, a fire rune sparking and sizzling across his skin. In the same instant the binding charm failed. Merry scrambled upright and saw Ronan sprinting across the ground to where Leo was standing. Her silver net had disappeared, and now Leo was lifting the sword and Ronan was reaching out his hand to take hold of the hilt.

'No!'

She raised her hands, but Finn was in the way again, casting some kind of protective spell, still yelling something about waiting, and she had to drive him out of the way. But he was good; he slowed her down and by the time she got past him Leo and Ronan together were vanishing into what looked like a dark, gaping hole cut into the dawn sky. Merry screamed out a last spell: it hit Leo and he dropped the sword, but then...

Then he was gone.

Ronan and Leo and the dark opening had vanished. She and Finn were alone, the landscape in front of them empty, apart from the lake and the sword, still lying on the grass.

There was a long, drawn-out crack of thunder, and it began to rain.

TWENTY-THREE

THE WITCHES ARRIVED in groups of two or three, those who could use the broomstick spell bringing others who couldn't. They ran towards Merry and Finn, casting spells at the spot where the portal had been. Merry didn't react. She couldn't remember how. She just stood there while the rain soaked her to the bone and Mum shook her, screaming about Leo.

But Leo was gone. That was the only thing she was certain of.

Her brother had been taken by Ronan, and it was all because of Finn.

Merry pushed her mother aside. Finn was sitting on a

fallen tree trunk a few metres away, his head buried in his hands. Rage burned through her veins. The familiar surge of power was running down the length of her arms, across her palms, waiting to explode from her fingertips. She made no effort to diffuse or moderate it, and she trembled as she looked at him.

Finn raised his head when she got close to him; she could see he'd been crying. He opened his mouth to speak. But before he could utter a word, Merry stretched out her open hands towards him, letting her power course through her fingertips, red sparks flying through the air.

Finn moaned and arched his back, slipping to the ground.

As he lay there, gasping, Merry walked forward until she was standing above him. She heard the voices of the other witches behind her, crying out in horror, yelling at her to stop what she was doing, but she ignored them. Her fingers burned and she hit him again with another surge of power, watched him writhe under the lash of her magic. She knew how much she was hurting him – and she was glad of it.

'Stop, please,' he begged. 'I didn't mean to – to…'

'To what?' Merry replied. 'To sacrifice my brother in order to save your own?'

Finn shook his head and tried to push himself off the ground. 'I never meant any of that to happen. We can still save Leo. There has to be a way.'

'Liar!' Merry attacked him again. Finn screamed and clutched at his shin. There was blood welling up through his fingers, and somewhere in the back of her mind Merry thought, *I've broken his leg.*

And for the first time she realised it was raining, and that she was freezing. She looked upwards towards the sky, reached out with her mind…

The rain stopped.

The air around her crackled and vibrated with her power. She could feel the energy rolling off her, sense the ancient magic of the landscape beneath her feet. And something else: *fear.* The coven were afraid of her.

Well, they should be.

She knelt next to Finn. Everything he'd said, everything they'd done together: it had all been fake. He didn't care about her. She'd just been… useful. Convenient.

'Tell me why you did it. Tell me what you were really thinking when you kissed me.'

The ghost of a smile touched his lips. He shook his head.

'What does it matter any more, Merry? Why don't you just kill me?'

And in that moment she was back under the lake, staring up at Jack – the King of Hearts – and saying almost exactly the same words to him.

Why have you stopped? Why don't you just kill me?

Shock left her breathless. She stumbled backwards, away from Finn. Her mother was right behind her.

'Merry, please – don't do this!'

Merry pushed her away again.

'How can you stand there and try to protect him, after what he's done?'

'I'm not protecting him. I'm protecting *you*. This isn't who you are, Merry. This isn't what you want to become. I've lost my son today. I can't lose my daughter too.' Mum dragged a shaking hand across her eyes. 'Please. Leo wouldn't want you to do this.'

He might. Leo couldn't stand Finn.

But then she remembered: how she'd forced Ronan to stop torturing Simon. How Leo – despite the pain and humiliation Simon had inflicted on him – had understood what she was saying. Had agreed with her, had asked Ronan never to do anything like it again. Leo pretty much always made the right choice. That was one of the things she loved about him the most.

Merry let her aching hands drop as the anger that had

been pulsating through her, sustaining her power, began to drain from her body. She looked past her mother at Finn. He'd managed to drag himself upright and was sitting with his back to the fallen tree, his broken leg stuck out awkwardly in front of him. There were streaks of blood on his hands and face, dark circles under his eyes. He looked terrible: defeated and beaten in more ways than one.

'I never meant any of this to happen,' he said quietly. 'I wanted to bring Patrick – Ronan – whatever that monster's calling himself now – I wanted to bring him home, to force him to tell us what potion he gave to Cillian. I wanted to help my brother. I know you won't believe me, but I never meant to hurt you. Or your family.'

He stared at her, before closing his eyes. His lips moved silently. He was muttering a spell.

'No! Wait—'

Merry took a step towards him. But it was too late. He'd disappeared.

Physical and emotional exhaustion caught up with her. The world reeled, faded, and her mother's arms were around her, pulling her close.

The rain began to fall again.

★

Merry was back at home. The numbness had returned. But it didn't matter – there was nothing left for her to do. Nothing left to say.

Eventually, people gave up trying to talk to her and she was allowed to go upstairs. In her room, she locked the door behind her and lay on the bed. She was finally alone. Grief and loss lanced through the numbness, slicing it open, and she started to cry.

Four days had passed since Leo had been taken. Merry had spent most of the time being interrogated. She'd wearily answered all the questions Roshni and the other coven members had put to her: about her battle with Ronan and Finn, about what Ronan had done to Leo. About when she'd realised that Ronan was the one murdering witches, draining their power. They'd gone over some questions more than once, as if they didn't quite believe her. And then Roshni had actually asked whether Merry had heard of something called a *Zauberzieher*, and Merry had almost laughed, saying, *yes, I know the stories, and I know about male witches and what we used to do to them, and did it ever occur to you that maybe we created Ronan, that we created our own monster* –

Denise – Flo's mum – nearly went ballistic at that point.

She already seemed to blame Merry for everything that had happened, because Merry hadn't dealt with the King of Hearts properly the first time round. Because she'd left its presence to linger on, trapped beneath the Black Lake, waiting for someone like Ronan to come along and free it. Roshni, and others, had leapt to Merry's defence, but Merry no longer cared what the coven thought about her. She didn't really care about anything any more.

Now she was lying on her bed in her room with the curtains closed, shutting out the afternoon sun. Getting up or getting dressed seemed like far too much effort. She turned over, kicking the duvet off the bed. Everything she'd gone through this year – defeating Gwydion, watching Jack die; without her brother, it felt like it had all been for nothing.

She gazed at the second hand of her alarm clock, edging her further away from Leo with every sweep around the clock face. No one knew exactly what Ronan had done, or had hoped to do, though Merry thought she could guess. Ronan was looking for a cure, for a source of magical power that would never run out. He believed that restoring the King of Hearts to a human body would give him that power. But how would he control it? By returning the King of Hearts to the shadow realm? Or by trying to take it to another place altogether? She didn't know. But somehow he'd managed to exploit the fragile, fluid nature of reality around the Black Lake to take Leo somewhere else.

'Ronan was trying to manipulate powers he didn't understand,' Roshni had said. 'What he was doing, trying to combine the ancient magic of the land with the evil of the shadow realm… I believe the spell must have destroyed both him and Leo. We're lucky – it could easily have destroyed all of us.' She'd told Merry – kindly, but with finality – that her brother wasn't coming back. That she needed to start grieving.

To let Leo go. But that was like asking her to get over the loss of a major organ. Without Leo, she just didn't work properly.

Roshni had also made the coven's position clear: no one was to attempt to replicate what Ronan had done. She believed any such attempt was bound to fail, but if by some chance it didn't, the risk of causing some huge magical catastrophe, of fracturing time and space around the lake, was too great.

No one person was worth that, she'd said.

Not even Leo.

Merry picked up the photo of her and Leo from the

bedside table. It had been taken at a fancy dress party last year: they'd gone as Luke and Leia. In the photo they were laughing together, and Leo had his arm round her shoulders. She thought about how he'd saved her when the King of Hearts was about to kill her. How he'd fought Mum when Merry was getting really ill in Northumberland. How he'd refused to allow her to face Gwydion alone. One way or another Leo always seemed to be the one holding her up. Holding her together.

If this was the other way round, Leo would already be trying to find a way to replicate Ronan's spell. He'd try to come after me. I know he would.

So what was she doing, wallowing in self-pity and despair?

To think beyond the immediate moment – that was too difficult. But perhaps she could just… begin?

Merry sat up. Swung her legs out of bed. Made herself stand and walk across her bedroom. Went to the wardrobe…

And there it was. *The trinket box.* Merry pulled it out and opened it, running her fingers across the parchment and the braid of hair. Leo's sword – the one that he had used to stab the puppet hearts, the one that Ronan had then used to summon the King of Hearts – that was somewhere in the house. Mum had picked it up at the lake. And gradually, the outline of an idea began to take shape in Merry's mind. Just a thought, its glassy bones so fragile that she felt they might shatter if she breathed too hard.

Excitement and nerves kicked in, making her hands tremble. Merry threw on some fresh clothes, then hurried to Leo's room. The sword was lying on his bed like some kind of damn funeral accessory. Merry took a deep breath, clenching her fists tightly, and turned away to drag Leo's old interrailing rucksack out of his wardrobe. It was large enough for her to stash the sword inside.

Back in her own room, she packed the trinket box and then threw in a few clothes and other bits and pieces. Within half an hour, she was ready to go.

Looking around her room Merry wondered – not for the first time this year – whether she would ever come back. Whether she should leave a note. Because she couldn't risk saying goodbye to Mum. If she tried to stop her, or if the coven found out…

Maybe I'd end up locked in a dungeon. Or worse.

That ruled out a note as well, in case Mum found it too quickly and sent Roshni after her.

But Gran…

Gran didn't know about Leo. Not yet. She was too ill,

too destroyed by what Ronan had done to her. She was still being watched around the clock by other members of the coven. For Merry to act without asking her advice, to leave without saying anything – it seemed like an act of betrayal. Another terrible indignity. And yet…

And yet, she had to act. Gran wouldn't want her to give up on Leo without a fight.

Merry checked the front of the house: the coast seemed clear. Swinging the rucksack on to her back, she climbed out of the window, clambered down the drainpipe and started running.

Merry was filthy by the time she got to the lake. Four days of rain had flooded every gutter and turned the baked earth to mud, and she'd slipped and fallen over a couple of times. But no one had seen her, and no one had tried to stop her. Once she reached the same spot where Leo had disappeared, she pulled the sword and her knife from the rucksack.

There was no point delaying. She crouched down, stretched her hand out above the sword, put the knife in position—

'I can help you with that, if you'd like me to.'

Startled, Merry toppled backwards into the mud.

It was Finn. Cuts and bruises gone, leg healed — fixed up, at least on the surface. His face was just as handsome, his grey eyes just as unsettling as the last time he'd kissed her. But the longer she stared at him, the more he seemed kind of... crushed. Like the spark had gone out of him. And then she felt terrible, wrenching grief.

His grief.

Merry put her knife down and got to her feet.

'What's wrong? What's happened?'

'Cillian. He, um...' Finn looked away from her, out across the lake. 'He's dead. It happened two days ago now. We don't know whether it was something to do with Ronan disappearing, or if his body had just had enough...'

Merry couldn't quite work out how to respond. There was shock and sympathy. But also, somewhere in the darkest recesses of her soul, a tiny, awful voice whispering: *Well, that kind of serves you right.*

Finn was watching her, waiting for a reply.

'I'm sorry. I wish... I wish Gran could have helped him.'

He shrugged awkwardly.

'At least I was at home when it happened. I got to say goodbye. Sort of. But then I came straight back here. I've been waiting for you.'

Merry narrowed her eyes.

'Why?'

'I've lost my brother. But we might still be able to save yours. I want to help.'

Merry shook her head and started to turn away. 'You lied to me, Finn. How can I possibly trust you?'

'Listen to me, please!' Finn was right in front of her, his hands gripping her shoulders.

'Let go of me.'

He released her, but didn't move.

'I don't blame you for being angry. For hating me. But think for a minute: you're about to attempt something that might affect the lives of everyone around you. But you don't care. Because the only thing you care about is saving Leo. You're risking everything for your brother, just like I was willing to risk everything for mine. Are we really so very different?'

Merry opened her mouth to argue, but…

But he's right.

What would she really have done in Finn's position, if she'd thought the only way to save her brother was to take Ronan alive?

Finn smiled faintly.

'You remind me of Cillian. Stubborn. Argumentative.'

'If you think I'm stubborn, you should get to know Leo. He – he—'

Sorrow choked her. The tears that she'd successfully held off for the last few hours spilt down her cheeks again.

'I'd like to get to know him, Merry. To prove to him that I'm not a complete waste of space.' Finn's fingers skimmed across the back of her hand. 'I want to help. Whatever the consequences.'

Merry dashed the tears away from her cheeks. But if she was to trust him, she needed the truth.

'What is this, Finn? Guilt? Vengeance? Or something else?'

Finn flushed and dropped his gaze.

'Of course I want revenge. And I have a lot to be guilty about. Even more than you can imagine.'

Merry stared at him, her insides knotting up.

'What do you mean?'

'I mean that there was another reason I came here, aside from tracking Ronan.' A fleeting expression of disgust twisted his features. 'I can barely stand to think about it. And now is probably not the best time to confess. But if, by some miracle, we survive whatever you're planning to do, I promise I'll tell you. I'll tell you everything. And if you never want to see me again, I won't argue. But the truth is…' He sighed. 'The truth is, I do care about you, Merry.' He brought one hand up, resting his fingertips against her jaw.

And alongside the pain of losing Cillian, Merry was aware of the desire and tenderness Finn felt towards her. It was intense. Intoxicating. And it was real. She stood on tiptoe and put both arms around his neck and drew him towards her…

And pulled away again. She wanted to kiss him, desperately. She wanted him to hold her. But there was still too much that she didn't yet understand. Secrets he was still keeping. And now… now was not the time for this. She had to keep a clear head, to focus.

'Finn, the coven…'

'I understand.' He bent his head down and brushed his lips softly against hers. 'Just tell me what you need me to do.'

Finn believed in her. Just like Jack had believed in her. So maybe it was time to believe in herself. To accept that she was different: not an ordinary person, not a wizard, maybe not even a witch, exactly. Time to see what she could really achieve, when she was completely and only herself. No expectations. No preconceptions. No… definitions.

'Right. Do you have any stuff with you? I'm not sure where we're going. Or how long we'll be gone for.' She glanced at the lake, grey and quiet beneath the clouds, its surface dimpled by the rain that had started to fall again. 'Or whether we'll come back.'

In answer, Finn dragged a large backpack out of a nearby bush. Merry swung her own bag up on to her shoulders.

'Hold out your hands.' She placed the sword across Finn's palms, wrapping his fingers carefully around the hilt and the blade. 'And whatever happens, don't let go.'

There was nothing else to say.

With her knife, Merry sliced quickly through her skin. She let the blood drip on to the blade of the sword, slotted the knife awkwardly into the side pocket of her bag, and placed both hands on the blade. And then she began to sing, to the land and to the sword.

She sang about roots, and family, and the unbroken ties of blood. About memory and time and the long years rolling across the earth beneath her feet. Words taken from spells and stories, half-forgotten fragments of songs and nursery rhymes. Phrases she just made up. And as she sang, she felt her power… uncoil. It was like when she'd been under the lake facing Gwydion. And yet, unlike. Then, the magic had coursed around her body as if it was electricity. But now it unwound from her like the roots and branches of a tree, delving into the ground below, stretching into the air and sky above, twining around her and Finn and the sword.

Her power collided with the magic that was held in the land. Light sprang up around them, encasing them, and she half closed her eyes, flinching from the brightness of it. Finn gasped as the sword began to twitch and shudder in their hands. And as her magic flared outwards the light grew heavy, weighing on them, crushing them, and her vision blurred and the blade of the sword was cutting into her hands…

Finn moaned and fell to his knees, dragging her down with him. The light vanished – and the darkness swallowed everything.

EPILOGUE

DARKNESS.

And silence.

And beneath her, something soft and cold. Merry moved her fingers a little. It was almost like…

Snow. She could smell the bite of it in the air.

None of her bones seemed to be broken. But her body felt raw. Like some outer layer had been stripped away. It wasn't exactly painful, but it wasn't comfortable, either. She risked opening her eyes a little.

The world spiralled madly, tiny patches of sky against tall trees. She dug her fingernails into the snow and waited until the images stabilised, and she was staring at bare branches, interlaced against a sullen grey sky.

Pushing herself up, she rested on her elbows and looked around. The Black Lake had disappeared. In its place was a dimly lit forest, densely packed with trees and vegetation, wild and overgrown. To her left was a stream, the water gurgling along past narrow, frozen banks. And by the side of it, just the hint of a path disappearing into the shadows. Other than the chatter of the stream, the forest around her seemed deathly quiet. No birds, no insects. Just a watchful stillness.

Merry scrambled to her feet. Her bag was nearby, but Finn wasn't anywhere in sight. Neither was the sword. She took a deep breath, ignoring the panic bubbling up in her chest. Instead, she dragged a jumper out of her bag, conjured a ball of witch fire, and started along the path between the trees.

It was difficult, walking through the drifts of snow. Every so often she tripped on tree roots just under the surface. To begin with she called out Finn's name. But the further she got into the forest, the harder it became to break the silence. She was about to stop, to throw her bag on the floor and give in to the despair that was gnawing at her, when somebody yelled out in pain.

She crept forward, hands raised, until she saw a flicker

of movement through the trees. Somebody was there, just ahead of her on the path. Merry broke into a run.

'Finn! Are you OK?'

She stopped.

There was the sword, sticking out of a clump of brambles. And there was Finn, kneeling on the ground, his face white and fixed with either shock or pain or both. But he wasn't alone.

There was a boy standing behind him, holding a long, angular knife to Finn's throat. The boy was wearing different clothes from the last time Merry had seen him. And he *looked* different: more wild. There were markings on the bare skin of his arms that hadn't been there before. But still, Merry would have known him anywhere.

'Jack?'

She took a step forward, and Finn gasped as Jack tightened his grip.

He was frowning at her, but there was no recognition.

'Who are you? And how do you know my name?'

ACKNOWLEDGEMENTS

AH, THE NOTORIOUS second novel. We started writing *The Witch's Tears* while we were doing the line edits for *The Witch's Kiss*, and had the same problems that most writers seem to face. Will we find enough inspiration? Will we be able to invent fresh and colourful ways of making our characters' lives difficult? Will we even remember how to write? If the answer to any of those questions is yes, it's due in no small part to the people listed below.

Lizzie Clifford, who wielded her editorial scalpel with precision, grace and humour, and left our writing all the better for it. We already miss you! We'd also like to thank all of the team at HarperCollins, especially Samantha Swinnerton and Siân Robertson, both of whom have been enormously helpful in the mad dash to the finish line.

Claire Wilson and Rosie Price at Rogers, Coleridge & White, for their ongoing support, advice and all-round loveliness.

Lisa Brewster at Blacksheep Design Ltd, for yet another extraordinarily brilliant and beautiful cover design.

Melanie Rietveld, who won the *Maximum Pop!* competition and gave Ciarán Hyland his name. Thanks also to everyone who entered.

Every reader who took time over the last four months to tell us that they enjoyed our writing: you probably have no idea just how much it has meant to us.

Our families, for their continuing love and forbearance. Endless appreciation especially to Neill (Spouse of the Year for the nineteenth year running), Georgie, Victoria, Rebecca, Sam, Dad, Frances, Gill, Andrew, Rebecca G, Nick, Linda, Dan, Sandra, Leslie, Greg and Sarah.

And a special mention this time around to Victoria. Her comment, that she'd like to see someone become 'the king of Leo's heart', led at least in part to the creation of Ronan. Though he's probably not quite what she had in mind…